ADVANCE PRAISE

"THE ART COLLECTOR'S WIFE is an exquisitely written novel. Susan Knecht's strong female characters are each distinct, full bodied, impulsive, dangerous, battling inner demons, and connected to each other with deep bonds of love and family that survive the treacheries of a hidden past. Her postwar Venice is not a bijoux destination but a real world. Tender yet propulsive, as if Elena Ferrante had written a thriller."

— PETER NICHOLS, AUTHOR OF *GRANITE HARBOR*

A beautifully and masterfully written page turner, THE ART COLLECTOR'S WIFE, replete with duplicitous villains and compromised victims, is much more than an art theft caper through the canals of Venice and streets of Paris. Nobody is completely innocent, but Lila Lesser, and her against-all-odds, concentration camp born granddaughter Isabel prevail, coming to learn much about themselves and their carefully guarded secrets. A story of family bonds and hard-earned love, THE ART COLLECTOR'S WIFE is in a class of its own.

— SIMI MONHEIT, AUTHOR OF *THE GOLDIE STANDARD*

THE ART COLLECTOR'S WIFE is a propulsive and deeply moving thriller populated by characters whose secret pasts come to haunt their present lives in Venice. In dramatic and unexpected ways, the love and loyalty of this unusual family is put to the ultimate test when the matriarch's priceless paintings (along with her granddaughter) go missing. An absolute must-read for fans of historical mysteries.

— VAL BRELINSKI, AUTHOR OF *THE GIRL WHO SLEPT WITH GOD*

Susan Knecht's *The Art Collector's Wife* is an emotionally rich, time-skipping novel that weaves together post-war trauma, intergenerational secrets, art-world intrigue, and the sharp edges of teenage rebellion. It starts in the horror of Auschwitz, then unfolds decades later in sun-drenched Venice, following the fractured legacy of one family—particularly the women who survived and the granddaughter determined to uncover the past. It's part historical drama, part coming-of-age, with a steady undercurrent of longing.

— LITERARY TITAN, 5-STAR REVIEW

THE ART COLLECTOR'S WIFE

Susan Knecht

Sea Crow Press

The Art Collector's Wife

Published 2025, by Sea Crow Press LLC
www.seacrowpress.com
Barnstable, MA 02630

Paperback ISBN: 978-1961864320
Ebook ISBN: 978-1961864337
Library of Congress Control Number: 2025935208

Cover image: Painting of standing girl in Venice Grand Canal Italy. Royalty-free stock illustration ID: 2449920929 by ChiliMili @Shutterstock

This is a work of fiction. All characters, organizations, and events portrayed in this novel are either products of the author's imagination or are used fictitiously.

For
William, Rick and Val who never wavered

THE ART COLLECTOR'S WIFE

PROLOGUE

Auschwitz-Birkenau
January 27, 1945

Each mark is a day. Lila runs her fingers over the cuts in the wooden beam, counting silently. These little notches that mark the time are made from the buckle of her shoe which she managed to save from the guard before it was taken along with all the other personal items, her blouse, her skirt, her underclothes, the embroidered handkerchief she had stuffed in the skirt pocket. They had arrived at the camp eight months ago to the day, Lila, Miriam, Leo and Ilse, and in all that time, her son is never far away. The men's barracks are just north of the women's; they spread out like cobwebs over the flat miles of the camp, and though Lila has searched for Leo in the glaring white of the snow and wind-swept yard, she has never seen him. Not once.

Lila coughs into her hand and then extends her arm, gently grazing the wooden beam. Her arm is the branch of a tree hanging over the dock, the bunk they sleep in is a giant barge, the dirt floor is the Atlantic Ocean. They sail across rough freezing waters towards the harbor in New York, the statue holds the torch that lights their way. Onward. Lila's cough rattles in her chest, and she snuggles closer to Miriam; they shiver into the cold hours of the morning, the icicles growing like daggers from the barracks doorway. The two women hold fast to one another in the bunk, legs intertwined. Shivering and trembling, puffs of breath floating in the frigid air. They have made it this far, Miriam because Lila wouldn't hear of anything else, and Lila simply to be with Leo once more.

It is too cold to sleep for any length of time, and every few minutes Lila checks on Miriam. Over the last month especially her friend has grown worryingly thin and so Lila makes sure she still can feel Miriam's warm breath on her hand. In a place of death, nothing flourishes, nothing survives, and yet, here they still lie, breathing, their hearts still beating, while beneath them on the dirt floor, the young girl, Ilse, writhes in pain, each contraction coming closer and closer together. Soon the contractions stop, but only for a minute. Lila gets up to tend to the girl: cold clammy skin, eyes wide like winter's horizon, Ilse exhausts herself with pleas for water, she needs water, her lips are dry parchment, her cries thin and cracked, but there is no more water, Lila shakes her head, a lump in her throat, they have given her the last few drops. Ilse was a piano student in Leo's class at the conservatory before they were deported and his first love; she is only fourteen years old and pregnant. Love came without warning like a comet and young Leo was besotted. That first day at the camp when news of the pregnancy was whispered in Lila's ear, there is no way of telling Leo and Lila doesn't see the point in telling him even if there were. At not quite sixteen, he can barely take care of himself let alone a small helpless baby.

To think, a baby! Still possible even during such dark times. For Lila getting pregnant had been an agony, a triumph of will over obstinate reality. After four years of trying to conceive and Albert indifferent throughout (he'd prefer a son was all he'd say), when they did finally get the good news, the doctor ordered Lila to bed for the duration of the pregnancy. To be safe. Their baby boy arrived on time, underweight and Lila nursed him for two long years, through bouts of colic and fever. After that he grew steadily like a reed. Leo was her greatest, her singular accomplishment.

At school, though, he struggled to read and write. Even as a little boy with his wild headful of defiant curls, stubborn like his father without a fraction of the intellect, Leo wanted people to like him. He was clumsy, brash. He never could make friends. The teachers wrung their hands. He didn't have the right words and could only speak with clumsy gestures and groans. At home he was frequently sick and sensitive to most foods. Boiled carrots and broccoli, a warm porridge made of rice and green peas, all of it left a scaly rash on his chest and cheeks. The doctors all said the same thing: the boy's a medical mystery. But a savant, nonetheless. A brilliant pianist at five years old, Leo was somehow bereft of both compassion and common sense. He scratched the startled little faces of the girls at school, pushed them down on the gravel, pulled their hair. Lila brought him cups of tea from the Chinese herbalist, to support his stagnant chi they said while he practiced his piano scales and mastered the Mozart concerto. In return, he slapped the teacup from her hand, scalding his own arm. Even then wrapped in gauze, he was sullen. Unaffected. She came to expect it. He never cried. Until he met Ilse the first day of class. "I'm in love, mama," he said with tears in his eyes.

Lila's arm is a branch. The bunk is a barge. The copper-green lady with the torch waits for them in the harbor. From somewhere nearby come hollow booming sounds, and then sirens begin howling in urgency. Even from inside the barracks, loud voices can be heard, German guards shouting orders and running back and forth, suddenly busy as field mice heading for burrows. Missiles shriek overhead and then reverberate on targets, and throughout the yard come cries of joy, of disbelief. It can't be! It's impossible. Lila limps to the doorway to watch open-mouthed as Russian tanks form a straight line through the snow, bulldozing everything in their path. The impossible has arrived. The camp's formidable front gates crash to the ground in one long solid piece, barbed wire and all. From the barracks one by one and then in clumps of twos and threes, the women prisoners crawl from their beds and gather at the doorway, straining to see. The ones who can still walk limp out into the yard, their hands held up to frigid gray skies. Mumbling prayers, they fall to their knees, swaying forward and back as the wind picks up.

Liberation. The soldiers shout the word like a toast to better days. Lila doesn't believe it. It isn't real, nothing is except Ilse's ungodly, intensifying screams behind her, beyond that nothing exists. Lila turns back to the task at hand, to the metallic odor of blood, as a little head emerges from between the girl's legs and then just as suddenly the afterbirth trailing after it. Lila bends down to grasp the slippery bit of life; there is only the tiny infant's first breath, first cry, more of a chirp really, her small pink fingers moving spasmodically like a wind-up toy.

"Ohhh," Lila says, her voice registering something close to awe. "Oh, this is something, isn't it?" she says to the exhausted Ilse, and to the now-roused Miriam crying softly in her hand. Lila covers the child in the torn jacket from her own prisoner's uniform and tries to stand. A sudden sound coming from the entryway startles her, and she turns around slowly.

Lila gasps. More frail phantom than human, Leo stands there thin as a page in a book, his gaunt frame barely filling the doorway. The shredded rags hang from him like loose leaves from a slender tree and his once brown eyes are now sunken black marbles. "Mama?" His familiar rasp rings out, at once question and declaration.

Lila tightens her grip on the little bundle in her arms. After a moment's breath, during which the world is swiftly rearranged, she falls weeping against her son's brittle shoulder. Her arm is a branch, his warmth is her baby's, she folds him into her chest, squeezes the bones of his back; she will never let go. "But you're here. You're still here. My son. My boy." She caresses his cheek, uncertain that he is real.

But the force of him when he pushes her away reminds her that he is as real as ever. The stubbornness. The tenacity. He has survived.

"What on earth?" He glances at the squirming lump still nestled in Lila's clothing. "Who are you, baby?" He takes the chirping infant into his own arms. Lila is at his side. She will never leave his side again.

"Lila?" Miriam squats by the new mother.

Before them on the cold wet ground, a widening black pool has formed between Ilse's spread legs. The girl is very still, her eyes are closed, the skin pale, bloodless. Miriam touches the girl's face. "Lila," Miriam says again, her voice filling with urgency.

Lila turns her widened eyes to her friend but says nothing. She is too busy watching her son smelling the baby's scent, kissing the little cheek. Softly. Carefully. He has never been so careful. And she is so tiny. Lila touches Leo's arm, and the flesh, once thick and muscular, is desiccated, it pleats like taffeta. But he is real. He and the baby are real, alive. *Liberation.* Leo takes off his prisoner's shirt and swaddles his daughter. His bare chest is concave like an empty pail, his ribs are the stairs of a winding staircase jutting out from his torso. His frail arms rock the baby back and forth, back and forth like a porch swing. "Little baby", he says, "little Isabel". At that, the infant's eyes open. He hums the German tune, the same one he hummed in Lila's ear all those hours on the transport.

Lila whispers a few words of encouragement, of advice. She repositions his arms, shows him how to hold the baby properly. Leo shrugs her off. He is not one to be taught. What he doesn't know, what Lila cannot explain, is that this little baby, her granddaughter Isabel, is nothing short of a miracle. Leo smiles, a shock of black space where his front teeth once were. He swings the baby faster, laughing. Lila admonishes him. Careful. Gentle. Isabel is small. Weak. He doesn't listen. Happy is too happy. Excitement is too exciting. Isn't life grand? Liberation! He spins around, and walks with the newborn in his arms slowly toward the doorway, Lila at his heels urging him to be careful. "Why isn't she moving?"

He stares at Ilse's inert body sprawled out just a few feet away, and before Lila can answer, there's a crack like a door slamming and as Leo's smile freezes, his arms go limp. On an instinct, as out of control as everything else, Lila springs. She lunges for the baby before any harm comes to her. The force of the crack sends Leo sailing backwards, and time slows down the way time does and there again is his breath in her ear on the train, his little hand in hers that first day of school. Leo lands quietly against the wooden bunk and sinks downward, his legs twitching nervy life like the baby's fingers, a tiny perfect hole in his forehead.

Lila cradles the crying infant and whispers softly. Kneeling down, she carefully places the bundle in the crossbones of Miriam's trembling arms.

At the bunk where Leo has fallen, her son has a smoothed, changed face like an angel's, with a blank calmness where the wild fury used to be. Lila strokes his hair, her fingers finding the place at the back of his head where the bullet has pierced his skull straight through. She stifles a sob and settles down on the ground next to her boy, as a wall of rancid, overpowering smoke filters through the barracks, and encircles them. She kisses Leo's cheek, and they lie together one last time on the cold earth, two spoons in a drawer, as Russian tanks inch across the yard and snowflakes swirl down like a blessing of hands.

CHAPTER ONE

Venice, Italy
The Lido
May 31, 1962

Lila Lesser places the wreath of dried flowers on the marble slab and watches the sea breeze buoy them aloft; they land several feet away on the tomb of a Jewish merchant from the fourteenth century.

"Miriam would you be a dear—?"

Lila gestures toward the wreath rolling away. She straightens her scarf. This year for the occasion of Leo's memorial the right outfit is somehow more important than ever, and Lila has chosen a light pastel peach silk scarf fashioned after Sofia Loren's in her latest film to compliment her sweater set and pleated skirt.

Miriam recaptures the floral arrangement, removes a stray leaf that's come loose, and resettles the wreath upon the slab. "There. Still intact." She looks glamorous, tall, reed-like, striking a tone of summer funereal in a black straw hat with a little veil.

The two women both stare at the headstone: Leo Abraham

Lesser, Beloved Son and Pianist: May 31, 1929-January 27, 1945. He was a consummate musician. Lila takes a breath. "Life–" She trails off.

"What's that?"

"I said 'life', it has a sick sense of humor."

"Well. To think it's already been seventeen years." Miriam adjusts the veil of her hat. She removes her eyeglasses, cat's eye on a chain. "Still, we've persevered, haven't we?" Miriam's blue eyes are the color of Delft porcelain, the color of a vase with delicate irises. Thank God for her. Thank God she is still here, and they have remained together.

"Have we, Mim?"

Lila envies her friend's certainty. If only she could be so sure. She would give everything. Albert's money, their former social standing, all of it. She wouldn't call what they have done perseverance so much as, absent any other choice, continuing to live. She covers her eyes with a gloved hand. She despises any show of emotion, even in the company of a good friend.

"Every year it's the same, isn't it?" Miriam swats a fly away and holds onto the headstone for balance.

And she's right. It is the same. Every year they come to the empty gravesite in the Lido to commemorate Lila's son's passing: they pay tribute, say prayers, leave flowers, a forlorn ritual between old friends. But this time it isn't quite the same thing, not really. On the seventeenth anniversary of Leo's death, everything has suddenly changed: Isabel has announced she's moving to Paris. Paris, of all places! Lila should have suspected as much, there'd been little signs all along, the missing money from Lila's purse, that unmistakable odor of clove cigarette smoke on Isabel's school uniform, books of illicit poetry spilling from her school bag (one with obscene illustrations!) and the calls and letters from school about unexcused absences.

Lila straightens the homemade wreath made from lilacs dried in a pot on her windowsill. Perhaps Miriam is right: perhaps nothing vital has changed. Maybe it's just another phase of adolescence, a normal phase, torturous but surely harmless. Surely. A bank of clouds swims across the sun and the fatigue of another bad night's sleep weighs heavy on her shoulders.

"Oh, why do we bother, Mim?"

"Because he was your son."

For all his faults he was. He didn't listen. He was rough and rude. He could not be taught. And then to have a baby when he himself was only a baby, well. But the shame of his behavior was eclipsed by the war and when the war ended, the shame returned like a bad memory. Still. Leo was everything to her. She thinks of her granddaughter Isabel, precious, incorrigible, and cannot help but see a shadow of something similar rising up from the past. Not if Lila has anything to say about it. It's been her constant mission to protect the girl from such gloomy realities, and a memorial ceremony for her father is no place for a child. She's at school where she should be.

"Shall we?" Miriam sniffles quietly into a handkerchief; she's never without one, allergies she says, but today is something else altogether, and, unlike Lila, Miriam is not one to hold back tears.

They bow their heads, but Lila doesn't pray and has refused to, in fact, since that time in the camp. Those last moments. And she would put the memory out, pinch the endless flame of that scene with wet fingers, but it still burns on. Every day and night. It's all that's left to her.

"Lila." Miriam nudges her.

"No, Mim. You start."

As Miriam mouths the words to the Kaddish, the two women sway in the breeze like the men in prayer shawls do in temple. It's not praying, not really, just a dance they do with the past. After a bit, Miriam lifts her bowed head. "Amen," she whispers. Her cat's eye glasses dangle from the chain around her neck.

"Amen." Lila mouths the word without sound.

She straightens her dress. The noonday sun aims like a searchlight on the cemetery and heats their shoulders, the tops of gravestones, and the grass at their feet. She dabs at her cheeks with a handkerchief.

"Are you alright, Lila?"

"I have something in my eye." Lila bristles. The least Miriam could do is pretend not to notice. "I should get back." She bends down to scoop up a perfectly round pebble to leave on the gravestone.

"Yes. Of course. Me too." Miriam squeezes her clutch purse under her arm.

A blackbird lands on the neighboring gravestone where the meandering line of pebbles runs across the top of the stone, Solly Hirschberg, it says; each pebble represents a recent visitor paying their respects.

"Leo's birthday, isn't it?" The familiar lilting voice from behind them is startling, out of place, and Lila turns around slowly. Arms folded across her chest, Isabel Lesser leans against an oak tree, the only one in the cemetery, the only one for miles. She doesn't eat enough, never has, and the school uniform falls around her thin frame.

"Again I wasn't invited?"

"Isabel! We—," Miriam puts her glasses back on. "Don't you have school? Lila?"

Lila stares down at the ground and says nothing. It's pointless. Because even if she wanted to talk, there's no finding her voice. No finding the words. Which is very unlike her, anyone who knows her, knows she always has something to say, in any given situation. Not this one. Lila bites down hard on her lip and feels the dry skin break open.

"School ended early today. Teacher's out sick. Really, nonna? I'm not a baby. I have every right!" Isabel places a gray pebble on the gravestone. "Happy birthday, Leo," she says, voice cracking. "Father, I should say. Guess that's it for another year, huh?"

Lila stares at her shoes.

"You never talk about my mother. Not once."

Lila clears her throat but stays mum.

"You have no right. That's my dad in the ground, isn't it? Who were they? Look at those dates," she points to the headstone, "he was only fifteen. She was a child. I need to know, Nonna!"

"Isabel please." Miriam tries to placate.

"I'll find out. You know I will. I'll find out about them and there's nothing you can do about it."

Isabel turns abruptly and marches back through the gravestones, her braids bouncing against slim shoulders. The pebbles fall through Lila's fingers as she watches her granddaughter walking away.

CHAPTER TWO

The cocktail dress in the window of the boutique on Correre Pugliese is blue and chic with darts at the chest and a girlish flair of taffeta at the knee. Isabel gulps at the stylish mannequin. It's nothing she could begin to imagine herself in, but precisely the kind of thing Antonia, a good three years older, could pull off with no effort. As usual her best friend is full of surprises. Trying on clothing was the last thing Isabel had in mind when Antonia invited her out after school, and this morning's bickering with Nonna had put her in a mood. It was always about money: Isabel pleading for a few lire, for a dress this time, arguing that her grades were excellent, that she'd been named valedictorian for the upcoming graduation, an honor very few students received. Still Nonna refused. She could be such an obstinate prig. Perhaps if Isabel hadn't followed them to the cemetery, Nonna and Miriam, and watched the entire strange spectacle at Leo's grave from behind a tree... Nonna was not amused. Well, that's on her too. If she ever did speak about her son, Isabel's father, or her mother Ilse, there wouldn't be such a mystery shrouding the whole thing, but she treated all of it like some kind of terrible secret. Sometimes it felt more like a punishment than a secret.

"With a little heel, am I right?" Antonia rolls up her mannish shirtsleeves, usually paired with a grimy apron. For this occasion she had left the apron at her father's cafe. "Come on, tell me what you think! I have to get back."

There were always customers to wait on. Her wavy auburn-colored hair is pulled back in a messy braid. Her fair skin is in reality a collection of pale freckles, dotting her smallish, very un-Roman nose, cheeks, and even her eyelids like fine dust. No one would ever guess she was old enough to run her father's osteria. But at twenty-one, Antonia is worldly and wise and her friendship has been the one bright ray in Isabel's daily Catholic school drudgery. To think they might never have been friends if Isabel hadn't wandered into the café out of sheer boredom two months ago to the day.

"Are you joking? I can't wear a dress like that."

"Do I look like I'm joking?"

The sea breeze paws at Isabel's unbuttoned sweater and flaps it open. Beneath the layers she is bony and boyish, flat-chested even at seventeen, and the familiar self-consciousness takes hold, the same awful feeling when the eyes of yeshiva boys drift over her in the Campo.

She bites her tongue not to snap at her friend.

"Come on." Antonia taps the display window impatiently: she has taken the rare day off and has no patience for indecision. "With your hair done up and a little make up? Perfection."

Isabel is not convinced. This kind of dress is for a grown woman with hips and breasts like Antonia's, whose body, even in the canvas apron, is a force of nature. Wherever they walk, heads turn and mouths open; to be honest, it's a bit much. Who wants that much attention, the wolf whistles and catcalls? And Isabel, all elbows and knees, never warrants a single second look. No. It's ridiculous and vain.

Still, what would it be like, she wonders. Especially now that there is a boy to consider. A boy whose opinion about such things matters. A little. She has been classmates with Niccolo Gritti since kindergarten but this year unexpectedly, their senior year, she has begun to notice his green eyes, his full lips, the way he shakes away his long blond locks each time they tumble forward and cover his face. He calls himself a poet and can back it up too, she's read one of his sonnets and it's not half bad. He's the one person she can discuss Dante and Gide with; sometimes they read Baudelaire's Fleurs du Mal in the Piazza San Marco and share an espresso from a demi tasse. No one else appreciates the same literature or smokes the same brand of French cigarettes. They are two of a kind, a rare pairing. He knows it too. He must. He would say the same of her if not for the fact that she saw him ride off last Monday with the dazzling Teresa, her voluminous red hair gathered high on her head like a prized stallion's tail. She had hopped on the back of his idling motorbike, and the two of them zipped past toward Ponte delle Tette, the red ponytail a victory flag waving behind them. Teresa! Of all the girls at school he could have chosen, a coquette who comes from money, who cheats on exams, and has never earned a good grade or anything else on her own, since her wealthy family gifts her with every kind of extravagance: gaudy earrings, an ugly bejeweled choker. Real emeralds, Teresa bragged at recess. It was stupefying actually. The sting of Niccolo and Teresa together is still the cold water dashed on a sunburn. No. Worse. It's enough to make her second guess why he shared his coffee in the first place.

"So, do you want this Niccolo person to notice you or not?" Antonia taps her foot.

"How did you know it was him?" The name spoken out loud makes her stomach flip over.

"I pay attention."

Antonia's smile hides more than she's saying, and suddenly her true intentions are clear. Their recent adventures in pocketing or nicking or whatever you want to call it when really it's just stealing, have become increasingly risky and this one would top them all. So far, their booty has merely included cheap lipstick and mascara from the local pharmacy, never expensive designer dresses.

Isabel's eyebrows rise. "It must cost over fifty lire!" But it would be lying to say she wasn't intrigued.

"So?" Antonia opens the door of the shop with her foot, the scratched brown leather of her shoes worn a much lighter shade at the toe. They enter, and nodding to the salesgirl, begin lighting from rack to rack like worker bees focused only on the most radiant, redolent flowers. There are a few other dresses, one made with silk and lace, one with a ridiculous crinoline skirt that catches Antonia's eye, like those Hollywood actresses in musicals, her tone captures the delight of an ingénue's first breathtaking society debut. But in the end, not one of them could work. They should go to some other girl who's curvier and more experienced with an ample cup size. A girl who giggles at all the right moments between sips of champagne.

They hover near the display window. Antonia points at the dress that started the whole thing.

"Really?" Isabel allows herself to be persuaded. If it takes this dress and all the risks in the world, she would have Niccolo's unwavering attention.

The salesgirl greets them pleasantly and brings them the blue dress, and Antonia waits outside the changing room as Isabel tugs the thing on and stands in the mirror, the sting of disappointment apparent on her face. The taffeta pokes out from her hips in all the wrong places and droops around her waist like a stretched out elastic band. The bust is enormous and the cups sag hopelessly on her chest.

"How are you doing in there?" The salesgirl's voice smiles.

"We're fine, thank you very much." Antonia pokes her head through the curtain. "Oh, dear!" she says, catching sight of Isabel in the full-length mirror.

"Not yet!" Mortified, Isabel grabs the nearest thing to cover up but Antonia pulls away the sweater.

"Let's see here," She gathers the dress material from the back. "Just needs a bit of taking in."

"More than a bit." Isabel lets the bust of the dress sag down revealing the childish graying undergarment with the front-closing buttons underneath, another practical birthday gift from nonna that still fits after more than a few winters.

"Have I taught you nothing?" Antonia balls the sweater up and stuffs it down the front of the dress. With a bit of tucking and pulling and pinching from behind, the silhouette in the mirror has a full bust and a narrow waist. "Behold."

Isabel gazes at this other girl, this woman in the mirror and almost wants to look away. It's too much, and not like her at all. With another sweater or two for stuffing she could be Sofia Loren debuting at Cannes. Niccolo would be spellbound at their graduation reception. Isabel lingers in his adoration and to Antonia's amusement, waves to her admirers with a cupped hand.

"Just one teeny tiny thing." Antonia peeks through the curtain to speak to the salesgirl. "Do you have one a size or two smaller?"

"I'm afraid that's our smallest one."

And back they come, the dark clouds ripe for a storm, and Isabel's smile fades. How stupid. Nonna would never let her out of the house dressed like that anyway. "Never mind Antonia. Please! Don't bother."

"What do you mean, 'don't bother'?"

"I mean don't bother."

"You're kidding, right?" Antonia elbows her. "Are you seriously telling me you don't see the exotic creature that you are? In this dress? You, my dear friend, are it. Now get dressed."

She darts back through the curtain to talk with the salesgirl about something. Isabel stills the rustling of the taffeta skirt to catch the tail end.

"No, the price is not the issue," Antonia says. "It's the style that doesn't work for her."

Antonia loves pouring out compliments like cups of espresso, and standing there, in this ridiculous dress Isabel feels like an idiot. In the changing room, she slips back into the school uniform: the plaid skirt, white blouse and wrinkled cotton sweater, back to the uniform of complete invisibility. Trying on expensive dresses, pretending to be a woman when she's really a girl? Completely ridiculous. Laughable. She wipes away tears and returns the blue taffeta to its hanger.

The little bell on the door rings as they leave.

"Now where are we going?" In spite of everything, Isabel is slightly curious.

"Come on! We'll miss the next boat."

"Right. Well let's just forget about that dress."

"Forget it? God no, I'm coming back."

"You're not."

"I am. On my own." Antonia's eyes widen at Isabel's protest. "It'll be quicker that way. And at the end of the week, that lovely bit of flounce will be yours, mademoiselle!"

They run down the quay with Isabel bobbing after her friend like a tethered balloon.

Flying about the kitchen, Miriam is a moving target and can never settle in one place. She stirs the water in the saucepan and winces when her fingers graze against the metal for a second too long. Besides being an excellent chef and skilled raconteur, she is a retired soprano who once sang La Traviata at Il Fenice, and now spends most days dusting a collection of unusual curios from her exotic travels around the world, all the while wearing Chanel couture. The morning sun edges past the curtain as she finishes up at the stove. A plate is placed in front of Isabel, and the hard-boiled egg rolls a little before coming to a wobbly stop in a sprinkling of paprika.

"Lila would never forgive me if I didn't feed you."

For all her fussing, Miriam is a welcome relief from Nonna, who can be an ogre in the morning with her endless directives about cleaning and wiping and putting away. Fortunately, Nonna has taken the early vaporetto to Santa Croce to see about some fish for dinner. But Isabel hates fish. The oily smell of it. The bones inside. And she certainly cannot stomach the food placed in front of her now. Breakfast is boring; all meals are, in fact. Life has only become tolerable since Antonia arrived. And since Niccolo invented the game of dares. Isabel shudders, a pleasant tingle running down her back. Nothing could possibly be as exciting, although she'd never say as much to Antonia.

"Oh, come on and eat! Just this once? For Aunt Mim?"

Isabel shakes her head with the usual guilt: she should indulge her, but hasn't the patience. Miriam still sees her as a little girl with a runny nose and bitten down nails. Nonna encourages it with the ridiculous idea that Isabel needs a child minder while she's working at the stationer's shop.

"Really? Not even a bite? You're practically wasting away!"

"Only people who have healthy constitutions eat the morning meal." Isabel pushes the plate away and sets the egg to wobbling again: the smell is beyond nauseating. "I suffer from anemia." A self-diagnosis, but it may as well be true.

"I see." The little frown lines around Miriam's mouth betray her age for a fraction of a second. When stone-faced and unperturbed, she could be Nonna's much younger sister and not, in fact, a full two years older. "How about a piece of dry toast? Or would that be too healthy?"

Isabel's eye rolling does not escape Miriam's notice.

"God, but you're just like your father."

"Am I really?" Isabel perks up at the rare mention. "What was he like then, Leo?"

"Oh, what was he like? I don't know. Leo was...an original." Miriam washes a spoon at the sink. "Yes, I suppose there's no better way to describe him. Did you know he never let me shake his hand? And hugs were definitely not allowed. Someday Lila will explain it to you. Although I never understood what the doctors were talking about. Savant was the word they kept using."

Savant. How curious the workings of genetics. Isabel can hardly stand social hugging, such public displays always makes her feel foolish, like a stage actor hamming it up or someone equally pathetic who craves constant attention; she has only recently succumbed to Antonia's insistence that they greet each other with la bise, in French fashion. No, if there's any touch she desires at present it's Niccolo's lips on hers. Her lips part and there's a moist flutter somewhere below her belly. A lovely tension. "And what else, Aunt Mim?"

Miriam pauses at the table to consider. "Well Leo never ate his breakfast." She shakes her head scornfully. "You can imagine how that drove your nonna crazy."

"Is that all?" Isabel pushes at the breakfast plate. The egg slides around, coated in red paprika.

"Did you know that once he painted the hood of your grandfather's Aston Martin? With oil paints Lila bought him for Hanukah. It's true! This was when we all stayed in Treviso that summer. Albert joined us later in the convertible. Brand new. Oh boy, did he regret it." Miriam laughs with fresh disbelief. "Leo's fingernails glowed with orange-red paint for weeks afterwards."

"Tell me more!" Isabel sits up in her seat.

Miriam's smile evaporates. "Please, sweetheart, you mustn't say anything to your nonna. She's forbid me from talking about it."

No surprise there. Nonna never talks about the time before the War. Never talks about the War itself. It's a dirty secret, a shame hanging over them all.

"From talking about what?" Isabel plays dumb.

"Isabel, dear, you must promise me!"

"Of course, Aunt Mim, I promise."

But it's a lie. Sort of. She won't exactly say anything to Nonna but she will find a roundabout way of bringing the subject up without giving Miriam away. It's a talent of hers. She has become a master of the circular conversation, as good as–no, better than–nonna. The temptation to know her dead father never goes away and has only grown stronger; Isabel will take whatever crumbs she can get. So far she has gleaned that Leo was secretive, quiet, and unlike Isabel, a piano prodigy at a young age. He must have been smart. Charming. Certainly capable of telling a few well constructed lies himself. Isabel smiles. So at least they have that in common. Miriam nudges the egg plate back and Isabel pretends to take a bite. When Miriam isn't looking, she slides the whole business into the napkin on her lap. The other questions will have to wait.

CHAPTER THREE

"Who told you you could smoke?" The short hirsute man swats the cigarette out of Niccolo's pursed lips. After the bell, most of the students have already filed into class but they are standing in San Polo at the open gates of Saint Dominica's as if nobody's watching. In Niccolo's hands is a tattered copy of "Lafcadio's Adventures," the Gide book they are reading in French Literature.

Isabel darts behind a tree. This Niccolo has a face she's never seen: the look of the fox in the trap; she cannot reconcile it with his other, more beautiful one. And this hairy little man doesn't look like any fisherman she's ever seen. He wears a pin-striped suit a size too small and the jacket strains against his wide-set shoulders. He grabs Niccolo's lighter and pockets it. "What kind of a son steals from his father?"

"I never stole from you Papa." Niccolo's voice cracks.

The short man scans the school in both directions, glancing toward the canal and then the dilapidated church at the corner that is held together by an ever-present scaffolding as old as the structure itself.

"You think you're such a big man? When the catch dries up, who feeds you and your brother? Who pays the tuition? Who? Your dear old Papa that's who." He grabs both lapels of Niccolo's school jacket, releasing them quickly when another straggler passes through the gates. "You stole from me, now you owe me. You get that?" His icy whisper cuts through the warm air.

A pebble skids off Niccolo's boot and lands near Isabel's hiding place.

"Was that the second bell?" she says, emerging.

"Who's this?" The short man takes in Isabel with a grunt.

"No one. It's no one, Papa."

The tall man smoothes out the front of Niccolo's jacket. "You! Remember what I said."

"I won't forget." The edge of sarcasm has returned to Niccolo's voice as the short man walks away and his 'forget' already sounds forgotten. The boy and girl watch the man leave the school grounds. "He believes a lie about me." Niccolo shakes his head ruefully.

"What lie?" She constricts a smile: she mustn't reveal how happy she is to be in the warmth of his attention once again.

Niccolo lights a cigarette, which he hands her. "What have you got for me?"

She takes a slow drag but her awkward attempt not to inhale leaves her coughing miserably, and she hands him back the cigarette, catching her breath. "Are you familiar with the five-fingered discount?" Her question hangs in the air next to his smoke ring. She fishes in her pocket for a second and then slides the thing into his hand. Let him see who's not an amateur.

Niccolo pulls the beaded chain to its full length and the ruby-encrusted crucifix sways through the air like a pendulum. He lets out a long low whistle like he can't believe his eyes, nor can she, really. "God help your immortal soul."

She shrugs. "I've always wanted to take it and now it's done."

It sounds about as mundane and matter of fact as deciding on a different route home instead of deliberately stealing Sister Angelica's prized rosary. Her heart still races when she thinks about the perfect timing: the good Sister had been called away early to take tea with the Monsignor Rinaldi, a cleric prone to rambling on about his younger days at the monastery. Isabel was in and out in a matter of minutes.

Every student at Saint Dominica's is familiar with it on sight; the rosary is practically the headmistress's calling card. A genuinely magnificent object, the beaded chain is strung with rubies and the crucifix is solid gold. That very first time in the chapel, five-year-old Isabel watched transfixed as Sister worried the beads through her fingers, her serene expression highlighted in the flickering altar candles. "Hail Mary, full of grace." Somehow seeing Sister Angelica's palms pressed together, Isabel suffered too.

"This is what you chose to steal?"

"Well your dares were pretty—" she stops short of saying it; an arc of cigarette ash is strewn across her shoe. But they were, his dares were lame. Hiding the groundskeeper's garden hose? Letting a bee loose in the canteen? With an impatient tap of her foot she dislodges the ash.

"What about swiping something we can sell?" He cocks his head.

"What do you mean sell?" Surely the game is about keeping the spoils.

"Um, sell. For money. We're not all born with silver spoons, you know."

"Who told you I come from money?"

"No one."

"Well, you shouldn't believe everything Teresa says."

"Think of something else, Isabella."

A bank of clouds overhead shaped like a great stampeding bull stretches out in uneven blues and purples, and all that comes to mind is the cheap reproduction hanging on the foyer wall at home, the celebrated painting Portrait of a Man, Albert's first wedding anniversary gift to Nonna. Isabel had stared at it longer than usual this morning while scrounging around for her house key and had to resist the urge to tear it down and fling it in the corner. They have no luxuries at home, other than a few worthless antiques and old reproductions nailed to crumbling plaster. Albert had the means; Nonna has none, that's the standard response to any of Isabel's requests for spending money.

She pockets the Sister's crucifix. "This is what I want." For once she will have the expensive trinket, the rare and costly thing.

"All right." He caves with surprising ease "Meet me after class, right here." He points to the balustrade. "I have something to show you."

But after class all that's left on the balustrade is a copy of "Lafcadio's Adventures" rippling in the breeze; Niccolo is nowhere to be seen.

In Math class, Isabel's legs are a revving motor beneath the desk. Fortunately, Sister Cecilia buys her excuse about needing the girl's room and she runs straight down the hall and toward the lockers. Her book bag hoisted on her shoulder, she eases the metal locker door closed with the softest click.

"Niccolo!" Her urgent whisper rises through the open door and echoes off the empty walls of the boy's washroom. She heads toward the lobby. Another missed class means another note to Nonna, but Isabel has become skillful at intercepting the mail.

On Calle di Preti the sea breeze rustles her braids as the church bell tolls the hour: one o'clock. Even without someone to share it, she savors the memory of the theft. There's a new strut in her step; the rosary chain in her pocket is only a hair's breadth between her fingers, and the beaded chain is warm: not from Sister Angelica's touch anymore but her own. As if it now belongs only to her.

Along the Grand Canal the air is thick and sulfurous from the petrol of motorboats. A construction worker's hammer pummeling the buttress of an adjacent palazzo drowns out her rumbling stomach. She counts her steps in the public garden where the weary arthritic branches of a sycamore jab the sky. Twenty in all to make it across. The glimmer of shame is the stitch in her side; it's Sister Angelica's benevolent smile in the web of branches and the 'A' at the top of Isabel's paper.

The rough plaid of her wool skirt chafes her legs as she boards the waiting vaporetto. She hadn't anticipated feeling this way. Drops of perspiration run down her spine and soak her dress slip as she slips into an empty seat. Teresa and her little cohort, the other so-called pretty girls, used to taunt her in the schoolyard. "Look at Isabel! She sweats like a Jew!" Not one among them clever enough to add two and two. But no more second thoughts. She is free. Saint Dominica's is on the shore behind the vaporetto and each bead on the rosary chain in her pocket is, or should be, a touchstone of adventure: the gold-leafed bible, the darkened study, the sister's fortuitous absence, the run of adrenaline electrifying every corpuscle during the taking.

The vaporetto lurches forward and the spray of seawater over the bow is some relief from the heat. The old man across the aisle is a stone-faced sentinel. Isabel nods in greeting but he doesn't respond. An old woman over-laden with shopping bags grips the railing for dear life and Isabel offers up her seat. Unlike Lafcadio in the Gide book who pushes a random passenger through the open doors of a moving train, Isabel is at heart a good girl. Nonna's rules of etiquette are second nature. Most times. Sometimes.

The old man has a blind man's walking stick at his side. An empty bottle of soda pop rolls from port to stern, and her mouth goes dry. She still can't understand what happened to Niccolo. He must have gone fishing with his Mafiosi father. She pictures it and feels the corners of her mouth turn up at the gruesome image: Niccolo and his bucket of chum, his fishing line hanging over the skiff, the bloated bodies floating all around them. The vaporetto rounds the corner, the purplish oil slick trailing in their wake like a greasy tail. On either bank aging palazzos huddle against the sun. At Ca' San Marcuola, Isabel is the first one to disembark. From behind the blind man's walking stick taps like the metronome during her piano lesson, and finally the gates open onto the Ghetto, the centuries' old Jewish quarter. A murder of crows squawk and take flight.

The peddler at the news kiosk calls out in newsman singsong, "Adolf Eichmann Executed!" On the front page, a man in a banker's suit hangs from a scaffold like the catch off a fishing line. His head slumps to one side in apparent disagreement with the verdict. Isabel flips past to the next page and a much smaller photo of a woman, tall and stately in a long flowery kimono. Four coal-faced little dogs are splayed at the woman's feet as she stands like Japanese royalty at the entrance to her palazzo. In small block print the caption reads, "Isadora Morgenfeld Returns to Villa in Venice."

Isabel drops some coins in the peddler's can and continues on with the folded newspaper tucked under her arm. "Shhh," she says to the yapping Maltese in the open window, and the dog defers, contrite.

At Goldberg's bakery on Rio Terra San Leonardo, the owner sorts challahs in the bin. When she spots Isabel her expression sours. Nonna puts it down to an old grudge but won't say any more. Nonna. If she knew what Isabel's just done, she'd never forgive her.

A group of yeshiva boys jostle past: the tallest of them ogles her, his face a morass of spots, the yarmulke slipping down his head rakishly. Most days she wears her hair in braids like the other olive-skinned Jewish girls in the ghetto, but the boy notices her Catholic school plaid with contempt. Eyes locked, Isabel dares him to look away first and when finally, he does, his cheeks are as fiery as the inflamed spots mottling them. It's the price you pay for your safety, Nonna insists when Isabel complains that her school clothes set her apart from the boys who tuck prayer shawls into trousers, satin tassels spilling over narrow belted waists, and from the girls who sport long woolen jumpers, somber black shoes and itchy tights even on the hottest of summer days.

Across the street from their building, at the stonewalled perimeter of the Ghetto and on the other side of the wall, is Antonia's café. Once Nonna gets home, Isabel will find an opportunity to sneak away. In the building's foyer in the mailbox marked Lesser there is an envelope with her name on it, but it's too dark now to make out the return address. Please be from Paris. She mumbles under her breath. During all these years of dutifully writing essays, she has wanted little else than to study the great French writers and poets in the city where so much of what was written took place. If this is the letter from the Sorbonne, it could be her one chance. But if it is the letter, surely it's arrived early: it couldn't have been more than six weeks ago that she had popped the application in the post. She begins to tear into the envelope but some rustling behind the closed door distracts her, and letter in hand, she races up the first flight of stairs.

"Isabel? Is that you?" A wavering voice, high pitched and cracking like the plaster on the stairwell ceiling calls out from down below. Isabel holds her breath and waits.

"Isabel, dear?" For someone who is hard of hearing, the old Signora has never once missed Isabel's arrival home from school, and, according to Nonna, her poor eyesight is a blessing. "She can't even tell that it's a Catholic school uniform you're wearing everyday. Blind as a bat, that one."

A bell-shaped woman in a house dress leans obliquely in the doorframe, catching the fringe of her shawl on the small nail securing the mezuzah in place. "Oh!" Signora Volterra runs her fingers over the little tear in the weave. The scratching of overgrown canine claws reaches a crescendo. From the edge of the open door, the wet black nose of the old terrier peeks out. "Beppo! Look what you made me do!"

"How are you feeling today, ma'am ?" The question must be asked: it's never wise to insult the concierge, especially a self-appointed one.

"Not well. Not well. I'm a little upset, if you must know. And those frightful workmen were at it again. An awful noise like the dentist's drill. Apparently a pipe burst down the street. I thought the sky was falling!" Signora Volterra waves off an imagined objection from Isabel, "But no need to worry. You'll have your bath." The nosy woman hears every little thing through the building's paper walls.

Isabel twists the envelope in her hands. Perhaps opening the letter in the hallway isn't wise anyway. What if it's bad news?

Mrs. Volterra points to the mailboxes. "Would you mind very much dear? My arthritis, you know."

Back downstairs the woman's mailbox contains a small stack of mail and thin packages. Isabel trudges back up one flight. "Here you are," she says, handing over the bundle.

Mrs. Volterra sorts through quickly, holding each envelope nearly a foot away to read the return address. "Bills!" she snorts until arriving at the small package. "Oh, it's from my son! Well, you should hurry. It's not polite to keep a guest waiting!" She closes her door with Beppo trailing at her feet.

On the sixth floor, Isabel fumbles at the lock with her house key. The flat is dark inside, Nonna insists that if they don't close the shutters during the day the sunlight will fade the deep mahogany to a shabby pink, and Isabel now switches on the light, throwing her keys in the shallow drawer of the spindly-legged table. Hanging prominently on the interior wall, the subject of Portrait of a Man stares back at her with suspicion. The school blazer and book bag hanging on the coat rack obscure the rest of the nobleman's bearded face. First things first. She rips open the letter and scans quickly. "Happy to inform you...you have been accepted for the academic year..." And there it is: she can scarcely believe it. Her future unfurls before her like an endless carpet.

She floats down the hallway to the kitchen on a cloud of euphoria. Through the glass pane of the cabinets, Nonna's china plates gleam in tight stacks and the rose-trimmed teacups hang from little hooks. Isabel fills a glass under the tap and guzzles the water in one long gulp, drinking in the Champs Elysées, the Jardin du Luxembourg, the palace of Versailles. A long shadow arches over her shoulder.

"Took you long enough." The voice is a shock. Niccolo stands in the doorway, a sinister cast on the blunt angles of his face.

Isabel blinks, as though slapped, the teacup still in her hand. "How did you get in?"

"The old lady downstairs." An object travels quickly, a flash of green from one of his hands to the other. "I followed you from school. Didn't you see me? Surprised to find you live here though. What could it mean?" He winks. "Six flights up! Why do the Jews have to build higher than everyone else?" The flash of green comes to a rest in his hands: it's Nonna's precious Murano glass apple.

Panic rises in Isabel's throat. He knows her secret. And she has never had a boy in the apartment. "Look, Niccolo, you have to go."

He continues tossing the apple like a circus performer, like a stupid boy who doesn't care that he has her life in his hands. God, but she wishes he'd put it down. The rare glass object was Albert's first wedding anniversary gift to Nonna. Her grandmother always bragged that while most women got platinum rings for their engagement, she got Murano glass. It was irreplaceable.

"I thought your family name was Volpe. That old lady downstairs kept calling you Lesser."

"Lesser was my grandfather's name." The practiced explanation is always at the ready but now it sounds lamer than ever.

"Makes sense. That's why you live in the ghetto, I guess." His words say one thing, his face another. He's gone off her, she's sure of it. Just like anyone at school would if they knew her real origins.

"Please put it down, it's precious glass. And my Nonna will be home any minute."

Niccolo's gaze seems to land and then pause on the white cotton blouse buttoned up to her neck. "Catch!" He pretends to toss the apple her way but instead sets it down on the kitchen table. His fingernails are grayish and a bit overgrown like an old man's.

"Anyway, I have something to show you."

He shrugs, pops his knuckles, waiting.

There's a bead of blood on her finger; she must have pierced the skin on the sharp end of the little rosary cross. She puts the finger in her mouth instinctively. He moves one hand along the contours of her cheek slowly, brushing away a loose strand of hair. The effect of his touch is beyond stunning: her skin has grown new receptors. Fiery. Electric, combustible ones.

But when his lips graze hers, Isabel recoils. This is not how she imagined it: so sudden, so void of any build up. Still the downy blonde hairs on her arms stand at attention at the soft pressure of his squeeze, his touch at once warm and cool like the dappled shade of the oak tree at school.

A gate rattles closed through the open kitchen window. Isabel steps back, forcing him to drop his hold. "You need to leave. This minute."

"Where do you keep the glasses?" He ignores her, brushes past, and the cupboards creak open. He drinks quickly from a rose-covered teacup and wipes his mouth on his shirtsleeve.

From outside the sound of a creaky stair. "Nonna." Isabel's chest tightens.

"It's my grandmother."

"Okay. You can introduce me."

She holds her breath, relieved at last when the sound of foot-steps grows fainter.

He points at the oil canvas perched high between the parlor windows, a portrait of a woman in Renaissance costume holding a rosary. "The fair Isabel, no? So this is where you got the idea."

"No! I don't know. Maybe. Don't!"

But he doesn't listen. He takes down the canvas from the wall revealing a square of white beneath the painting; the rest of the wall is grimy with age.

Isabel is gob-smacked. No one has ever dared to remove the painting except to dab at the frame with the feather duster on Sundays; even this is done sparingly.

He returns the painting to the wall, and the canvas dips off center to the right. "Very impressive for a girl who doesn't have a silver spoon." She breathes him in: tiny blond hairs dot his chin and upper lip. "This is what I was talking about. Selling something valuable. Like the one in the closet."

Her face burns hot. "You've been in my nonna's room?" She straightens the canvas a jot.

"Don't get apoplectic. I wrapped it back up."

Apoplectic. She loves his words. But how dare he? Rummaging all over the flat like a common thief. She stifles a grin. The painting on the wall was the one thing in the flat with any value, that and maybe the one hidden in Nonna's closet; no bigger than two feet by two feet, it was a portrait of a sixteenth century noble woman her bowed head wrapped in a scarf, a shawl covering her shoulders and her hands clasped in supplication. Isabel came across it once while looking for loose pocket change. The paint was thick and textured and smelled of linseed oil and the gardenia scent that was everywhere in that room. Isabel wrapped it back up exactly as she found it. She could never be a painter. Too much time spent staring at white canvas when life should be inhaled all at once, its thousands of flavors wafting in the breeze.

"You know, my father is acquainted with the best fence for stolen art in town."

"You've been watching too much film noir."

"I'll take that as an invitation."

"What?"

"To the movies of course. Fellini is sublime," he whispers, once again pressing his mouth against hers. She jolts at his darting tongue, the sweet taste of tobacco, the prickly edge of his cheek, but her legs, heavy as sandbags, and the magnetic force of him anchor her to the spot. When he finally pulls away, her mouth is swollen and tingling.

"It's a date then." He runs a hand through the lock of blond hair that veils his eyes, and it's the best thing anyone has ever said to her. "Monday after school at Cinema Dante."

"Is it also a dare?" Her voice is small, tremulous.

"Yes." He smiles; he is tremendous, exotic and mysterious.

To think if she had waited just a few seconds longer in the garden before heading home she might have missed him. She might never have felt the roughness of his fingers. He is Baudelaire and Lafcadio combined. "Whether you come from heaven or hell, what does it matter, O beauty!"

He blows her a kiss at the front door. She promises herself to tell Antonia about the blue-green flowers at the center of his eyes.

Passing through the dining room on her way to the parlor, she notices an eerie difference: the center of the table has a vacancy. But that's right. The glass apple was left in the kitchen. She rushes down the hallway back to the kitchen, and the rose-covered teacup falls from her hand shattering into pieces on the floor.

The apple is gone.

CHAPTER FOUR

On Monday, Isabel wanders outside the cafeteria at Saint Dominica's, away from the tinkling spoons and the grating of chair legs, and into the courtyard for a smoke. At the sight of the familiar figure outside the gate, Isabel sucks in air, steadying herself against the balustrade. Easy does it, she tells herself, no sense in panicking. Nonna could be here for a variety of reasons. Surely it's about Isabel's unexplained absences from school, the telephone calls and letters that have gone unanswered, and nothing to do with the missing rosary.

Unlike the nuns who saunter and glide, attuned to a higher purpose, Nonna marches a brisk business pace through the main gates in her linen skirt and sensible lace-up shoes. Isabel continues to watch helplessly as her grandmother walks into the main lobby and the heavy doors close behind her.

Regardless, until Niccolo's crumpled note bounces off Isabel's leg, the hour hand on the wall clock in Sister Cecilia's class remains stuck in place for a good thirty minutes. She unfolds the scrap of paper, "Wait for me after class!" is printed in tiny block letters.

After the bell they linger in the crowded hallway.

"My nonna is here," Isabel whispers in Niccolo's ear, noting the edges of his cologne: cinnamon or maybe cardamom.

"So?" He is a monument to indifference.

"So, we could be in big trouble."

"We?" He is implacable. "Hey, are you in or what? The painting?"

She nods. "Yes, but I think you may have something of mine already, I mean my nonna's. The glass apple?"

His grin, white teeth and dimples, cuts her off. He squeezes her hand, his is cool against her clammy skin, the contact is electric, and all urgency melts away. "Let's talk later. Cinema Dante?" He calls back over his shoulder, a confident hitch in his step.

"I'm not kidding! She'll kill me if I don't get it back!" But he's too far ahead. She should run after him, insist he return the apple or else, she'll never speak to him again, she'll turn him in to the carabinieri and confess everything to Nonna and the sisters and to God. But her knees are putty and it's everything she can do not to collapse on the spot.

After school, Isabel is the coward for anyone and all to see walking down Calle dell'Ovo. At Ponte di Guglie a pair of seagulls perch on the dock posts like suspicious palace guards, and she savors the aroma of baking bread, never tires of it even as her boredom with the whole place has grown in recent months. The canals of Venice swarm with cruise ships full of tourists snapping family album photos, their eagerness to soak in all the sights a sharp contrast to her own wanderlust, the ever present desire to move to Paris. A desire that was crushed the day before yesterday when she asked Nonna for help with tuition and the flames were instantly doused with a word: no. Now there's no chance of bringing it up again: onceNonna finds out what's been stolen at home, Isabel will never hear the end of it. A solid cover story for the missing apple and cutting class is what she needs. As if those two things have the same weight; they don't, but either one is a definite step down from Valedictorian. Sister announced the names last week and Isabel won the coveted spot. She cannot pretend she isn't pleased.

Antonia's café is at the intersection of Rio Terra San Leonardo and Calle dei Preti, and Antonia is the queen of cover stories.

Not twenty yards ahead, a woman, wearing an ochre nubby wool sweater over a black crepe dress, lumbers toward her, her swollen ankles busting out of the thick-soled laced brown shoes. At her side, a wiry brown terrier the color of standing water pulls her along with his nose glued to the gutter: Signora Volterra, on her afternoon constitutional. Isabel hurries inside as Beppo drags his mistress past the café window, the old woman muttering, while the dog continues on his scent trail and strains at the leash, winding it tightly around the well curb. That was too close. Signora Volterra cannot be trusted not to blab. No one from the Ghetto would dare frequent the cafe, least of all Nonna, who finds it vulgar and prefers her Campo where the steady flow of familiar characters dominate: the rabbi's bearded unwashed brother who davens in the square, Signora Goldberg and her well-loved, egg-washed pastry.

Inside the café, the low din of conversation is punctuated by the occasional clatter of dishes. Two men in gray flannel jackets slouch over bowls of pasta fagioli and trade insults between mouthfuls. A woman in lined silk stockings, a strange choice for this heat, claims the last available table and with an angry gesture exiles Isabel to the one remaining counter stool. It's a quarter past three, according to the clock on the wall, and only a few minutes remain to beat Nonna home and help with dinner, but Antonia is nowhere to be seen. Suddenly, a thunder crack of raucous laughter erupts from the back room, and Antonia sweeps in, clearing dirty plates and pocketing the lire of a departing customer as she goes.

Catching sight of her friend, Antonia salutes her. "Isabel!"

"Antonia, hello." Isabel peels off her jacket, the familiar shyness descending. As always her friend insists on La Bise, and they kiss the air at either cheek. The oversized apron gathers the excess of fabric around Antonia's slender waist like twine wound tightly around a narrow bouquet of gardenias. Otherwise she smells of cooking grease and is not really pretty, not in the conventional sense: her eyebrows are too full, her cheeks too round and the jaw line too male and severe. Even her hands are far from dainty with the long fingers and gangly knuckles; but because she insists on wearing rubber gloves when washing stacks of dishes, her one concession to the feminine, her skin is soft as a lamb's; in all she is a coquettish tomboy like Pippi from the children's books. The two girls met only three months earlier on a rainy shopping day at the fish market, but have been inseparable ever since.

"What happened? You look like you swallowed a bee."

Still caught up in loud conversation, the two slouching men in the corner rise from their seats and throw crumpled bills on the table. "Thank you, gentlemen!" Antonia shouts after them. With her elbows resting on the counter, she cups her chin in her hands. "Okay, then. What is it? Tell me every little thing."

A heavy pan comes crashing down from the kitchen. Antonia holds up a warning hand and darts away to sort the problem; moments later she reappears with a rag, which she uses to polish the counter top. A clean spoon is set down in front of Isabel, and a small steaming cup, which splashes black coffee down the sides and into the saucer.

Isabel brings the demitasse close to her lips and blows the steam across the surface. Scalding. She sets the cup down. "I may have stolen something from school."

Antonia waits cautiously. "And?"

"And it belongs to the director."

"And?"

"And? And it's her fancy rosary. With rubies." She waits for a reaction. "Rubies!"

Antonia's puffed-out cheeks explode in a big stream of breath. "You, my young Jewish friend, are going straight to hell." She makes a swift sign of the cross.

"Yeah, that's exactly what he said."

"Of course that's what he said. He's right! Wait, who?"

"Niccolo." Isabel chews on a fingernail. "From Math class."

Antonia's laugh is all irony. "Of course. Niccolo from Math class."

Their game of dares was not supposed to go this way. First it was just for a laugh, hiding Sister Cecilia's megaphone and Niccolo running bare-chested through the courtyard after lunch, the lean muscles of his back rippling and not once getting caught. But he was never supposed to sneak into her flat. Nonetheless, Isabel's belly flutters at the memory of him in the kitchen, Nonna's rose-covered china teacup in hand.

Faced with her friend's ridicule, Isabel tries in vain to affect an air of seriousness. "You should see the rosary, it's really something."

"I'll bet." But far from approving, her friend's face is a mask of restraint, her lips morph into a thin straight line. "His idea?"

"Actually it was mine. Not bad, huh?" But the old surge of adrenaline isn't as quick to arrive, the pride of a few days ago is already wearing thin. Deflated, Isabel takes a sip of espresso and grimaces in pain, her lips burning. "He'd probably take credit for it. Although he was as surprised as you when I caught him in the parlor."

"Hold on." Her friend pinches the bridge of her nose with a thumb and forefinger. "Are you trying to tell me that this Niccolo from Math class broke into your flat?"

With fresh misery Isabel recounts the part about the missing apple, the discovery of the painting at home, and finally the sighting of Nonna at school. She drains the espresso all in one gulp like a shot of strong whisky. Ignoring her blistering tongue, she sets the demitasse down and feels oddly proud of herself.

"There's a painting?" Antonia refills Isabel's empty cup.

Isabel can scarcely believe it herself. If Niccolo hadn't told her he had stumbled across it, Isabel would never have suspected him of doing so. He had re-wrapped the canvas and stashed it back in Nonna's closet expertly. Selling it could yield a tidy sum of cash, he told her. Think what you could do with that money. She did. It would definitely be enough to live and study in Paris.

Antonia's eyes cloud over like they always do at the mention of the French capital. "Oh, Paris. My Papa used to take us to visit friends on Rue des Vinaigriers in the Tenth after the War. He always complained about the prices and the filth. But I loved it. The chic women, the Beaujolais, the music in the street along the canal. I told you, didn't I?"

"Yes, of course you did." Isabel taps her friend's arm warmly. Antonia has a tendency to repeat her stories endlessly like an old woman who chats incessantly while knitting and often forgets which bit she's already shared, a little tic that's easily forgiven. "Think about it: with that kind of money I could buy Nonna a new apple just like that." Isabel snaps her fingers. "And still have enough for tuition at the Sorbonne. Nonna refuses to pay."

"But stealing her precious painting?" Antonia raises an eyebrow.

Even if her friend disapproves, Isabel and every good reader of French literature knows that picaresque heroes survive by their wits and cunning, by seat-of-the-pants plans made on the spur of a moment. Clearly this painting in the closet had never seen the light of day; why should Nonna ever discover it was missing?

Unconvinced, the worry lines deepen in Antonia's forehead.

"Would it help if I were to tell you that Niccolo's father might know someone who can fence the painting?"

"And what does Niccolo's father want in return?"

Isabel shrugs. "I suppose he'll get something for his trouble."

"Indeed." Antonia smirks and undoes her braids; her loose hair wreathes her face in a halo of flyaway strands. "Like you're not the one taking all the risk here. I'll be honest with you Isabel," she gathers her hair back in one hand. "This isn't like pinching a little mascara."

"I know that!" Isabel continues to sip the espresso absently, bitterness pooling in her throat.

"And if this Niccolo is so great, why does he want to get you in trouble?"

"Couldn't I say the same about you?"

Antonia stiffens and Isabel regrets the question instantly. She would never fault her friend for initiating her into the five-fingered discount. Their forays into shoplifting have been some of the sweetest memories of her young life. "Of course I don't mean that."

"No, I suppose that's fair."

"Don't be silly."

"I'm just trying to watch out for you, you idiot."

"I know, I know." Isabel reaches out and briefly touches Antonia's arm.

"I mean, why do you think I pinched that blue dress by myself? Well now it's out." Antonia shakes her head. "I was going to give it to you as a surprise for your graduation. I can't have you getting in trouble with the law. Just tell Niccolo to give you back the apple and we'll all sleep better at night. And then return the damn rosary to Sister what's-her-name and everything will be hunky dory." Antonia claps her hands together like problem solved.

Isabel swallows hard but cannot budge the lump in her throat. The blue dress was a dream; she never thought she'd get to wear it again and as sweet as that was of Antonia to worry about her wardrobe, she should never have done it. Isabel grips the counter with both hands. "His name's Niccolo, and he's not a total fool. He reads. Books and everything. He asked me out to see the new Fellini."

"Tell me you didn't...."

"I said yes." There's no reason to feel guilty but somehow Isabel does.

"So because he's charming and fashionable and he reads, you're swooning? Why don't you just start saving that posh allowance of yours, instead of stealing your way into the big house."

"Big house?"

"I guess you don't read crime novels."

Isabel shrugs. Her allowance is far from grand, a few lire for chocolates and the vaporetto, but it's a few lire more than Antonia ever got from working at her father's café since the age of eleven. Isabel never should have mentioned it; it only made her look like a child.

"And what happened to my Valedictorian? The pride and joy of Saint Dominica's?" Antonia clicks her tongue derisively. "She can't be a felon as well, you know."

Isabel slumps down on the stool. Suddenly it all seems like a bad dream. Antonia never cared about Isabel's grades at school just as Isabel never cared that Antonia worked a boring job for a living and lived off the pocket change left on bistro tables. They had a deal. It was unspoken but nevertheless. It was true that they led different lives, and their prospects were completely separate and unrelated; but that was the beauty of their friendship, that they remained united in spite of their polarities.

The two friends sit silently, neither wanting to trouble the waters further. As the lunch crowd thins out, the woman in the mink stole lingers one last moment, the long arc of her cigarette ash suspended above an empty plate, and starts when a short man in a straw hat stands up unexpectedly. He catches his chair before it falls backward. A clatter of dishes once more from the kitchen is followed this time by the muffled sound of a man swearing.

"Well that's me, back to work." Antonia throws her dishrag in a bin of dirty dishes.

"Yeah. I should get home."

Antonia lifts the bin of dishes in her lean sinewy arms. "Hey, but what do I know? I didn't even finish high school. Thank you Signora!" Antonia's face transforms into sweetness as the woman in the floral dress adjusts her mink stole before leaving. "Anyway in the not so distant future you'll be living the life, right?"

"If you mean I'll be working as an office secretary, then yes, I certainly will."

If Nonna has her way, that's exactly what the future holds. How did they end up down this road? She shouldn't have mentioned Niccolo to Antonia. She is a fierce friend certainly and protective to a fault; but she never means any harm.

Her friend's gaze penetrates the chill between them and is ardent and bright when the younger girl finally looks up. "You know I'm just trying to help, right? Look if you want to go to that French school so badly then you will. Of course you will. Or another school, just as good. We'll find a way."

But Antonia doesn't realize. The Sorbonne is the only school Isabel has ever dreamed of, and always has, ever since primary school when Sister Agnes first mentioned it.

"This one is smart enough for the Sorbonne," the Sister said, and Isabel didn't know where that was exactly but from that moment on she was destined to go.

"You know what though? They may have music and Beaujolais and Camembert at your French school but they don't have me." Antonia winks.

"And I'll miss you like crazy."

"Just say the word, Signorina Lesser, and there's a job for you here."

Isabel smiles in spite of the pit in her stomach.

"What's so bad about working for a living?" Antonia pockets the change from an empty bistro table and slings the dripping rag absently over her shoulder; a wet spot widens on her blouse.

"Nothing." Isabel mustn't insult her, and lately lying has become as easy as drawing breath. "Don't you remember the last time?" Antonia had asked Isabel to help out at the café a month earlier, and she was left alone with Antonia's apron and order pad for an unbearable hour while her friend ran off without any explanation. The whole experiment was an unmitigated disaster. Not one customer received the right order and an old man received half a cup of espresso in his lap. No extra charge. How can Antonia not understand? Surely Niccolo's kiss is an invitation to a completely different perspective; a wider vista with an endless horizon line. How can the answer be anything else but yes to a life of sensual and intellectual pleasures? If working means anything other than writing or working in support of her writing, then the idea is unthinkable. "An artist's life is all I'm fit for really."

"But how will you eat?" Antonia's eyes are fierce and determined. "And who do you actually know in Paris that will feed you?"

It's not like Isabel hasn't asked herself the same question. For all she knows they may still have family left in the City of Light. Once or twice Nonna talked about an estranged friend who settled there later after the War but never gave a name. Otherwise, all that's been said about her late parents could be scratched on the back of a matchbook: her father was a piano prodigy and her mother his student, and that they both died young at Auschwitz right before the war ended.

At the clatter of pans once more from the backroom, Antonia unties her apron and tosses it on the floor. "Alright. Let's get out of here."

"But what about work?"

"How can I work with your face like that? Come on."

CHAPTER
FIVE

The meeting with Sister Angelica went on longer than expected and, by the time she arrives home, Lila is tired and peckish. Good God, but those Sisters loved the sound of their own voices, eternally droning on about this or that. Lila had sat semi-conscious in the director's study for a good five minutes of meaningless pleasantries, the cuckoo clock striking the hour in ridiculous dramatic fashion before the news finally came out: ten missed classes in as many weeks, Sister Angelica said. And then later in the vestibule, Lila heard the sisters whispering something about a missing rosary. Gone from the director's desk from one minute to the next and who would do a thing like that?

Inside the apartment now, she pulls back the heavy damask curtains and the late afternoon rays rush into the dining room. On the hutch, the morning newspaper has been left out, and she catches the headline in the giornale: the heiress Isadora Morgenfeld has moved back into the Palazzo di Beneficio. Lila's nose wrinkles in distaste at the grainy photograph of the limestone façade, two gargoyle masks affixed to the stone wall lining the Grand Canal. The first and only time she'd been asked to accompany

Albert to one of his art exhibitions, the celebrated heiress hovered near the great vase of orchids in the Gallerie dell'Accademia, her sanctimonious smile and white manicured hand offered in greeting in royal fashion. Isadora had oohed and ahhed at Lila's husband's every observation, declaring Albert Lesser a genius collector, as Lila demurred behind him in the lace and chiffon graciously on loan from Miriam, full of worry that her own silk stockings, just washed for the occasion, had sprung a run. In one meeting Lila had had more than her fill of that woman. The bluster, the extravagance. She was convinced that the citizens of Venice would fare better if the Palazzo were made into a museum for all to enjoy. Alas, that was not to be.

Lila slams the paper down and catches sight of the obituaries on the back page. A name jumps out from the rest: Stella Goldberg, age 60, died from natural causes. The baker's wife, proprietor of the only kosher bakery in the Campo, that surly woman whose nasty temper was well known in the quarter had passed from among them. May her memory be a blessing. Lila kisses her hand automatically and looks toward the ceiling. The baker's wife had survived the camps but her husband, an affable man with a sweet smile who was forced to put up with a difficult wife, wasn't so lucky. Lila shakes her head. There was nothing natural about Mrs. Goldberg. She always treated Lila and Leo with contempt, choosing the smallest of the challah breads to give them for the Sabbath and the rejects among the mandelbrot, the ones with hardly any raisins. But sixty isn't that old. Is it? Lila's own 60th is barreling toward her like a freight train this May. She scratches at the rash on her arm, little pink bumps that appeared weeks ago and never went away. She would pay her condolences to their grown son, Meier, who had taken over the bakery and continued to dole out their perfect challah. Yes. It was the right thing to do.

Lila glances at the dining room table. Isabel laid out the place settings in her typically rushed fashion that morning. Two china plates have been set out for Sabbath dinner without glasses, linen or silver, and something else is missing. The room is too white;

and there is an odd vacancy between the crystal vase and the candelabra. She scavenges inside the settee cupboard but comes up empty. Disoriented, she rests a hand against the chair back. The day the newly-weds first arrived in Venice, Lila's new husband presented her with the Murano green glass apple. Lila's young husband was especially coy that late April afternoon, his slicked hair glistening with pomade and his mustache neatly trimmed. They had spent a wonderful day, a picnic in the park with sparkling wine and cucumber sandwiches until it started raining and they ran back into town and ducked into the glass boutique off the square. "To our life together," Albert said, placing the sparkling green apple in the palm of Lila's hand and kissing her wet cheek. He was beaming with love for her and full of promises and Lila took him at his word. She meant to keep the harmony between them. If ever Albert was cross or withdrew to his study, she forgave him; he was a prodigy after all, as gifted in business as in arts and letters and was allowed his dark moods. She made his favorite meals, darned his socks and brought him his tea on a little Japanese tray. When the baby was born, she thought he would be pleased, but Albert barely held the colicky infant and soon began spending more time away on trips. Lila could not say when exactly her husband stopped loving her, but the chill between them grew like an advancing winter that never quite dissipated.

The apple was all that remained between them. If not for Miriam's opera patron friends who agreed to stash it in a palazzo attic on the Grand Canal, it would have vanished in all the looting.

Lila rushes down the hall, but nothing in the girl's bedroom appears to be out of the ordinary: the bed is made, the sheets pulled tightly, the pillow fluffed and the dresser dusted. The writing desk is tidy too. She pulls on the cord in the closet illuminating a single bare bulb overhead, and a dilapidated shoebox tips over from the shelf up above. Several small, unopened packages and a tangled knot of necklaces spill onto the floor. But not an apple among them.

"What's this about an art collection?" Isabel moves the potato around her plate as she glances at the newspaper headlines. She is skin and bones these days but not for lack of nourishment. Lila always prepares a good dinner, red meat usually and potatoes, boiled vegetables and sliced bread in the basket, like the French, with fresh butter.

"What now?" Lila raises her head from her own plate, distracted. She has no appetite, hasn't had one all day and this new interrogation from Isabel's isn't helping. "I'm sorry, but who told you that reading was allowed at the table?"

"But isn't that a photograph of grandfather?" Isabel points to the black and white picture of the heiress looking stately in her clumsy fashion next to a well turned-out man in a clever three-piece suit.

Lila's stomach turns at the sudden image of her husband. Albert was always impeccably tailored. But Albert's wardrobe is the last thing she needs reminding of. She flourishes the gold-flecked Kiddush cup in her hand. "Come now Isabel, have you really forgotten? These are strictly for the Seder. We never put them out for Shabbat." Since Albert died, they haven't hosted a Seder since, well Lila can't remember the last time, but still.

"Sorry, Nonna. My mistake."

"My mistake, my mistake. According to Sister Angelica, you've been making a few too many these days. Ten unauthorized absences Isabel? Ten?"

Isabel draws in a deep breath. "I can explain."

"Please." Lila waves away the attempt. One of the linen napkins has a wine stain and must be attended to immediately with a little seltzer water, and besides she doesn't care to listen to fiction. Rising from the table with the gravity of someone who has won this round, Lila takes the stained napkin to the kitchen with Isabel following close behind, still reading from the article from the paper.

"Signora Morgenfeld presides over one of the premiere collections of twentieth century art." Isabel stops mid-paragraph, her eyes wide. "I swear that that's grandfather."

Looking at any photograph of Albert is always a kick to the gut. Lila turns on the faucet at full blast and begins scrubbing at the stain on the linen napkin with gusto, spraying water onto her housecoat and drenching the linoleum. Yes, Albert collected only the best pieces, but, unlike that poseur of an heiress, he was never one to make a fuss. That long-ago evening at the soiree, Signora Morgenfeld peeled off a silk glove revealing immaculately manicured fingernails, polished delicate mother-of-pearl. Lila shuts off the faucet and assesses her own nails, bitten to the nub. She wrings out the linen napkin and hangs it on a little line outside the kitchen window. She has useful hands, has had them all her life. Strong knuckles and gnawed-down nails. Someone with such hands could never compete with the likes of a truly cultured person. After attending that first soiree with Albert, she never accompanied him again, preferring instead to install herself at home, keep the flat in perfect order and put their inquisitive little boy to bed. "Where is papa?" little Leo would ask and each time Lila would make a fresh excuse: Papa has a very important business meeting or he's having a drink with friends. She hated even mentioning the collection for fear the poison of Albert's passion would spread and Leo would become contaminated with it and cease loving her too. Why bother with a mother so plain and boring when one could stare at the beautiful art? Indeed, next to such exquisite gold-leaf frames hung in such rarefied settings as the heiress's palazzo, Lila faded into the cracked plaster. Surely Leo felt the same, what with her nagging him to practice the piano every afternoon (he should have one foot in Albert's cultured world) and her constant vigilance that he keep his stranger "interests" in check.

"Didn't grandfather collect art?"

"He did."

"So that is Albert in the picture!"

"What? Don't be absurd. Don't you have enough to worry about? Like that little shoebox? Hmm? The one in your closet? And the Sister mentioned a missing rosary too. What about that?"

"Shoebox?" Isabel's blank expression betrays nothing.

Lila slips a little on the wet floor as she barges past the girl and heads down the hall to her granddaughter's bedroom. Straining on tiptoes in Isabel's closet, she rummages around the top shelf. "But it was just here...I saw it!"

"Honestly Nonna, I have no idea what you're on about."

And there it was. Her granddaughter's little tell. Lila cannot count the number of times Leo began his lengthy explanations with just such words: honestly Mama, I never touched that kid in class. He hit me! And later to visit the headmaster's office and there his little classmate sat, a shiner and a fat lip and the mother fuming. It was nothing you could smile and nod away to the neighbors, or blame on an adolescent phase. Leo's impulses were constant and intractable. And Albert, as ever, was no help. After the umpteenth incident of his son beating up a child at school, he never bothered looking Lila in the eye. When Leo brought home little Ilse, only just fourteen, Albert said: "Honestly Lila I don't know how you can look in the mirror" and walked out of the room. Honestly...Well, the truly honest have no need to begin their sentences with such a word. And anyway what could she have done? I love her, Leo said, and there was no reasoning with him.

Lila opens her mouth to speak and then thinking better of it, says nothing. The girl tries her patience like no one else since Leo, but in spite of everything, she longs for nothing more than to help save Isabel from herself, from the rotten strand in their Ashkenazi ancestry. Something she could never succeed in doing with Leo.

"You only notice the bad, Nonna, never the good." Isabel frowns but stops when Lila glares at her.

"I notice the good. I notice. I've been very happy with your accomplishments at school, Isabel. I encourage you to keep up the studying even after you graduate. While you're working. It's only reasonable."

"While I'm working?" The girl's face falls. "But what kind of life is that?"

A decent life, Lila wants to say, a real one, but something in the girl's expression is too sad, too forlorn and Lila holds back. "Come on. Earning your living is not so bad."

Isabel's mouth is a thin line. "That's what Antonia said."

"Who?"

Isabel just shakes her head at the question. As impenetrable as ever.

"Well, my little shop has been a godsend." Only this isn't quite true. Not recently anyway. There's no use pretending: she's never had a head for business. That was Albert who was both charming and adept at math. In the meantime, Lila has over-ordered again, and ten boxes filled with reams of paper and pens lie untouched in the store aisles, while sales this season have been lethargic at best. With bills from the business mounting and vendors to pay, Lila has had to economize in little ways, nothing Isabel would notice. A chicken instead of a roast for Shabbat, fresh bread every two days instead of each morning. It's just a little bump in the road. That's what Lila wants to believe. She bites at the tip of her nubby fingernail, a small bad habit that grandmother and granddaughter share, and winces a little when she goes too deep. A drop of blood springs to the surface of her calloused fingertip. Albert always said that she was too enamored with her own pain, that she reveled in it. But Lila doesn't believe it. Not really. It was always simply there, the pain, parked in the rain like a stalled-out car. Not going anywhere. It was the terrible ache in her knees when she descended the staircase and the tightening in her shoulders when she hoisted the little fishnet shopping sack at the market. A bit of discomfort in the space between the joints, in the space between the frightening scenes from long ago that still niggled at her every day. Surely it was far better to play at catastrophe than to be genuinely caught up in it.

"Are we wealthy then?" The girl is relentless tonight, trained on Lila like a floodlight on an escaping inmate in the yard.

"Wealthy?" Lila huffs. "Not likely. Look, if you won't finish your dinner, at least help me clear the table." She grabs her granddaughter's untouched plate while Isabel begins collecting the dirty silver. Before the Germans came to ransack their flat in the Cannaregio, Lila, Albert, Miriam, Leo and the young Ilse went into hiding within the Italian countryside where a farmer acquaintance of the heiress's hid them and Albert's precious collection in a secret cellar beneath the stables. For weeks, they breathed in stale air and survived on gray potato soup and bread crusts. The darkened space smelled of mold and horse dung, and anywhere Lila has gone since, the acrid fecal odor has followed. No. Isabel doesn't need to know about the collection. Albert entrusted Lila to safeguard it and that's what she has always done. You must show them but never sell them, Albert said long before the SS discovered her and the others pale as ghosts beneath the horse stalls. Stupid soldiers. They never did find the paintings. One small bright light. Afterwards when they were separated on the cattle cars heading east, Lila never saw Albert again. She had only her dear friend Miriam by her side, and now her own withering body and those bloody paintings. And Lila hasn't sold the art, not ever, not even to repay her business debts, but she hasn't shown the collection either, having wrinkled her nose at each museum offer, the phone calls and handwritten letters. What does she know about the art world? She couldn't tell a Kokoschka from a Schiele. She would be in over her head. Always has been.

Lila scrapes the untouched plate of food into the bin under the kitchen sink. Everyone had thought her too ignorant and too plain to marry into the great, renowned Lesser Family. And yet. Albert had married her. Why exactly, she had never understood. Perhaps because her figure was trim in those days with a bit of curve at the hip, and her smile was kind, or so she was told. She pauses for a moment to hear the girl's shuffling from the dining room as she sullenly gathers the cutlery. Well, whatever Isabel is up to, her sudden interest in the art is both new and troubling. Up until now, her granddaughter has never been the wiser, too caught up in adolescent drama to understand that, in a sense, they're sitting on a fortune, and standing on a legacy.

With the last plate cleaned and put in the dish drainer, Lila wipes her hands on her housecoat and sits down heavily on the little wooden chair. A strange thing to be both wildly rich and hopelessly destitute, and all in one endless afternoon. Elbows resting on the kitchen table she cradles her head, rubs at her temples, but no quick remedy to her troubles is forthcoming. Well. The time has come to make some decisions. Surely if the Morgenfeld woman hadn't reared up again, Lila could have put off any plans for the bloody paintings even longer. It was like an ongoing bad dream.

The daisies in the pitcher in front of her are dead and wilting. Lila pokes at one and rusty yellow petals rain down on the kitchen table. After the war, only Lila and Miriam emerged with the baby Isabel, everything and everyone else having been scattered to oblivion. And now, seventeen years later, the Lesser Collection lies dormant, all but two Titians still unaccounted for. But it wasn't the Germans who took them. The culprit has always been obvious since all of the solicitor's letters to the heiress went unanswered and returned unopened. Lila unclenches her fist to find Isabel's uneaten piece of challah bread. She pops the crust of bread into her mouth and without chewing, gulps it down. And now that awful Mrs. Goldberg has passed away. Lila scratches at the itchy rash on her forearm and pulls down the sleeve of her sweater. Well, there's an end to waiting. Incomplete or not, the collection must be shown. It was time. Lila would not fail Albert in death as she had in life.

She startles at a sudden tinkling noise: Isabel standing in the doorway with a fistful of silverware and the newspaper folded in half. A little sneer at the lips, her hips jutting out like a public school girl, the girl is impertinence itself.

"I have a right to know if we own an art collection."

"A right to know?" Lila rises from the table. She throws out the wilting flowers from the pitcher and pours the rancid water down the sink. "From where I stand, you don't."

Isabel's expressions shifts. "I didn't mean that I had a right, exactly. I simply want to know more. About our family, I mean. Don't you think I should?"

"Don't you have homework to finish?"

"It's not due til Monday." Isabel pouts.

Lila waves her off. The sighing and carrying on. The girl is nothing if not dramatic.

"Fine. But you still owe me my allowance this week." Isabel covers her mouth but it's too late. "Nonna, I didn't mean it like that."

"I owe you?" The heat from Lila's itchy arm travels upward and a warm pulse strobes in her neck. To think of everything she's given her granddaughter, a home, a safe school, life itself, for God's sake. "How ungrateful... "

"I'm sorry," Isabel wails.

"And now stealing from the nuns!"

"I'm not! I mean I haven't! Honestly."

Yes. Honestly. The girl's acting is good, to the point of conjuring the appearance of tears. "And please tell me where you have put my Murano glass apple. Apparently it's vanished into nowhere."

From the foyer comes the crisp call of the telephone. Lila answers it on the third ring. "Hello?"

"Lila?" Miriam sounds breathless. In the background there's the ambient crackle of tourists and the bright church bells of San Marco.

"Oh Miriam!"

"Did you forget—"

"Of course not! I'm on my way!"

Lila never ventures out at night, with her nighttime myopia and unease in crowds, so when her friend first brought it up, the rendezvous at the café seemed like a distant possibility, something they would never have to actually make good on. Miriam was more mysterious than usual, hinting only that it was a special occasion but wouldn't say more. Usually Lila could read her like a book. Not this time. But she had agreed anyway even though it was Erev Shabat. Oh, who was she kidding—Lila was never that observant, only putting on the spectacle for Albert's well-to-do family.

"I'm hanging up now, Miriam!"

In the foyer, Isabel blinks up at her expectantly. "Would you like me to mop the floor?"

"Just finish your homework." Lila rushes past toward her bedroom. She'll need to change, put on some lipstick, fix her chignon. She cannot be seen in a housecoat all her life. The vanity mirror catches Isabel hovering in the doorway. "The dishes have been washed, Isabel, you'll just need to dry them." Lila sighs: her closet is full of absolutely nothing to wear. She must rummage through the dresser instead.

"Where are you going? Nonna?"

Lila stops in her tracks and turns around to face her granddaughter. "How about this? I'll answer your questions when you decide to answer mine."

CHAPTER SIX

The stalls of the Campo della Pescheria market, usually crammed with piles of cod and sea bass—their silvery skin shimmering, their indifferent eyes trained on the curious droves of shoppers–have been washed clean with a garden hose, and are now vacant with not even a fish bone left behind. The vendors' tables are bare: gone is the impressive ziggurat of neatly staggered fillets destined for the stew pot; the smell of sawdust and brine all but eradicated. Lila walks through the empty space of what would have been an animated crowd of white-haired ladies clutching baskets and netted shopping bags, pushing relentlessly toward the fishmonger's table. She had missed her chance to shop that morning, all that to-do with Isabel's school hadn't left time for much else, and she feels suddenly gutted like the fish, drained like the watering can on the kitchen windowsill. She should never have agreed to an evening out, but it's too late: at the center of the piazza a tall elegant woman waves vigorously at her. Lila waves back, more of a twitch of the hand, really; Miriam is overly dramatic with her greetings. Always has been. And she hasn't aged much since before they remained glued to each other's side on trains bound for Auschwitz. Today, as ever, Miriam's Valentino skirt suit and lilac silk blouse is tailored and impeccable, her dyed hair red and glossy as robin's feathers, although a bit receding around the temples; even as a girl she had a French duchess' upwardly migrating hairline. The two women have known each other since primary school in Lublin, since the day the schoolmistress marched a tow-headed Miriam into the classroom and sat her down, sniffling, in the empty seat next to Lila. The two girls became instant friends.

"How was the white fish today?" Lila can think of nothing else to say and kisses Miriam on both cheeks.

Her friend shrugs. "The market was an absolute zoo. I left after two minutes. Shall we?"

Arms linked, they head into the smallest of the bistros overlooking the piazza. The light is weak but they find a table and sit down. Miriam motions for the waiter, a little bird-like man in a cummerbund and bow tie who acknowledges them with a flourish of his hand.

"So. You sounded so mysterious before." To be fair, Miriam always sounds that way on the phone. Lila stuffs her graying gloves in her purse, glad to be rid of them while her friend unbuttons her jacket at the neck and reclines on the banquette. Her friend tries to signal the waiter again but misses him on his way past. Caffè Florian used to be Lila's favorite before the war, but now it's tables and chairs, shoddy at that, too many Americans and inattentive service.

"Unseasonably warm today, wasn't it?"

This is how they always begin: Miriam insists on small talk: excruciating minutia about the weather, her latest couture purchase (a two-tone Vuitton purse), and the like. Lila sighs heavily. It's all pretense, this attempt at being quaint, civil, a part of the quotidian. After the war she could only go through the motions, smoothing starched white tablecloths at home and arranging doilies at the backs of armchairs, all the while, the bombs continued to go off down every pleasant street and always at the corner of her eye the splinter of the barbed wire fence trailed her. She never thought she'd hum a popular tune again, let alone sing a full-throated song. But Miriam, a contralto at Il Fenice in her younger days, never stopped singing afterwards. How quaint, Lila would think each time, when what she really wished was that Miriam would shut up and cut out the endless pretense, the living as though nothing of import had ever happened to them. Something had really happened. It really had.

"Hasn't it?" Miriam eyes Lila as though she's a ghost hovering above the table and not sitting across from her at the overpriced tourist bistro.

"Hasn't what?" The light is weak and the little candle-lit tables are filled with animated diners clinking glasses, celebrating, always celebrating, something, anything, God-knows-what. Lila picks up her steaming teacup but hesitates to sip, too hot; she'll scald herself.

"I was just saying how lovely it is to see you and hasn't it taken too long to make this happen?"

They were always telephoning, making plans, more often broken than not and, it was true, usually by Lila who had been finding it more and more treacherous to venture out, even in the campo.

"Yes, yes you're quite right, Mim." Lila stares dejectedly at her napkin, uncertain of how to bring up the subject of the paintings. Maybe Miriam hasn't seen the paper, the article about that insipid old what's-her-name. But Lila should bring it up, the subject, Miriam has connections to the art world and might know a trustworthy curator. It doesn't help that she'll need to ask for a loan to pay for the curator. Not that Miriam would refuse, but the shame of it. No. It doesn't help at all.

"Well don't worry! You look positively aghast! I only meant how lovely it is to spend time again. You know, just the two of us. How long has it been? Weeks? A month? So much has happened. I suppose that's why I insisted we have tea."

"Well, out with it then." Lila smiles weakly and pushes the steaming saucer away. Miriam should go first, she has been pressing Lila to meet up for days.

"Let's order something to eat first." Miriam lifts a slender hand to attract the waiter once more. "Yoo hoo!" She gestures sweetly, but playing demure simply will not do.

"Signor!" Lila barks and the waiter stops dead in his tracks. They are never used to it, these little men: the authoritative voice of a woman.

"A moment please, Signora." Disgruntled, he dispatches steaming bowls of seafood stew to a group of Americans erupting in laughter.

How pointless it all is. Lila has no appetite for conversation or the frivolous gaiety of strangers. There are things Lila must discuss with Miriam, but lacks the courage. She is a giant sack of nothing in her waist-less dress and too-large sweater.

The evening synagogue service has let out in the piazza, and through the windows a cluster of men in black suits and flat wide-brimmed hats clamor, their curled side-locks frame pale bearded faces.

"Finally." As the waiter arrives, Lila slaps the menu down on the table.

"Signora?" He waits without pad or pencil for their order.

Lila dares not order the prosciutto even though she is tempted to each time they go out. She may not observe the kosher laws but eating pork is out of the question. "The cheese plate please, signor, and a sparkling water."

"And the insalata for me." Miriam hands the waiter her menu. "Oh, and an espresso please."

"But you'll never get to sleep!"

"So?" Miriam giggles like a little girl with a secret.

"Honestly, Miriam."

"I know. I know. All in good time." Miriam removes a compact mirror from her purse.

"Well, you eat like a bird. That hasn't changed." In the camp food was all they used to dream about. At least Lila did. If Miriam had been fashionably thin before the war she became gaunt later on. Lila gave her half her rations just to keep her alive.

"What? I ordered a salad." Miriam dabs at her lipstick with her pinkie in the compact mirror.

"Yes, a salad." Lila pouts. Doesn't it ever get old, this desire to be pretty? She cannot be bothered anymore; but secretly she misses the days when it took little to no effort to turn a young man's head. She would emerge from her father's little house in Lublin and pass through the garden gate to be greeted with approving stares in the road, her curvy figure accentuated by the little wool coat, a subtle grin at her lips as though to say, "yes you may admire."

"Don't you remember?" Miriam fluffs the silk flowery cravat tied in a loose knot around her neck. "My birthday gift from you last year."

"Is it?" Lila absently butters a crust of bread from the basket. "I think Isabel has been stealing from me." Her pronouncement sounds less like conjecture and more like a verdict.

"I'm sorry?"

"The Murano is missing."

"The Murano...you mean the green apple?"

Miriam pulls at the end of her scarf and it falls open. The skin on her neck is lined with wrinkles like taffeta. But it's true: everyone, even Miriam, is growing old. How could they ever be the same people from before? Hurtling through the same universe, living out the same lifetimes? That this old frumpy Lila was the very same young girl with a handsome wealthy husband and a shiny glass apple? That life was ever sound and sure? It isn't possible. Yet there Miriam is, ordering a salad with herring.

"Albert must be rolling over! And you really think that Isabel—"

"Yes."

Miriam's eyes squint in concern. "But why?"

Lila shrugs. "Who knows why teenagers do what they do? Did I tell you I found Sartre under her bed? Not the philosopher, obviously. His book."

Miriam giggles. "Were you snooping again?"

"That's not the point. It was Sartre, Miriam. Who has time for ennui and nothingness? This generation is spoiled with luxury."

The waiter shows up again, this time with a tray. Limp lettuce leaves hang over the edge of Miriam's plate.

"And my espresso?" Miriam asks too late. The waiter has darted away once more.

"I found a stash of costume jewelry and cosmetics in her closet. I mean unopened packages."

"You didn't!"

"I'm telling you, Mim, it is very likely that our Isabel is a thief. I would never allow her to wear make up." There's more besides, but Lila hesitates to share it: just the other day while sorting through the laundry, there was the pungent scent of men's cologne like ripe onions on Isabel's school blouse, the same fragrance that lingered on Albert's collar after his museum galas, and under Isabel's bed along with the indulgent Sartre there were two smutty French poetry books with dirty pictures scrawled in the margins. Lila takes a long drink of sparkling water and sets down the glass, eyes fixated on the bubbles ascending upwards in long straight lines.

"Do you think, Lila," Miriam is careful with her words, "it might have something to do with school?"

Please, not again. "And why should it?" Lila tires at the prospect of having to entertain for the umpteenth time her line of reasoning for sending Isabel to Saint Dominica's.

"She's forced to play the part, isn't she? Pretending to be the good little Catholic girl with all those nuns running around."

"She has it far better than you or I ever did." Lila wrings the napkin. She and Miriam are walking miracles, the sturdy weeds that somehow pushed through the dead Polish soil. Isabel, on the other hand, would never have made it out. And if it were to happen again (and who could say it wouldn't) then Saint Dominica's was the only solution, and a clever one at that. Lila always said: better a Catholic granddaughter than a dead one. She pats the sheen of perspiration on her upper lip with her napkin. "Anyway I'm not a fool, Miriam."

"Of course not Lila."

"Our good little Catholic has been cutting classes. And it's something more. I just don't know what yet." Lila shrugs; talking about it is no help at all. "So." She pushes away the untouched cheese plate. "What's your big news?"

Miriam leans back and breaks into a wide grin. "It's not a 'what,'" she refills her water glass and Lila's as well. "It's a 'who.'

The Dorsoduro is strange at this hour, at any hour really; every time Isabel's visited, the houses have their shutters closed and their curtains fastened and always seem to be looking in the other direction as if anything could happen and all of it would go unnoticed. Against the late evening chill, she buttons up her sweater. The last time at the chemist's, she forgot to mention Niccolo's invitation to Antonia who, she's sure, would have had an opinion or two. Her friend, she's been surprised to discover lately, seems to have a jealous streak, and their last heist was less than exciting, yielding more lipstick tubes in Antonia's pocket than she'll ever use and not one new thing in Isabel's pocket just her house key.

Standing in front of an old, dilapidated house, gray paint peeling and roof shingles hanging sideways, Niccolo waves her over, and a familiar shade of embarrassment descends. Why would he ask her out on a date and then have her meet him at home? But his bluster had allowed for few questions. "Seventeen Rio Terà Canal," he said in the hallway outside of math class, which was halfway across town from the movie theater, but she agreed nonetheless. With his posture slumped, Niccolo appears unusually small, his back to the rundown house. Out front, a group of workers are digging up the gutter and making a racket the likes of which she has never heard of in the Campo. The noise of the drill rattles her eardrums. Perhaps it was stupid to be so agreeable.

"Hey. You made it." Niccolo says over the din. He holds open the front door for a hirsute stocky man who moves slowly past them; the same little man who was in front of the school the other day. He has on an oil-stained sleeveless T-shirt, the kind gardeners ball up on the floor for their wives to wash, and his arms are pale and pudgy as though not quite used to heavy lifting. A bulky parlor chair follows in his wake: he plops it down next to the widening hole in the sidewalk. At the armrests and along the sides of the once regal chair, the periwinkle blue silk upholstering is shredded, the telltale sign that a cat has claimed it for its own. He sits down with a grunt, his cold black eyes assessing Isabel from beneath a slouchy cap. A long raised scar twists the length of his cheek like a river.

"Papa, this is Isabel."

"Who's that now?" The man's natural volume, a thunderous smoker's voice, pierces the ruckus.

"That girl I told you about. With the Lessers."

The man's face clouds over for another moment, a deep crease in the bridge of a wide bulbous nose. Absently, as though his arm has a mind of its own, he begins pecking the finish off one leg of the chair with a small pocket knife, one cut after another.

"Take it back this way!" The workman in cover-alls directs the slow moving excavator digging a three-foot wide crater at their doorstep.

"No, back the other way, Graziano!" Niccolo's father swings around in the chair and attempts to light the old cigar stub perched on his thick brownish bottom lip. "I don't authorize any of it!"

"You don't need to, Gritti. This is from the city." The man in coveralls waves the work slip in the air. "The pipes are old. You're lucky we're replacing them."

"And how am I supposed to concentrate?" Signor Gritti points to the litter of chair arms, legs, seat backs and gray stuffing scattered across the stones in front of the house. In the window is a faded sign Gritti Upholstering. He inhales deeply on the cigar but no smoke comes out. He turns toward Niccolo. "So you're going to fill me in?"

"Papa, I told you."

"You told me. You told me a lot of things. I'm a man of action. What have you got to show me?"

"A painting. She's got a painting."

"Is that so?" He turns to Isabel who shivers in her buttoned-up sweater, her stomach sinking. She should have guessed as much. Of course this was not going to be just a date.

"Actually it's just my—,"

"It's just what?" The stocky man shakes his head slowly.

"We have a plan, remember?" Niccolo glances over at Isabel, desperate.

"You better not be winding me up, Nico." Snorting, the man gets to his feet quickly, pulling baggy trousers up over a stout middle. "And as for you, Graziano, my man at city hall will hear about it!" He coughs up a wad of spit and sends it flying just missing the foreman's shoulder.

"Gritti, you son of a bitch!" The foreman gestures back rudely.

His father leading the way, Niccolo takes Isabel by the hand into the darkened anteroom and in spite of it all: the drawn curtains, the unconscionable odor like unwashed armpits and days-old cooking, Isabel recedes into his warmth.

Signor Gritti turns on the light: a gold velvet couch, covered in plastic and piles of newspapers that extend over the cushions, sits in the middle of the room, along with all manner of detritus: broken frames, mangled arm rests, chair legs, dirty clothing, and unwashed cooking pots. All of it littering a threadbare Persian rug. In the corner a stiff gray mouse is stuck in a trap, dead for days; there's no cat anywhere in sight.

"So?" Signor Gritti forces a lopsided smile like a man with better things to do and stubs out his still-unlit cigar in an overflowing ashtray.

Isabel shakes the pudgy hand extended to her, brownish skin like the stain on his lips. The sinking feeling is not to be ignored; surely Niccolo feels it too, though perhaps he's grown used to it.

"What have you brought me?"

"No papa. I wanted you to meet her first."

He puffs air, dejected.

"Sir?" Isabel avoids eye contact: the blacks of his eyes are more menacing than the stench, which wasn't as noticeable outside.

"This painting, you have it or not?" He taps his boot, old scratched leather, shoelaces missing, something you might find in a garbage heap.

Niccolo gestures emphatically. Isabel reads his eyes: Tell him, tell him what you have.

"Look, you're good at math, right? You have a painting, I make you money; you don't, and my boy here just lied to me." He turns to Niccolo, pocket knife in hand and traces a line down his son's cheek. "You must really want us to look alike, huh son?"

"I..." Niccolo's face is flushed, no answer at the ready.

Gritti laughs an off kilter laugh. "I'm kidding! Niccolo tell her." He nudges his son.

"I have a painting," Isabel says without thinking any further.

"Good." Gritti's smile dries up. "Now let's talk."

"His name is Carlo. Carlo Bianchi." Miriam lights a cigarette and holds her breath.

It's not as though Lila hasn't been expecting something equally ludicrous but her belly contracts from the impact all the same. She searches her purse for a tissue, playing for time. "You were saying?"

Miriam blots her lips on the napkin, leaving a raspberry lipstick stain. "Isn't this silly! I don't know why my heart is pounding so."

Lila snaps her purse closed in frustration. It was always the same story with Miriam. And always about a man.

The espresso finally arrives and Miriam stirs the demitasse with the little silver spoon, breaking the coffee's oily blue-black surface before taking a sip.

A boyfriend at Miriam's age? Lila bristles. But there it is, unmistakable, the sparkling eyes, the little singsong in the voice, her gestures even more dramatic than usual: her dear friend has for the millionth time fallen in love.

"That's not even the big news. Lila–" Miriam pauses for dramatic effect, "he's asked me to marry him."

Lila's hands clench. Of course he has. Miriam is the perfect mark for just this type of con artist.

"Did you hear me?" Miriam returns her cup to its saucer with solemnity, her long slender neck bare like a Modigliani without the scarf, her lips pinched and thin even with lipstick.

"Yes Mim. I'm only taking it in."

It was bound to happen. Even at Auschwitz, Miriam was always too quick to trust. When she was shorn like the other prisoners, the fuzz of her auburn hair still glowed strawberry-blonde in the sunlight, and the guards laughed and said she could pass for Aryan. She soon became the commandant's pet.

"Please, Lila. The suspense! Tell me what you think!"

But it's obvious what Lila thinks, ridiculously so. Miriam doesn't need another husband. It's only been three short years since the last one. And he would have frittered away all of her savings on gambling if he had been able to stay away from the liquor cabinet. In any case, Miriam was spared when he drank himself to death, and there was still enough savings from her years singing at the Opera and the reparations from the Polish government to carry on.

"But your nest egg!"

"What? Don't be silly! Money is not at issue, Lila: Carlo is retired with a good pension."

Lila shrugs; she would die for a savings account that was not tied up in the exigencies of her husband's estate. And she, herself, has never seen one penny of reparations from the Poles, not even after years of pleading her case. If Miriam didn't choose to ruin her own life with unscrupulous men, she could be quite financially comfortable indeed.

"What does he do? Or what did he do?"

"He was in the shipping industry."

Shipping. Lila wrinkles her nose. The omens pointing to her tragedy with Albert are inescapable, but you cannot explain what sight is like to the blind. She stiffens at the flash of light from the diamond on Miriam's finger. "Oh, but you haven't said yes! This Carlo person is no more than a stranger!"

"I have, and I'm ecstatic, thank you very much." Miriam offers a better view of the ring to Lila, the diamond glinting pink and blue in a shaft of sunlight. "Honestly I feel like I've known him all my life."

"You always say that, Mim."

Miriam slumps in the chair, the flowery scarf falls from her lap. "I'll be sixty-five in a week, Lila. Sixty-five. I don't remember the last time I received a proposal of marriage. Do you?" The question hangs in mid air, and the hair at the nape of Lila's neck prickles. "Oh Lila! You know I meant nothing by that!"

"You needn't bother, Mim, no offense taken." Lila huffs. "I'm simply asking you to consider the seriousness."

"You don't think I have?"

Lila waves the smoke away from Mim's cigarette. A mind that's already made up is not worth wasting time on. Experience is an exacting teacher, handing out each lesson one student at a time. In her own case, once Albert realized that the Lila he had rescued was an administrative assistant from the university and not a cum laude graduate, their rose-colored glass apple days were over. Nevertheless, he still expected his dinner served by five thirty sharp, his shirts steamed and pressed and laid out for that evening's party.

Miriam stands up and pushes her chair toward the table. “Well, I love Carlo. And he loves me.”

Lila watches her friend walk to the powder room. Long and lithe even in her sixties, she would have an almost youthful gait if not for the subtle limp, a souvenir bullet from the Gestapo’s raid on their Polish village. But love? Please. Love was the least of things; love was a whim like choosing a nail color or a stylish pair of shoes. And Miriam was a dear, dear woman, more sister than friend and generous to a fault, but somehow, she had lived this long without understanding that the aftermath of a betrayal in love never fully goes away, not really. Once hung out to dry in the public square, there is no moving on from the humiliation. No one, unless by absolute necessity, and least of all a very sensitive person, should enter into the bonds of holy matrimony. Lila should know, she had spent a lifetime finding out.

Cinema Dante is cavernous and cool; mildew leaks through the porous wall it shares with the pub next door and the air is stale with alcohol and old spirits. A few more moviegoers file in for the last show of the evening. She and Niccolo settle on two seats at the center of the fifth row, too close for Isabel’s taste, but Niccolo happily sinks into the crushed velvet of the seat, motioning for her to do the same. The last time she visited the theater was years ago when Nonna brought her to see an old Hollywood picture with a starlet who giggled all the way through her own performance, and they shared a popcorn. Isabel’s stomach growls, but she has no appetite for food. Not after seeing that house. But here the two of them are, somehow extricated from that frightening hovel, somehow on a date.

A hollow sort of silence separates them. The top three buttons of Niccolo’s school shirt are unbuttoned and a small pendant hangs from a little chain: orange gold.

"Saint Anthony." Niccolo notices her attention. "Do you like it?"

Isabel shrugs; she prefers not to flatter. Boys like Niccolo receive more than their share of compliments. How inconceivable and how at odds with the world that such a boy could come from such a father. Signor Gritti was not only a smelly troll, but a tyrant as well. And yet. The glow of the heavy, gold medal against Niccolo's bare chest, his collarbone defined even in shadow.

"You don't believe in the saints?"

"I don't know." But in fact, she didn't. According to Nonna, the Jews have always had troubles and yet no saints ever interceded for us.

"It's my father's. Saint Anthony's the patron saint of lost things."

Isabel re-imagines the piles of stuff in that room, like endless monuments to chaos. "Seems like your father's found a good deal more than he's lost."

"That's because he's a collector."

And so is his son, she thinks, although she hadn't spied the missing glass apple amidst the scatter of debris.

"Something you want to ask?"

She shakes her head, not wanting to remind him of his theft. Not yet.

"Look. I'll go get us some popcorn."

When he returns, she smiles in appreciation as he hands her the little bag, but doesn't eat one kernel. His Roman nose in profile is that of the leading man, and she can never eat with a handsome boy watching. An old gentleman in a fedora makes his way down the row and slumps down in the seat directly in front of her without removing his hat. The lights go down, and the opening credits of Rossellini's Open City flicker on the screen. From the first moment, she is enthralled, as the film's shadows dance like bird's wings across Niccolo's white shirt. At this, her very first Rossellini, all the worry about Nonna's apple, the painting, or the uncertain prospect of walking the boulevards of Paris evaporate, and the memory of their first kiss in the parlor envelops her, the taste of cinnamon and cloves, the force of his lips against hers, as if to say take this, take more. More is what she desires, at least she thinks she does. At night in bed it comes on strong, in fact, she cannot remember what life was like before this urgency, before she had the constant wetness in her underpants at the mere thought of a certain boy, and seeing him in person, and this close, is almost intolerable. She tenses, pulls away. She is here for another reason too. Gritti had said to bring the painting by tomorrow. It was obvious that the crazy old man would think nothing of hurting Niccolo if he didn't get his way, and she cannot let that happen. Her hand softly brushes against Niccolo's on the armrest, and in the darkened theater she cannot tell if it's his arm exactly or the light grain of the velvet upholstery, until his fingers curl around hers. He leans in, a lock of hair falling across his eyes, it's silk against her cheek. The salty taste of his mouth is there once again, familiar, wonderful. She kisses him back, slowly, languorously. For the moment nothing else matters, and she will find a way to accomplish the challenge set before her. Somehow, she will have to smuggle the canvas out of the house and bring it to Gritti by tomorrow, this coveted painting that may not even be authentic, and all without Nonna catching on. She almost laughs. Impossible. Impossible she thinks, twisting towards Niccolo, impossible, as she moans a little, a familiar sound, not movie kisses this time but real ones that blend in with the action on the screen. Niccolo's tongue caresses first her lips and then plays along the inside of her open mouth as if to say anything, anything is possible, my love. She closes her eyes and floats in dark flickering space.

When Miriam returns, her rose bonbon lipstick is refreshed, a garish pink that brightens her lips at the cost of her complexion, which suffers in contrast. She drains the cup of cold espresso, leaving traces of rose bonbon at the rim. "I should tell you that

Carlo is taking me to Greece." She glances up at Lila warily. "For our honeymoon."

Lila stares through the plate glass windows of the bistro: the seawall frames the square, and the clouds hang heavy, white tufts of wool against azure blue. As she watches, a gull bullies a flock of pigeons feasting on scattered bread crumbs along the balustrade, before taking off in a great cackle of flight.

"I've told Carlo so many things about you." Miriam places her hand gently on Lila's fingers resting on the table. "That you're my best friend. That you saved my life more than once. That without you—," she trails off.

"You've gone outside the line a bit." Lila points to her own lips, the red stain of her lipstick is cracked and faded, but Miriam presses a handkerchief against her eyes instead.

"Are you all finished, Signora?" Hovering by their table once again, the waiter points to the untouched plate of cheese.

"Please."

The waiter picks up Lila's plate first, then Miriam's, and balances them both skillfully on his forearm. "And we'll take tea as well." With an officious nod he turns and snakes back through the crowd.

The voice of the man at the table next to them rises above the fray. "I never thought I'd live to see it: Eichmann executed. Can you imagine? The architect of the final solution, hanged!" There are gasps and headshakes all around. But hanging was too good an end for such a man. Lila fumes silently. That monster would have stolen all of Albert's paintings if they hadn't taken so much trouble to hide them. She glances at her watch, and impatiently smoothes her chignon before clearing her throat.

"I have something to ask, Mim." Lila's hand trembles a little. This should not be so difficult. She curls her fingers in her lap. "You know that the subject of the art collection is not an easy one."

"I know that, Lila."

"Well I have something to ask you."

"Yes, you've said that, Lila."

"Here. Read this." She hands the letter to Miriam who searches in her purse and, finding her opera glasses, perches them at the tip of her nose.

The invitation arrived two weeks ago from a certain Signor Agresta, the director of the renowned Biennale dell'Arte, and Lila had noted the prominent return address with mounting anxiety before slipping the letter into her apron pocket. She never forgot about it, but until this week, she hadn't been able to give it a second thought.

Miriam re-centers her glasses. "It's for the retrospective of Arte Informale...doesn't that usually include the Spatialists like Lucio Fontana...and the Abstract Expressionists?"

"Yes! How impressive that you remember."

"Of course I remember. But is this good news, Lila?"

Lila huffs. "Who can say? Anyway, I've decided."

When her eyes widen, Miriam has the look of a raccoon with dark thick lashes. "But you said you would never..."

"I said. I said. I know what I said." Lila recoils when the waiter appears with the tea. "Thank you," she says with annoyance at the interruption. "I've made my peace with it, Miriam. Life is both too long and too short, isn't it?"

Lila sips at her tea. She hesitates to mention it, even to Miriam; lately, aside from the forgetfulness, something else has been off. Nothing too drastic, the sky above Venice is still blue only less so, but something about life and living has waned. Not that she's one to fret over physical ailments, unlike Miriam who worries over every scratch and hangnail. Death would come sooner or later to them all whether they prepared for it or not.

"I don't expect we'll get invited again. And the Biennale dell'Arte is the perfect venue to exhibit the collection. Don't you agree?"

"Of course it is!" Miriam gasps.

"But there is a wrinkle." Lila clutches her purse in her lap. "I can't do it on my own, Miriam. The business is in shambles and

I'm broke." She takes a deep breath and manages the words in one quick exhalation. "I need to ask for a loan."

Miriam snaps open her hand bag and in seconds produces her checkbook and a pen. "How much do you need, dear?"

"I don't have any idea. But enough to pay for the services of a professional, I would think, a top notch curator."

"Say no more! I already know who."

"Do you? Oh Mim, really that's such a help! How much does a private curator charge these days?"

"I couldn't say, but the gentleman I'm thinking of would have an idea."

Lila's eyes well up. Miriam is the best of all people, beyond generous. In spite of her erratic decisions with men, the learned helplessness at times, she was a real friend and a mensch. They should all aspire to be more like her.

"It's nothing." Miriam pats her hand warmly. "But do you suppose..?" Her voice trails off.

"What is it Mim, dear?" Lila dabs her eyes with a handkerchief.

"Do you suppose you could consider meeting my Carlo?"

Lila gulps at the knot at the base of her throat. These introductions to Miriam's gentlemen friends are always so awkward, not least because whenever she has a man in her life Miriam becomes someone else. Fawning. A bit docile. There but not there. And now this talk of a wedding. So rushed. So ill advised. But it's not Lila's place. In any case there's no avoiding it.

"Of course I will. How's next Wednesday, 4 pm sharp?"

"Wednesday?" Miriam asks.

"Yes, for tea! What else?"

"Yes, tea. Of course!" Miriam clasps her hands together, beyond pleased.

"And have you set the wedding date?"

"June twentieth. That's a Saturday."

"Isn't that next month?"

"It is. Carlo says he'd marry me tomorrow, but I needed a bit of time to plan." Miriam giggles. "You know me, the party is the whole point. From there it's off to Greece!" Miriam takes her wallet out of her purse.

"Put that away dear," Lila removes the crisp lire from her bill-fold. "It's my treat."

"Nonsense!" Miriam's forehead wrinkles.

"No, no dear. I insist. Consider it an early engagement present."

It's only fair that Lila pay for the small things. She tries to squelch her tears but they well up again. She's no fool: Miriam will leave her eventually; it's down to serendipity that they have lasted this long, a blessing that they didn't lose each other during the brutal trek in the cattle cars. They held onto each other like frightened mice; they never let go. But Lila always knew that only a man could separate them. The marriage proposal may as well be from this Carlo person as any other.

Lila hands the bills to the waiter who thanks her with a short bow of the head. "I should get back." She claps her hands together. The sudden smack is more abrupt than she means. "Alvise is useless without direction. And I've over-stocked again."

"Well I don't know how you do it. I'm only too happy not to bother with working anymore." The crease at the bridge of Miriam's nose causes a slight crack in the outer layer of her face powder and foundation. "Did I mention that Carlo was a banker in Rome? In another life, he says. Tomorrow he's taking me out on his boat. Around the Lido." She reclines in her chair, the satisfaction on her face evident, her spindly legs stretched out in front of her as though she's already on the damn yacht in the Aegean. "With our combined pensions, God willing, we'll have a few years of travel ahead." Miriam kisses her fingers and holds them up in the air. A nervous Italian tic that Lila has always refused to make.

The waiter returns with Lila's change. At least they're through the worst of it, and the conversation is over. Things are never as bad in actuality as dread makes them appear.

"Well, let me know what time we should be there. Can I bring anything? A bottle of champagne? We must make a toast." Miriam beams.

"Why not?" Lila jumps and pats at her chest at the sputtering of a nearby engine. "Wretched motorboats! You check with—." As usual the name escapes her.

"Carlo." Miriam grins like a teenager.

"Right. Carlo. I'm flexible." The words sound a little contrived but no matter.

"And I will call you with that name." Miriam kisses Lila once on each cheek, an affectation picked up from French films. "The curator. I hear he's tremendous. A Signor De-something or other." She adjusts the scarf around her neck before heading off across the piazza with new energy in her step.

Love-sick little Miriam. How many times must the carousel go around? Lila tucks her wallet back in her purse and rises from the table then quickly sits back down. Hidden beneath Miriam's water glass on the table are three folded bills, enough for two dinners and a generous tip for Signor Hummingbird. Lila's loud sigh stops the man at the next table stops mid-sentence. She waves him on. Pocketing the bills she knocks over the water glass in the process and rushes off in the opposite direction from Miriam. No sense in paying twice.

When Isabel opens her eyes from the kiss, the Nazis march past the Trevi Fountain in cinematic black and white, and Niccolo is fumbling with the pearl buttons of her blouse, his hands exploring her breasts. A rush of exquisite sensation unlike anything she has felt before envelops her, like flying or running swiftly in a dream, her feet barely touching down through the alleys at dawn. So then. This must be what all the fuss is about. This is love.

"Ouch!" Her whisper is too loud and someone in the front row shushes them. She swats at his hand when he pinches too hard, but her nipples remain at alert. He is undeterred, his fingers search for a deeper place between her tightly crossed legs, and her body pounds softly in response, but she wants to go back a step or two to the kissing, the clasping of fingers, the holding. Somewhere above the projector light, Nonna is frowning down on them and Isabel is not at all sure anymore if this is the thing to do, if she really wants to find out. Niccolo reaches his fingers beneath the undergarments while the old priest in the film accused of hiding Jews, begs the commandant for his parishioners' lives. The Gestapo beat him viciously for his trouble but Niccolo doesn't care. He caresses her inner thighs, kisses her neck and runs coarse, cool hands along her spine as the Germans drag the poor fellow into a waiting sedan. In the row just ahead, the old man in the fedora snores gently as the black Mercedes races away and Niccolo squats beneath her his head in her lap. His mouth between her legs is swallowing her whole, and when he pushes his finger inside her, the searing flesh begins to burn her like a lit match against her bare skin. She tries to see them lying in a field, chaste kissing and cuddling but that's quickly dashed because as she reclines in the seat the pulse of his finger becomes faster, deeper until like a miracle, the pain finally transforms into a warming tingle running down her legs. She tries to imagine that the crunch of the Mercedes' tires on wet pavement is the rush of a stream and the clicking of the projector, the music of crickets. Her back is arched, the sigh that escapes her barely audible. The credits run down the screen and Niccolo holds onto her unraveled braid until finally she wrests free. When the lights come up, the crickets disperse, the velvet seat is damp and the theater is empty. In the dim house lights Niccolo's handsome face is cast in shadows. A stranger's face. Unrecognizable.

She rises too quickly on wobbly legs, the fiery pounding below has not stopped though she wishes it would, and her mouth is inflamed and swollen from the rough sting of his beard. When she glances down her blouse is undone and her skirt unzipped. Cringing, she quickly finishes dressing.

Niccolo squeezes her hand. "What is it?"

"It's nothing. I just need some air is all." She heads down the long aisle toward the light of the lobby, light headed with a few bits of popcorn clinging to her sweater.

Outside in front of the theater marquee, Niccolo shields the match from the gentle wind off the water and lights up a cigarette. "Didn't you enjoy the movie? We can go again," he says, "to the movies I mean."

"The movies?" Her voice is hoarse but she takes a drag from his cigarette and hides her distaste: syrupy cloves.

"Yes. Don't you want to go to the movies with me, Isabella?" He reaches for her sweater to pick off a piece of popcorn and her mouth goes dry. "Next time we could do more. I mean I think you've got what it takes."

"Have I?" Her throat burning, she hands him back the cigarette. She shouldn't have inhaled. She never inhales.

"I should say so." He places his finger on her lips. "Don't you think?"

She doesn't know. His cloves and his warm breath, the searching fingers, the burning. It's all a bit bizarre. She thought this was what she wanted, to be his girl on the motorbike. And she does want that still. But what about this painful strangeness afterwards? Like she's become one of those girls, the ones that break some unbreakable law. Like she's swimming too far out at sea. And what was it that Antonia was always saying? "Don't go to the bars at night unless you're with me. And don't trust any men, especially the young ones," she said. "They'll love you all right and then..." She'd drawn a line across her bare throat.

"Knock, knock." Niccolo grabs both of Isabel's hands. "Hey, where'd you go?"

"Me?"

"Yes, you." He laughs. He pulls her toward him for another kiss.

"I can't." She steps back.

He crushes the cigarette butt under his shoe. "So...you don't want to..."

"Don't be stupid. I'm late, that's all."

His mouth finds hers again, his fingers gathering the hem of her skirt and inching upwards but the next sound grates with the force of two trash can lids clanging together.

"Isabel Lesser!"

And the city returns in full, the smell of fish in the smoldering water, the dilapidated palazzos gathering around like concerned relatives and Nonna, livid blue in her dress coat and sensible shoes, as out of place as two young students at the theater on a school night.

CHAPTER SEVEN

What a debacle. Isabel was grounded, forbidden from going anywhere but school and home, and not even a stop at Signora Goldberg's bakery in between. After Nonna's long speech about not leaving her a cent and this after saying they had no money anyway, Isabel endured a sleepless night in twisted sheets, her lips still tingling from Niccolo, her body still quivering. Right. They were penniless but somehow there were beautiful paintings covering the walls and one extra hidden in the closet. It never really made sense but she never questioned it before. Until now. There's little to lose since she's already lost Nonna's trust. Not that Nonna truly trusted anyone. The only thing to do was to cut class and head to the library. At this point another missed class wouldn't matter. And the devil was in the research or however that saying went.

The Biblioteca Nazionale Marciana sits off to one side of the Piazza San Marco, an imposing framework of columns, grand windows, and arches. Instead of turning right toward Calle dei Preti, the usual route to school, Isabel crosses the square and heads toward the great monolithic building. The fine art section is housed in the east wing, a few steps from the Grand Canal, and the gondoliers' songs drift in through open windows. Two winged cherubs greet each visitor at the top of the wide marble staircase, their stone faces undoubtedly privy to centuries of tawdry secrets. The great center hall is cool, etched in shadow; sound travels by echo and the clicking of ladies' heels in the adjacent rooms bounces against the walls. Inside the study hall, book carts squeal as librarians in tweed skirts and eyeglasses, perch on step ladders to re-shelve old texts detailing the frescoes of Rome on towering bookcases.

Venice has never changed. Not for centuries. But after yesterday, everything has been altered, and Isabel most of all. Her dreams of university in Paris are dashed. No help from nonna will be forthcoming. No help at all. It's as strangely exhilarating as it is frustrating. The tickle of Niccolo's lips nags her like a waking dream, his probing touch still tender between her legs and his offer still front and center: fencing a painting would yield a tidy sum, he said. Still, she never got to ask him about the Murano. The green glow of the glass apple now replaces the picture of his face smiling back at her. Of course he took it. He takes everything. Especially what's willingly given, as Nonna would say. And Niccolo has given her a small gift box she must not show to anyone for fear that it will be seized and stolen away. Surely Nonna would understand if she ever had some fun in her youth. How could anyone live this long and avoid pleasure altogether? Of course, there was Albert or someone before him. There must have been. But in the photo album grandfather looks as stuffy as a dusty old upholstered chair and never has a smile. My God, how austere and lifeless he must have been, even in his prime! Isabel sighs. One thing is certain: Nonna has been through too much in this life. She is stingy most days and usually irritated, but she didn't deserve to lose grandpa's gift.

Her future in the crosshairs, Isabel leaves her book bag on an empty table and hangs her sweater on the back of the chair. In the stacks, her fingers run against the gold-leafed lettering on the book spines. All the masters of the Italian Renaissance are present and accounted for: Leonardo, Raphael, Boticelli, Tiziano. One oversized volume lies on its side: a retrospective of the period including both major and minor works. With the unwieldy book in hand, she heads back to her table where one glossy page after another offers too many paintings to take in at once, each one more beautiful than the last; passionate scenes of lust, greed and death playing out in somber palettes. What luck that she was born in a different era, one with mini-skirts and technicolor, strawberry gelato and passion. By all means, bring on life and the living! If the nuns don't snatch away all the fun beforehand, that is.

She reads on about the great Tiziano Vecellio or Titian, and one wizened face catches her attention: Mater Dolorosa. "Our Mother of Sorrows" is a woman in profile cloaked in blue robes, a brown scarf covering her head, her hands clasped in supplication, and just like it said in the newspaper, the tiny print under the lithograph reads "the Albert Lesser Family Collection." Isabel gasps. It's Nonna's painting, the one sitting in her bedroom closet this very minute—unseen and unknown—except by Isabel, of course, and a certain beautiful boy.

According to the book the collection is comprised of at least thirty valuable works targeted by the Nazis for looting, but when war broke out, many of the works were rescued. Further down it says that the heiress Isadora Morgenfeld once hosted some of the paintings in her gallery. At the dinner table nonna looked her straight in the eye and acted like she had never heard of the heiress. Isabel blinks slowly. Surely Signora Morgenfeld and Albert must have known each other! It's the only reasonable deduction. And the Lesser Collection must contain an authentic Titian. Like the Titian in the closet. The edges of the page blur a little and her feet float a bit lighter off the floor under the library desk.

She slams the book closed to the dismay of the man reading the newspaper at the adjacent table; they trade scowls. After all these years of frugal living and never even to be allowed a whole pastry from Goldberg's; thanks to her grandmother, each cake was always rationed into uniform small slices and no more than one handed out at any given time. And never mind Isabel's former paltry allowance, which Nonna in her miserly judgment, had now ruled against. And how could Isabel forget thrift store shopping for weekend clothes (Nonna called these frumpy pieces "antiques") and only after Isabel pleaded loud and long enough for a new jumper? God bless the school uniform, Nonna said, since it saved a fortune in fashion. A bike was out of the question, This is not Amsterdam Isabel, and why bother when the vaporetti and walking were the best methods of transportation. How dare Nonna, when all this time they owned a bona-fide Titian?

"Everything okay, miss?" The librarian squints at her through half-moon glasses.

Isabel nods, suddenly embarrassed. "I see you're reading about the heiress Morgenfeld. Have you seen the recent article?" The man at the next table closes his newspaper dramatically and the librarian moves on.

Isabel's chair squeals on the marble as she rises from the table. In the periodicals room, she rifles through a recent edition of La Republicca and finds her way to the Arts section. There's the article she read to Nonna, and another earlier posting entitled, Isadora Morgenfeld Saves the Lesser Art Collection. Several images follow the heiress's photograph including a painting by the German Expressionist Oscar Kokoschka, his portrait of a paper-thin woman entitled "Lotte Franzos." The subject is fortyish and familiar, wearing a high-necked buttoned dress. The resemblance is uncanny, seated there she could be Nonna's dear friend Miriam: the long, heron-like neck, the reedy arms crossed loosely in her lap. And there are other German Expressionists too, like Egon Schiele and the female painter Gabriele Munter, whose landscape, "Countryside Near Paris" is featured. Isabel eyes a Munter landscape, the countryside outside of Paris rolling out like thick sumptuous carpet, the blues and greens and milky overlay of forest, ocean and air. "Lesser Collection, Venice Biennale 1932," says the caption below, and Isabel imagines her grandfather and the heiress arm in arm that momentous day, sauntering the emptying halls of the exhibition, two celebrated collectors vaunting their best new prospects. In the photograph, however, just as in Nonna's recollections of him, Albert's face remains obscured by the shadow of his smart fedora hat while Signora Morgenfeld's glows radiantly, invitingly.

A robust signora embarking at the Accademia vaporetto stop barrels past, her oblong face sallow and etched with years of household worry. In her arms are too many parcels. With three feisty little children in tow, she hustles up the ramp and promptly drops a netted bag full of fruit. A runaway orange rolls down the plank and bumps into Isabel's foot, and she stoops to pick it up while the children clamor around their mother, throwing apples and oranges this way and that in a lively game of keep-away.

"Basta! Enough!" The signora shouts, but her children don't listen; the point of everything is the game after all. They run circles around their mother, immune to her threats while the other passengers chuff in complaint and find their way through the sudden chaos. Isabel collects several apples from the ground and, with the orange, hands them back to the woman. "Thank you signorina. You are very kind," the woman says through her tears, stuffing the bruised fruit back in the sack. They find seats on the bow of the boat and the children reach greedy little fingers through the rails to wave at Isabel on the dock. "Goodbye! Goodbye!" Their twinkling cries burst like streamers as the vaporetto makes its sluggish trajectory down the Grand Canal.

The signora could be Nonna after the war except with two extra little ones to look after. Why not? It's as right as anything else. Other than the few short phrases Isabel has heard about that time, her childhood is a blank, one long blurry page after another, with little real memories of her own until she is four years old nibbling an apple core in the Lido in a bathing suit two sizes too big (for growing into, Nonna said) and later heaving her lunch over the side of a skiff on a windy day at sea. They had gone fishing with

Aunt Miriam and her boyfriend, Another old fool, Nonna whispered, and it didn't make sense to a little girl, the whisper, the disdain, Nonna's endless bad mood. But it could never have been easy for nonna, always saddled with one nuisance or another. First, of course, it was Leo. Her grandmother never let on, but Isabel always suspected that something was not right between her grandmother and her father. And in recent years, she thinks of the rosary and her shoebox stash, it's been his daughter. Isabel frowns. Perhaps she is just like her father. She quickly shakes off the notion. How much influence could a man she's never met have over her life?

The pathway along the park is edged with flowers, and a wasp hovers inside one of the open tulips planted in single rows along the path, its wings slick with pollen. If that painting in the closet is the only thing of value left to Nonna, technically, that makes it Isabel's inheritance. She laughs out loud, and the wasp flies off. Her grandmother would sooner give the canvas to Miriam or loan it to some museum or other. The only thing Isabel can count on without any means of her own is that this floating sewer of a city will never let her go and here she will remain, rooted to the ocean floor like the rotting mossy planks that dot the lagoon.

The light has shifted across the canal and rather than a real structure, the Palazzo di Beneficio resembles a Giorgione, the white vertical lines of the cypress trees point upwards to painterly clouds and the thick strokes of titanium smeared against a cerulean blue sky. Sell the painting. The echo of Niccolo's voice, gravelly but certain, fills her chest with warmth; her breath quickens. It's a bit crazy but ever since their date she feels his gaze everywhere even in her most intimate moments, in the bath, when she's washing. In fact, his eyes are on her right now. She looks around her and can't help but smile. It's embarrassing, exhausting, a new kind of life. A pebble buffets off the toe of her shoe and hits a peeling tree trunk. Antonia said no stupid moves, and maybe she's right: stealing a rosary is not like swiping a pressed powder compact, and stealing a painting is...well, stealing a painting is something else altogether.

A middle-aged woman leans against the balustrade in front of the palazzo. Wearing bulky gardening gloves she stretches to clip a stray twig off the tree. "Good afternoon!"

"Good afternoon," Isabel says, disoriented. She had meant to take a left at the park and avoid the canal altogether but apparently never followed through with the plan. "Isn't this...?" She points to the villa but thinks better of asking. "What a lovely myrtle." Nonna's lessons on plants have seeped in and she can name this tree and many others. Perhaps the woman will be impressed.

"Thank you." The woman cranes to clip another small branch. "It's grown like gangbusters this spring."

"They have them in Paris, too." Isabel speaks with the authority of someone who's been to the City of Light and more than once, and not an armchair traveler with her cup of tea and dog-eared Madame Bovary.

"Careful, there." The woman gestures, "You're on uneven ground."

Isabel must have passed by the famous villa dozens of times. She avoids the next few loose paving stones to take a better look. It's the same one from the photograph in the paper. But this is the first time she has ever seen anyone out front. From this close she can peer over the hedgerow, only a few of the great houses facing the canal have one. Prestige pays for exclusivity. The woman's rubber gardening boots are covered in dried mud, and the wide brim of her floppy sun hat peeks out from above the bushes. At her feet, three small, sand-colored dogs chase each other in frenzied circles around the myrtle.

"And good afternoon to you as well, my lovelies!" she says to the dogs as they lap at her ankles. If her Italian is flawless, it's not native: the 'r' is too flat and the consonants sound like the actors in Hollywood movies. No doubt the heiress brought along her American assistant on this trip back to town.

"Are they yours?" Isabel points to the panting dogs.

"Actually they come with the villa. Piccolo! Off this minute!" The woman whistles to the pug scratching at the azalea bush. A shade falls over her face but the easy smile remains, a failed attempt at seriousness as though no obstacle is too daunting for the truly robust. "What a shame. We've only started growing them again." She laughs. "We can never stay angry at these terrors for long."

"Do you know the woman who lives here?"

"I should say so." The woman nods.

Isabel shields her eyes from the sun. "A real patron of the arts from what I read."

"Well, the Italian papers like to exaggerate," The woman removes the clumsy gloves. "But in this case I'd say they got it right."

"This may seem strange..." Isabel leans against the branches of the hedgerow to steady herself. "Do you think she might spare a moment...to talk with me?" Her voice is louder than she intends and she blushes.

"Oh I couldn't say. She's a busy bee, that one, with her meetings and her phone calls." The pug at the azaleas commences scratching at the soft roots in the potting soil. "Piccolo! Enough!" She stoops to scratch Piccolo behind the ears. "He's a little unsure of the pecking order as you can see. The runts of the litter always are." She props her shears against the tall mounted stone vase. "Why don't you come through? I'm sure you'd be welcome."

Isabel steps between two high plantings. Beyond the hedgerow it's quite a different world. A quadrangle of chaise lounges face the water, in the center of which is a wrought iron table with a glass top. Along the perimeter, manicured bushes brimming with pink and coral-colored roses sway in the breeze.

The enormity of it all. The magnificence. Isabel almost forgets what she came here to find out in the first place.

"Please." The woman points to a chaise. Tall like that famous pilot, the woman who flew an airplane around the world, she wears a loose-fitting smock with mud stains at the elbows. Isabel sits down, setting her book bag on the paving stones beside her, while all three pekingese descend upon her at once, sniffing and licking her bare legs anxiously with darting little pink tongues. Isabel laughs uncomfortably at such intimate attention.

"Don't mind them. They're curious about new people. You must be parched." The woman pours a long drink of lemonade from the pitcher on the table and hands it to Isabel. Her fingers are narrow, surprisingly smooth for a gardener's hands, with mother-of-pearl polish on perfectly rounded nails. On her ring finger is a little cameo inlaid with ivory. "Do you like it? A gift from an admirer." She smiles.

"How long have you worked here?" Isabel doesn't drink: the clink of ice cubes is thirst quenching enough, and the beads of condensation running down the glass are cold against her skin.

The woman takes a long sip. "Most of my adult life, I'd say."

"It's wonderful." The sunlight on Isabel's face and bare arms is the golden light of a Leonardo. She basks in it, willing herself and the woman and the three little dogs to be the royal subjects of a lush Renaissance painting, warmed by the sun, the daffodils around them in thick brush strokes.

"Do you live here in Venice?"

"I do. On the other side. Forgive me. I'm Isabel. Isabel Lesser." She holds out a moist hand.

The woman's eyes widen and she sets down her glass; Piccolo, who has been nestling comfortably, grumbles in her lap then circles around before settling in once more. The woman studies Isabel's face for a protracted moment, as if her visage is the first page of a good book. "Lesser. As in Albert Lesser?"

"Yes. He's my grandfather."

The woman gasps, and the drowsy lap dog straggles to attention. "Of course he is."

"That's what I wanted to talk to Signora Morgenfeld about, in fact."

The woman sets her floppy hat down on the table, her expression conveying equal parts kindness and disbelief. “And here I was thinking today was a day like any other.” She extends her long fingers. “Isadora Morgenfeld. Lovely to meet you.” She places the drowsy pug on shaky feet on the paving stones and unbuttons the soiled gardener’s smock: the embroidered red kimono jacket underneath is vibrant as poppies.

Perched at the end of her lounge, Isabel enjoys a descending wave of vertigo that makes the chaise lounge beneath her feel aloft. She hovers just inches above the veranda and tries to take another sip from the glass as if drinking lemonade on a pleasant sunny afternoon in the company of *the* Isadora Morgenfeld, were the most normal thing in the world. The one and the same art collector who’s lived all these years in the grand old Palazzo di Beneficio surrounded by famous painters, musicians and dilettantes. All of them loafing about this same terrace and calling the villa home for a few fortunate days, weeks, or months. To think of the many absinthe parties and the numerous romantic entanglements that revolved around the engine of that storied world, Isadora Morgenfeld herself! Isabel shivers a little, unable to believe her good fortune and, with the glass perspiring in her hand, feels hopelessly rich if only by sheer association.

Even though the Isadora Morgenfeld in front of her doesn’t look precisely like the photos in the library books. Clearly. How could she when so many years have passed? The graying hair, the delicate lines etched around deep-set eyes, put her squarely in the ranks of Nonna’s generation. Even so, Isabel would never have pictured Isadora Morgenfeld as a mature matriarch pruning trees amid a trio of scampering pekingese.

“Would you like something to eat? Some sliced fruit?” The heiress gestures at the front doorway to the villa, and a petite wiry woman in a white apron returns moments later with a tray and sets two bowls filled with strawberries, cubes of pineapple and green melon on the table. The sweetness of fresh fruit evokes real summer, and, smiling, Isabel dabs at the pink juice dripping down her chin with the starched linen napkin. A propeller plane overhead drags a banner: Cinzano, and the woman in the apron returns to the house with an empty tray.

"So. Tell me what you know about your grandfather."

Not surprisingly, Isabel is stuck for an answer. Nonna only keeps the one photograph from Albert's student days at the university in her top dresser drawer. He looked shy and small like an awkward adolescent even in his suit, and not quite the heir of a successful textile business. Isabel shrugs. "Not much, I'm afraid. I was hoping I could learn a bit more."

"Of course you were. How can I be of help?"

Isabel's pulse quickens: finally and after all these years, she would find out everything, the correct chronology, how grandfather met Nonna, the story of her own origins. She gasps, stumbling over her own words in her eagerness to get out her hundreds of questions.

The heiress laughs kindly and holds up the hand with the cameo ring as if to say, there now, breathe, one at a time.

Isabel takes a deep breath. She begins again. "How did you first meet?"

"How did we meet?" Signora Morgenfeld's gaze settles on the flagstones. "Well, at the time I kept a little gallery. I should think we first met there." She squints as if the answer lies somewhere in the earth between the stones. "Yes. It was there, in fact. How is it possible so many years have passed...and yet here you are." When the heiress looks up, Isabel feels like a phantom, made of air and memory instead of solid fresh.

"So, he came into the gallery?" Out over the water, the flap of a seabird's wings and its vocal cry almost drown out Isabel's words.

"Oh, yes. Many times. It was a little space and smelled of gin but we sold the work of some of our brightest stars." Signora Morgenfeld sets her drink down on the ground. "Can I ask how old you are?"

"Seventeen." Isabel grins. It's surprisingly agreeable to say her age out loud, especially to someone so celebrated. She swats absently at a passing fly.

"Yes, that sounds right. You were born right at the end of the war, weren't you? We heard that Lila survived, there were rumors, but nothing about a granddaughter." Her eyes shine as if to say such a baby is nothing short of a miracle.

In her childhood, the slightest question about Albert would send Nonna into spasms of tears and after a few uncomfortable attempts at the dinner table, Isabel learned not to delve any deeper, and she basks in a strange contentment at hearing some news, any news of her family's past.

"Now where did our sun go?" The clouds through her uplifted glass cast a deeper green shadow on the terrace, as Signora Morgenfeld finishes her lemonade and buttons the top button of the magnificent red kimono.

"What was my grandfather like? As a person I mean." While the heiress recounts the details, Isabel indulges in the portrait of Albert forming in her mind. He was shy, yet dapper, a charming man, intelligent, wealthy, an industrialist and a patron of the arts, a sampler of exotic cultures; in all, a Jewish man of means who ran in the same circles as Isadora Morgenfeld. So satisfying was this new rendering of her grandfather that Isabel was content to linger there. Slowly she would work her way up to asking about the paintings.

"Once after returning from a scouting trip to find new artists in Morocco he insisted on saying 'Inch'Allah' at the end of every sentence like a native speaker. And he kept saying it ever since!" The heiress's laugh is still more ingénue than matriarch, crows feet and grey hair aside. "Naturally Albert and I hit it off right away. He was funny and extremely brilliant. But there was a kind of humility to him, too. Something I've been accused of lacking, I'm afraid. Truly, he was a solid sort of person." Signora Morgenfeld smoothes the line of her skirt, trying in vain to conceal the tears. "What a lucky girl you are to come from such a mensch. Did your Nonna teach you Yiddish, too?"

Isabel nods, but it's a lie.

"Mine did too. Inch' Allah." Signora Morgenfeld winks.

"Inch'Allah," Isabel says, noting with irony they've gone from Yiddish to Arabic without a second thought. Nonna would be scandalized. Isabel had heard her grandmother whispering in Yiddish on the phone sometimes, long distance calls cloaked in secrecy, and she occasionally exchanged a few Jewish words with Miriam, but that was the extent of it. Consequently Isabel had never envied anyone who spoke the language, thinking it antiquated and inelegant. Until now.

"What do you mean by solid?"

"Well he would never take credit for his own hard work." The heiress dabs at her nose with the napkin. "He inherited money from his father, then built the family textile business into something ten times more profitable. Not everyone can do that. I certainly couldn't." Signora Morgenfeld sets her napkin down on the table. "Did you know that your grandfather only agreed to lend his name to the art collection at my insistence?"

"Yes, an art book I found in the library referred to The Lesser Collection." Isabel beams.

"Are you doing some research?"

"I am. About the stolen artwork during the Third Reich." Another lie, but with practice the telling of them seemed to get easier and easier.

Signora Morgenfeld gazes down at little Piccolo who has climbed back into her lap and fallen asleep. "Yes." Her voice is quiet and thick. "So many masterpieces were looted."

"Yes, but—" Isabel gathers her courage. "I read that most of the Lesser Collection was saved from getting into German hands... by Isadora Morgenfeld."

The heiress laughs awkwardly. "That might be overstating it."

"So you didn't have the paintings shipped to America?"

"I did not as a matter of fact."

"But the book said that —"

"You mustn't believe everything you read in books, my dear. I simply put a few paintings aside." Signora Morgenfeld purses her lips in thought. "But contrary to what you read, they remained in

Europe." She nods at the sycamore and myrtle trees surrounding them.

The woman in the apron retrieves the dishes from the table.

"With the Germans only days away and Albert not returning my calls I made the decision I thought he would want. After the war, most of the collection was returned to your family. I haven't looked back. It was the right thing to do."

The clouds overhead huddle together darkly and the myrtle tree sways in the draft of wind. The gardener's smock on the lowest branch dances like an otherworldly spirit. Isabel cradles her head in her hands and tries to slow her breathing. All of it was true: the paintings in the parlor, the one in the closet, all of them were genuine.

"What is it? You look positively haunted."

Isabel nods. "I...I am."

"You mean Lila never told you—," She stops short, shifts in the chaise and the pug with her. "I've tried so many times to let her know. All of my letters were returned, unopened."

"I don't understand. Why...why would you risk so much?"

The gravity of that time settles on the heiress's face like a shadow. "Do you know how many people will use you for what you have? Use you up and leave you with nothing? I knew countless painters, art dealers, ambitious gallerists, the most talented writers and celebrated journalists, and every single one wanted something." She sniffles. "Well that was never Albert, never your grandfather. He would have given as much as I gave. More."

"But what do most people want?"

The heiress shakes her head soberly. "I don't have a good answer for you, I'm afraid. But I hope when you find out for yourself, it's not as painful as it was for me."

The heiress gently strokes the dog in her lap and the afternoon sky shifts back to what it was, sunny as before.

What did she mean by painful? The new information flies about Isabel's head. She can barely keep track of it all. She must try to think straight, however, not squander this chance chasing details. "You said most, most of the collection was returned?"

"Everything but two paintings. Two priceless paintings are still hidden away. I tried to return them as well. As I said, Lila —"

"But that means—," Isabel's mind overloads. Is it possible?

"Yes." The heiress waves again towards the swaying myrtles and sycamores. "They have been right here, right here all along."

CHAPTER EIGHT

At Goldberg's Bakery, rather than the typical queue that snakes through the doorway at noon each day, only three people wait in line ahead of Lila. The air inside is different too. Though warm with the aroma of baked bread and honey cake, a certain dark energy has been purged, as if, rid of the baker's wife, the walls are free to breathe again.

Lila coughs in her handkerchief, her breath escaping her for the moment, what Isabel said still fresh in mind. That somehow she met up with that Morgenfeld woman. They had tea. They talked about the collection. It's too strange to be believed. After years of Lila avoiding the celebrated Isadora Morgenfeld, her own Isabel is invited to tea.

The cashier accepts cash from the patron before her and the cash register rings. Panicked for a moment, Lila opens and closes her purse and breathes a sigh, thankful that her wallet is inside. She would lose her head if it weren't attached. The baker's son Meier, still gangly and still as at odds with his height as an adult as he was in adolescence, welcomes the man in front of her, a well-dressed type in a seersucker suit. Lila peers around him to get a better view of what is on offer. A handful of fresh breads and a luxurious stack of Linzer tortes line the display window next to rows of Mandelbrot and stacks of flaky chocolate and cinnamon raisin rugelach. Albert's favorite.

"What can I get you?" Meier asks the well-dressed man who pointes to a tray of babka.

"Might I have a taste?"

Meier cuts a snip off the spongey cake and hands it over.

"Miraculous. Simply miraculous." The man in the pin-striped seersucker jacket and panama hat licks his fingers, his well-trimmed mustache fringed with crumbs of torte. The way his darting blue eyes take in the whole display case he could be a bird watcher surveying a flock of wild geese from close up. "I'll take five."

"Two?" Meier Goldberg wipes the back of a floury hand across his temple.

"Did I say two? No. You're right they are rather small. Make it five. That's the magic number, isn't it? Too much is always better than too little."

The baker's son stammers an incoherent reply. Never one for small talk, Meier Goldberg prefers the logic of common tasks. He places each little cake in an open cardboard box, constructed hastily from a flattened stack next to the bread slicer, but the last of the pastries flies from his hands and lands on the floor. He mumbles an apology and picks up the stray cake to toss it in the bin.

"No, no." The man gestures toward the casualty.

"But sir it's—"

Reaching over the counter the man snatches the fallen pastry from Meier's hands and, without so much as a second thought, takes a generous bite. He pulls a mote of something from his mouth, a piece of fur or a moldy crumb from ancient bread, it is too distasteful to imagine, and closes his eyes, alone at the head of the queue in complete and perfect privacy. "Delicious. Truly. My compliments, young man."

After the large box is wrapped with string and tied in a clumsy bow, Meier hands it over along with the correct change. "Thank you, sir."

The man turns around still licking his lips and fingers, tips his hat to the long suffering queue and leaves with his bounty, clearly off to even more important matters.

"The usual, Signora Lesser?" Meier eyes Lila with a slight grin, his usual sign of recognition. Meier brandishes the braided egg-yellow challah in his gangly hands.

"Yes. Please."

On Riva di Basio, thin ribbons of late afternoon light filter through the large plate glass window; outside the old sign, 'La Carta Fine' hangs high above. Except for the clock's muffled ticking, the shop is quiet. Lila tugs again at the cord; at the third attempt the blinds flap upwards like startled pigeon wings. She sets down the netted shopping bag containing one small, sad challah next to the stack of bills on the mahogany counter, an antique vestige from the shop's previous incarnation as a trattoria. That strange fellow in the bakery had bought the last of the Linzers and now they would have nothing for dessert. Sighing, Lila runs her fingers along the bumpy facets of the wooden counter rail. Signora Bertollini, the former proprietor, had perished in the camps, and her eldest daughter had explained when they sold the place to Lila that the one-of-a-kind counter had been salvaged from an abandoned ship in the harbor. She said her mother, if she were still alive, would have instructed Lila to keep the mahogany polished at all times like precious wedding silver. To this day, Lila has kept her word to a woman who had died before she could ask, polishing and tending to the wood every week and worrying after every scratch and imperfection. She never had the heart to replace the magnificent piece with something more practical and modern. If the signora hadn't survived the atrocities, Lila had and every day since, and surviving was tiresome work enough. Besides everyone knows there is no avoiding what has come before. The past continues to grow up like a weed through the cracks of new cement.

From her doorway, Lila watches the green grocer across the way, Signor D'Agostino, balance on top of a teetering ladder. Every Friday he scrubs his storefront windows with a soapy rag. A portly man with belted trousers hiked up to where his waist should be, he returns Lila's greeting with a salute Mussolini would have been proud of. The sopping rag back falls into the bucket with a little splash as he climbs back down.

"Signor D'Agostino, hello! How's business?" Lila manages the usual polite smile.

When the fascists ran the country, this rotund little man would have denounced her to the authorities in the heartbeat it takes him to draw breath, but today, as long as they avoid awkward subjects like religion, history, and politics, they tolerate each other amicably. Never mind that along with fluffy heads of lettuce, red ripe tomatoes and celery stalks in his window, his Italian flag remains a constant staple and everyday a new nationalist politician's poster is taped up. Never mind that he hates her and all her family and her ancestors before them. A good neighbor must spend a few minutes passing civilities on a warm spring day. Lila pulls out her best good neighbor smile.

"Hello. Signora Lesser. Hello. It's a slow time. You too, I'll bet. With that pazzo prime minister, who has money for my vegetables or your fine paper?" This is pure flattery: everyone knows what people would buy in a crumbling economy if it came to a choice between writing and eating. There'd be no contest. The grocer coughs heavily, a baritone smoker's cough. Lila looks away. The vulgarity of the man. "It's okay. As long as they come for my potatoes, I'm not complaining."

Finally: a little honesty. Nodding, she pulls off a few dead leaves from the wilting plants in the patch of dirt in front of her shop. "Do you think we'll get rain this week? My geraniums could use some help."

The grocer shrugs. "What do I know? I'm no weatherman. Why

not water them yourself?" He points at something in the distance. "Expecting company?"

Down the street a tall elegant woman in high heels walks towards them like a tentative soldier navigating a minefield, haltingly but determined. A man follows a step behind, costumed in pin-striped seersucker, light blue and white stripes, and straw hat. He has a wide flat face and strong jaw. With his fair hair and complexion, he could be a Swedish tourist vacationing at the Lido with his Italian mistress. Lila blinks slowly. It's the man from the bakery.

"Yoo hoo!" Miriam waves a gloved hand. By the time they arrive she is breathless.

But wasn't that later today, the meeting that Miriam had gone to such great pains to set up? "You'll forgive me, Signor D'Agostino —" But when she turns around, the green grocer has already disappeared inside his shop.

"We're a few minutes early I know." Miriam peels off a white cotton glove and fans herself with it. "This is Signor Davoglio, Lila. The art curator."

Is this the picture of an art curator these days? A smug Swede carrying a bakery box? Lila rubs her at her lower back, trying to mask her disappointment as just the usual aches and pains.

"Signor Davoglio, Lila Lesser." Miriam is beyond pleased with herself.

"Enchanted, Signora Lesser." Signor Davoglio offers his hand. His voice is as smooth as Neufchatel cheese, and the gold cufflinks and expensive leather loafers sparkle with the kind of polish that's a bit too shiny for Lila's taste. "Please. It's Marcello."

Lila shakes the soft white hand grudgingly. His fingernails are evenly buffed into squares.

"Have we met before?" The smile lines fold in around his eyes.

Obviously they have. He was the buffoon at the front of the bakery line, but Lila won't let on. Instead she shakes her head, a sudden timidity falling like a protective shawl around her shoulders. No. She knows something he doesn't and for the moment this is how she'd like to keep things. "Would you excuse me for a moment, Signor Davoglio? Miriam, a word?"

Lila motions her friend over and whispers urgently. "This is a mistake."

"Whatever do you mean?" Miriam persists in her perplexed fashion, unaware that her famous curator eats cake and who knows what else off the dirty floor. "We've come all this way! And I don't need to tell you I pulled a few strings. Marcello is a busy man."

"Marcello, is it? Look, all I can say is he's not the right one."

"Lila, but you haven't even —"

"Is there a problem, ladies?" Signor Davoglio has removed his hat, and his hair slicked with pomade is a few shades darker than his natural blonde. The hairstyle, even if it suits him, and it does, Lila must grudgingly admit, is an anachronism, nearly three decades too late.

"Not at all." Miriam laughs uncomfortably. "It's just that... would you mind terribly if we munch on something before we get down to business?"

Signor Davoglio hoists the little bakery box tied with string. "I have just the thing."

———

"But you keep the paintings here?"

Davoglio's steady tenor betrays more than a hint of covetousness. Miriam eggs Lila on with a little roll of her hand. Tell him Lila! But Lila says nothing. It was a bad idea to show Albert's collection. A stupid idea. Someone will surely steal them away. The paintings inspire envy and greed, and people are always taking things that don't belong to them. History remembers that the Germans tried and failed. No. She must tread carefully. Caretaking the collection is her lifelong obsession. They hadn't been hidden in the Italian countryside for months under stables that smelled of horse dung, the boxes of paintings buried like royal cadavers in the dirt beneath them, just to have some dandy in a smart hat come along and get his hands on them.

"Can I help?" Davoglio looks on as Lila slowly unties the string of the bakery box. She shakes her head.

The counter in the storeroom is laid out with the embroidered placemats kept for a rainy day, little porcelain teacups and saucers placed carefully in a row as the kettle whistles away on the burner, and the box of Linzer tortes is opened, the smell of butter pastry and jam scenting the musty aisles with better ideas. There will be tea and civilized discussion because no impulsive decisions are ever made over tea and cake. But no sooner is the table laid, when the door bursts open and Alvise, Lila's shop assistant, stands unsteadily in the threshold, pained and bewildered, a line of blood meandering down his arm. "Could someone please—" He collapses against the open door.

"Lila, call someone..a doctor, an ambulance!" Miriam rushes to the boy's side, now a heap on the floor, frozen with shock and adrenalin.

Miriam manages, with Signor Davoglio's help, to sit the boy upright and drape his arm like a limp ribbon around her shoulder. "We shouldn't move him. Call for help!" Davoglio nods at Lila. "Let's wait for the ambulance."

As Lila dials the number for emergencies and then responds with wooden answers to the operator's questions, she cannot help but fixate on the line of blood running down Alvise's arm, staining his white shirt purple-red and now the curator's pinstriped jacket. She blinks slowly, unable to look away: it's the perfectly round hole in Leo's forehead again, his legs twitching, his hands still warm in hers.

Miriam and Davoglio are talking to the bleeding boy, asking him questions, his answers come back slowly, one syllable, a groan, and then one more. Stabbed. Davoglio holds the injured boy's hand while Miriam grabs her sweater and wraps it around the boy, the little mink collar a strangely comical sight around Alvise's pale face. The news comes in spurts: a burglary, his billfold taken, hold on Alvise, they implore, they're coming in five minutes. Lila some water! Lila rushes to the sink and holds the glass under the faucet, willing the perfect black hole in Leo's forehead to recede into oblivion.

A non-life-threatening flesh wound, Miriam reports over the phone. But, will he be alright? Lila asks. Of course. Miriam's sighs and curt responses are darts missing their target. And the meeting with the curator? Miriam will not let the matter drop. Yes, yes, we will reschedule. There's irritation in Lila's voice. Another time. Nothing is as important as the boy's recovery. Certainly. Miriam agrees. They will reconvene. Still Lila cannot shake the feeling that this Davoglio is a strange man, an odd fancy man. But an odd fancy man who saved the day, Miriam says. Enough to be trusted with the collection? Miriam wants a definitive answer, but for once Lila has no fixed opinion. She puts down the receiver, clears the plates, tosses the untouched tortes in the bin, and pours the teapot's contents into the storeroom sink, a long high stream of yellow not unlike a dog peeing in the street. Once upon a time, she wasn't useless in an emergency.

The ticking clock, the passing vaporetto outside, none of it is any comfort. The shop is too quiet when she's all alone. The sight of all that blood is something she cannot unsee. And the smell. Miriam had given her what details she knew: a man with a knife on Calle Zen. Alvise's money taken, the wages he was trying to save for his mother's rent and living expenses, and the boy himself, completely shaken. It's disgusting, the crime in the city. Especially to one so kind-hearted, a son on leave from university to care for his ailing mother since her husband passed away. Such a son is a rare gift. For other people. Never for Lila. But she will not feel sorry for herself. Time is short, and she must take up a collection. Yes. Lila brightens. As soon as she feels a bit more steady, that's exactly what she will do. Alvise can buy himself a new starched shirt for work and not worry about his mother's groceries. A little bit of compensation will soften the blow. But her mood darkens after the phone rings: this time a creditor she's been avoiding threatens her with a lien against her business, instructs her to pay off the entire debt if she wants to avoid foreclosure.

Long after the clerk hangs up Lila hears the dial tone through the open window of the shop. A horrible empty sound that banishes any other real music of the day— the birds, the passers by, the complaint of children at play. Quiet as stone, as a statue, she sits next to the wooden counter, trying her best to imagine real blackness, the only possible solace. The stationers shop is lost. She covers her mouth. Sometimes anguish is a muting thing.

Perhaps, she thinks disconsolately, buying the trattoria from the late Signora Bertollini after the war had been a mistake. After the death of their mother, the old signora's family had wanted to unload the failing restaurant and Lila could have it for a song. Swiftly, with more hope than forethought, she signed on the bottom line. Only a few strokes of a pen would finally give her an occupation, a profession, something Albert, wherever he was, could smile down on. Something he could finally be proud of. During their marriage she was never good enough for him, no matter what she did to make a home: the incessant tidying up and organizing the shelves, the ironing of bed sheets, and stirring of sauce pots, and all of that was considered cheap, insignificant domestic work; and their family life always a disaster. Dear sweet Albert. He laid all of Leo's problems like a thorny martyr's wreath on Lila's head, as though she alone had given birth to such a strange, intractable child. And when her husband had the nerve not to survive the war, he did what many people of means often do: he used his last will and testament as punishment. A posthumous thrashing for her sins. Sure, there was the initial modest distribution, enough for Lila and the baby to start over in Venice and to send Isabel to Saint Dominica's, but afterwards, there was only a meager stipend left over for living expenses. And the reason is simple enough, although it pains Lila to admit it: Albert was stingy, although she couldn't say selfish, he could give when he wanted to and he made her feel like a fancy woman with a priceless art collection, but to be honest, he was stingy, exacting, controlling with money. At least he'd been right about Isabel, stipulating that she wouldn't be able to come into her inheritance until she turned twenty-one, and considering her granddaughter's recent behavior, that had been a wise, almost prescient decision.

So. Lila had made a business decision all on her own. A widow raising a baby alongside the handful of other Venetian Jews who reclaimed their homes after the war, she would also be the proprietor of a paper shop. Now she had her inventory to count, her papers and pens to showcase. Every day since, and for the first time in her life, she imagined herself clever and independent. A stationer's shop suited her; it was far simpler to run than a trattoria. Lila knew next to nothing about the restaurant business, whereas she had spent her whole life adjacent to paper and pens. Albert was an occasional writer who dreamed of setting down his memoirs which was, like many grand plans, never realized. Nevertheless Lila went about her new project with unusual vigor and single-mindedness, spending long hours at La Carte Fina, arranging the displays into works of aesthetic balance: a range of ballpoint colors spread out like a rainbow, with a fresh sheet from each ream tacked to the wall for the customer to sample the ink on high quality paper. In the first year after barely any merchandise moved from the shelves, and when the years afterwards followed suit, she would not allow herself the luxury of dismay. Giving up was not an option. After all, there was the occasional tourist who fancied himself the next great American novelist or the wide-eyed student on a random splurge. The years went by in this way, and with age and experience things became very clear: the business was a complete and total failure. But this recent money trouble was the executor's fault, a gangly man who speaks in a cold monotone and never listens, only waits to speak. If he hadn't refused Lila any additional monies from the estate, she would never have had to take out the business loan. One can only economize so far on sugar and bread and coffee. And asking Miriam for any more help was beyond embarrassing. The humiliation. But foreclosure. Such an ugly word.

Lila locks up the shop. Across the way Signor D'Agostino is back on his ladder teetering like a wobbly egg at the top rung as he carefully peels off last week's fascist from the top of the display window and replaces it with a fresh corpulent mustachioed face. When he notices Lila, he quickly loses his balance.

"Oh!" She rushes over while the grocer hangs on, panting like Signora Volterra's little dog and steadies the ladder before he can fall. Grateful, he sends her off with a salute, a trickle of blood on his knuckles.

Lila places a lavender-scented handkerchief on the last rung before leaving him to his postering. A good neighbor doesn't let a neighbor bleed to death.

The next morning before school Isabel blows a strand of hair out of her mouth, and feigns interest in the toast on her plate. "So, Signora Morgenfeld was grandfather's friend?"

"Again, you're asking?" It takes every bit of will not to spit in the soapy sink water at the mention of that woman's name; it's relentless, the girl's need to know about the past at every turn. Lila continues scrubbing the pan vigorously.

"So what if I am?"

But Lila refuses to talk about that woman. Talking about her means picturing the two of them together, and she won't see it, not again, her husband and that floozy in the coatroom at the gala, his arms around her back unzipping the periwinkle sequined gown and Lila hovering like an uninvited ghost, a clumsy pathetic witness to their gasping and moaning.

Lila closes her eyes, carefully dries a glass with the kitchen towel and when she opens them, the image slowly circles the drain with the dishwater. Nonetheless. None of that was Isabel's fault, and Lila must keep that in mind. Not her failed marriage, not any of it. And she would not do what her own mother had done to Lila, blame her for the terrible violence her stepfather wrought upon their lives. Unlike her mother who was weak and self-interested, Lila has tried at every turn to be fair, even-handed, and as kind as she can be, without spoiling the girl. She has in fact been siphoning away a little of her own monthly allotment from Albert's estate, a few lire she dutifully deposits in a coffee can hidden in plain sight on the kitchen shelf. Some pin money for a rainy day, not enough for university, certainly not, but for the girl's incidentals after graduation.

Isabel waits, a hand on her hip, for an answer to her questions about that woman, something Lila absolutely cannot give her, before finally turning heel and heading out, the front door slamming.

Let her go. A good hour later Lila startles from folding linens at the loud knock and drifts toward the foyer. She opens the door, a pillowcase in one hand, "Signor Davoglio!"

"Good afternoon, Signora Lesser. Miriam gave me your address. I hope this is alright."

Lila smiles her usual good neighbor smile, but it isn't alright. No one outside her extremely small circle ever drops by unannounced. With the exception of Signora Volterra who, lonely for conversation, brings up the mail once a week.

"I've heard from the doctor with Alvise."

"Yes, the doctor. Of course."

"Miriam told you? Well then you know your boy will make a complete recovery. I had hoped to be the one to deliver the good news." He clears his throat, sheepish. "There's something else, a small matter. May I?"

Lila crosses her arms, unconvinced but steps aside anyway. "Please."

When he enters the foyer, the little space is made even smaller as he spins around taking in all four walls, his gaze finally falling on the painting next to the coat rack. He coughs quietly into a handkerchief, a little purring sound so unlike his earlier bluster.

"Well this one is no reproduction."

"It isn't?" Lila plays dumb. Of course he is right. But if he is the expert he is said to be, he will get no extra help from her. Let him prove his worth. And this Titian hangs in pride of place in the foyer for a good reason: other than the pieces they were able to hide in the countryside, it was the only one Lila had been successful in having returned to them after the War. Still. There is no sense in announcing this to the world.

"The scope." Davoglio regains his composure. "His vision never fails to impress. No other master could ever surpass him."

"Titian, you mean?"

"Portrait of a Man. The one and only." He peers at the painting very closely. "I wanted to set your mind to rest," he says, stepping back.

"About what?"

"We may have gotten off to a less than perfect start yesterday." He gestures as though her stationer's shop is right behind him. "I can be a bit, shall we say, enthusiastic, and for that I must apologize."

"Really Signor, there's no need—,"

"Please." He holds up a hand the way a maestro does in that delicate second before the orchestra plays. "There are a couple of things you may not be aware of, Signora Lesser, and the first is you would be well served with me as your curator. I know Italian Renaissance Art better than most, and for that I will not apologize."

"And the second thing?"

"The second is I can say with complete certainty that this is no reproduction." He turns and hangs his jacket on the rack.

Lila eyes the coat rack incredulously. She in no way meant to suggest he stay a while. She decides to continue with the lie. Best to keep him on his toes. "I assure you that it is, signor. It belonged to my husband."

"That part is true. I imagine Albert Lesser was better acquainted with it than almost anyone. But I assure you, signora, I have seen this particular painting before."

"I'm sorry, but that's perfectly impossible." Lila is insistent. The painting was lost for years. How could this man know that it was among the few works that were returned?

For a second, he gazes down at the floor. When he finally looks back up, his voice has taken on a new tone. A strangely intimate one. "I was there, too, you see."

Lila cocks her head. "What's that?"

"There. In the camp. That's where I saw it."

He rolls up his sleeve with the efficiency of a doctor or a workman as the apartment walls begin to close in and the unmistakable stench of piss and excrement wafts off the plaster, that airless gasp when human bodies are packed too tightly together. With the last roll of his sleeve, Lila cannot look away. There seared into the man's skin is a mark no longer than a common garden worm. A blurry line of blue numbers, pale, but permanent as death.

CHAPTER NINE

The boatyard in the Dorsoduro sleeps. Its glossy black gondolas and smaller vessels, the pupparini, sandoli and sciopòni remain stacked under the wooden roof of the main building which is tucked into the canal like the little houses nestled in Cadore's mountainous valley, a place Isabel has only ever seen in pictures.

"Anyone there?" she calls out, a catch in her throat. "Hel-lo?" A skinny tabby cat settled on a stack of crates at the shed entrance opens a sleepy eye and stretches once before leaping down from the crates and disappearing into the building. A flurry of wind breathes hard and warm against her bare neck. In her haste this morning she somehow still managed to dress carefully, taking pleasure in tucking in the thin white blouse and zipping the plaid skirt. Today the school costume had even more significance than usual; today she would for the first time in her life meet a fence, a real sort of criminal. And she must look the part: naive, trusting, the least likely girl to be sitting on a fortune, but a girl whose family had, however unlikely, because Isabel had given the matter much thought, retained a treasure. Nevermind that the truth was even more unbelievable! Nevermind that Signora Morgenfeld had two Titians that Nonna knew nothing about. Two! Who in the world could claim such a thing? Perhaps luck was on her side. Finally. And if that were true, there was absolutely no more time for classes. Such boredom was well behind her.

On the phone, the heiress said to rendezvous at the villa at noon to pick up the art, and Isabel cannot help the flutter in her belly and uptick of her heartbeat at all these machinations. There's still enough time to meet with Signor Gritti's man and determine his worthiness for the job. Luckily, she had gotten out of bed early for once, the one benefit of sleeping badly and waking throughout the night from too many bad dreams: the terrible quicksand on the stairs, the falling and never landing, the giant dark wave rising and swallowing the seashore and all the children and families playing on the beach and then her father's face from an old photograph Nonna had saved in her bedside table drawer, looking at the camera like it's the last thing he'll ever see.

A last tug at the zipper of her skirt had her tripping over her book bag and its contents spilled out across her bedroom floor: notebooks from language studies, textbooks from math class, but soon without all that bother, plenty of room to carry the incredible windfall from Signora Morgenfeld.

In the Gritti's boatyard now, Leo's black and white photo face is seemingly everywhere. He's hiding behind the stack of gondolas that drag American tourists along the canals for exorbitant sums, snickering like a schoolboy. He's teasing the cat, a delinquent's grin on his face. Isabel glances around, impatient. Niccolo should have arrived by now. Yesterday, his crumpled note had bounced off her shoe in math class. She read the scribbled message quickly, and after the bell rang he admonished her on the school steps. Don't forget, my father's squero! The Dorsoduro! A squero? She had called out after him as he ran through the gates. I thought your father was a fisherman! Too late. That boy was gone; he never even looked back. Well, Niccolo can come or not. She doesn't need him. With all the proceeds from the Titians she could be an heiress herself, in fact she would be one already, if not for Nonna, and her lies and half-truths.

If Nonna seldom spoke about Leo, she mentioned Ilse even less. The thought of her mother stabbed in Isabel's chest like a chronic malady. Ilse was a stranger and yet the most important person at once. But she didn't bother to stick around. And then both of them had perished like the paintings, her young parents. Why not enjoy the rewards for them both? Do the things they could never do. Become her truest self, a young heiress with too many cats, who gathers artists together like Signora Morgenfeld did. She would publish novels under a nom de plume to preserve the mystery. No need for university. No need, in fact, for much else. Well, on second thought, university is essential, inheritance or not. She could not be deprived of higher education, after all.

A bead of sweat slides down her back. Damn that Niccolo and the curve of his lips. Perhaps it was a mistake to let him kiss her. A little rattle from the stack of crates at the shed entrance distracts her: just the cat resettling on his perch. Besides the two of them, the boatyard is unoccupied. They could be a painting. Still life with cat. She grins.

"You're nice and early."

Isabel spins around, knocking over a pair of oars leaning against the shed that then clatter on the stones. By the door, looking every inch the surly giant he surely believes himself to be, is Signor Gritti. He can't be more than a few inches taller than Isabel, and in his shabby coveralls, worn presumably for a day's hard labor, a thin sheen of sweat shines on his face and balding head. His narrow dark eyes give him a chronically perplexed expression. She rights the fallen oars and stands mute.

Signor Gritti gestures toward the book bag hanging limply from her shoulder. "What have you brought me?"

The warm sea breeze tickles her bare legs. She could run. Be gone in seconds and catch the next vaporetto back to the campo. Forget the whole mess. She stays put.

"Who are you anyway? You don't look like any Catholic school girl I've ever seen. Come now. Don't be offended. I know my Jews is all." He grins. "Can always pick one out in a crowd."

Of course. Isabel seethes. Niccolo! That lying little...he must have told his father her secret, and probably more besides, like their date at the movies. My Jews. Antonia was right. Men do love to brag. Isabel buttons the top button of her cardigan.

"Aren't you a little deer in headlights?" Gritti steps closer, his is the worst kind of odor: cigarettes and alcohol, unwashed sweat and the putrefying grease of days-old fried sausages; the kind the old people in the Dorsoduro love to eat so much. He extends a hand. "Let's shake.Yes? Good. There. Pleased to meet you." The little meaty palm is calloused and moist like the rough stones at the seashore, and Isabel recoils, wishing in vain she could wipe her hand on her skirt.

"Down to business?" He licks his lips. "So. Show me."

But she waits uneasily. If it's a test, and the shortness of her breath tells her that it is, surely she has passed. He'll see nothing, not from her, not just yet. Even an unseasoned criminal knows enough not to come to a strange meeting place with the goods. "Shouldn't we wait for Niccolo?" She cocks her head.

"Niccolo?" Gritti laughs, a thick roiling noise like an engine turning over. "Not if we want this to happen today." He lights a cigarette. "And I'm a busy man." He gestures at the stack of gondolas. "Any second now, signorina, the crowds will be lining up." He nods his chin, a nervous tic.

"But he said he would come."

"Who Niccolo? Look, your boyfriend's not coming. Besides he'd just get in the way, right?" His eyes lock on the school bag.

"Well I don't have it with me." Any pretext of a plan flutters out of her head as her heartbeat thrums in her throat and her mouth has gone quite dry. Niccolo, that coward! He promised her she wouldn't be alone. Gritti takes a deep drag of the cigarette and his narrow eyes widen, solid black like a lizard's. He laughs again and she sees he is missing an eyetooth, something she hadn't noticed before. Wrapping an arm around her shoulder he pulls her in toward him. God, but the stench! If she could plug her nose, she would. She scans the perimeter around them, forgetting for an instant where the exit is.

"I'll come back with it. Later."

Gritti shakes his head. "No way, princess. This isn't the marketplace. No one else is buying." He drags on his cigarette before launching it with a flick of his fingers toward the shed door. The cat hisses, its back arched as the embers fly past. "Don't you worry though. You'll get a fair price. Your people always do. Unless ...," he trails off.

"Unless?"

"Unless we need to have a little talk with the nuns at school. You'd be surprised how fast news travels."

The rosary. Niccolo must have told him. The blue sky above, the sea breeze at her back, the world takes a vertiginous tumble and she would fall over, flimsy as a paper doll, if somehow her legs weren't still holding her up. Isabel stiffens. She won't let him do it. She won't let this little troll give her up to Sister Angelica and force her expulsion. "I will. When Niccolo's here. And your guy. I'll come back then with what you want."

"Not good enough."

Gritti slides one hand slowly into and out of his jacket pocket and flicks his wrist. The open switchblade gleams in the dim light. She can't move. Can't back away. Not until the tinkling of little bells breaks the spell, and they both spin around. The workman at the front gates has a jangling set of keys in one hand and a bucket in the other. He freezes at the sight of them. "What the—how did you get in?"

Gritti has his dirty fingers around her arm. "My house," he whispers, "three p.m. And you'd better bring it this time." He runs the blade lightly against her wrist, and she freezes, her agency gone. He could do anything. He would do anything. But his blade is a tease: light enough not to break skin but with the promise of pain to come.

The workman gestures. "Hey you! This is trespassing!"

But Gritti is already making his way toward the exit as quietly as he came. Time, for her, becomes an abandoning thing; somehow she's pinned to the earth. The boatyard grows twice its size as she becomes very small, a little lawn statue, a stone vessel for water, and there is only quicksand and waves and never getting away.

"I'm calling the police!"

What would Leo do? Her problem-solving mind kicks into gear, and quietly, slowly gaining in volume is the knowing voice, the one beneath everything else, beneath the static and self-doubt, the disgust and fear. The one that says she must move too. She hoists the empty book bag on her shoulder and flies past the still-dozing cat, the workman's threats and curses echoing from behind.

The villa is quiet, the shutters are closed and the pekingese nowhere to be seen. A few flowerbeds have been dug up in the garden and the tulips flop over, defeated. As soon as he left the squero, Gritti had simply evaporated, smell and all, like mist. Isabel swallows hard, she must concentrate, be logical. A man like that would find her soon enough. She lifts the thick ring in the lion's mouth and lets it fall against the tall wooden door. "Anybody there?" she calls out timidly.

She clams up, suddenly embarrassed. It's a young voice, a girl's voice, not a young woman who does business with fences and criminals. The steady zip-zip of motorboats crosses the canal but nothing more. Surely a groundskeeper, the housemaid, someone must be at home. But there is only the hum of boats and occasional squeal of laughter of tourists from the not too distant quay. Isabel knocks again harder with her fist this time, the whole plan falling down around her like the old scaffolding against the palazzo. She chokes back tears. The stupidity. The bad luck. But she should have expected it. She has nothing, comes from no one, and this city will never give her up.

A ship's horn blows hollowly in the distance. She wipes her eyes, knocks one last time just to say that she did in fact try her best. The front door flies open.

"Oh Signorina Isabel!" The housemaid catches her breath. "Sorry I was—is the Signora expecting you?"

Isabel gulps down her panic. Surely the heiress had not forgotten.

"I'm sorry, but Signora Morgenfeld was called away."

"She was supposed to leave something for me? A package."

The housemaid's eyes light up. "One moment, signora." The door closes and seconds later she reappears in the doorway holding a small box.

Isabel slips the little package into her bag and thanks her. Finally, a bit of good luck. It's a good sign, she's sure of it. A different kind of life is surely waiting on the other side. But it's a line in a book and she's not sure she believes it just yet. Gritti's blade still plays on her arm and leaning against the tree trunk, the package in hand, she steadies herself for the walk back down the path through Giardini Papadopoli. She pulls up her sock. She's come this far, there's no going back. Of course Nonna would tell her to go back, Antonia would too. From behind comes a strange, hollow sound like the beating of a stick against a thick carpet. *Thwack.*

Sometimes pain doesn't register until later, sometimes not at all. A streak of brilliant, burning, yellow light, then blackness.

Cold water bleeds through the dank porous walls of stone and mud. Isabel's head is pounding, and her vision clouded. From the thin shaft of sunlight far above she can make out her enclosure's shape: a tube. A vertical tunnel. She writhes against its damp embrace, a straitjacket of space, she is barely able to move an inch or two in any direction. Her arm, she discovers, is lifeless, pounding. When she does try to move, her socks squish in her shoes. She turns her head and a jolt of electricity runs through her temple, trailing down her spine. Water drops rain down from above, and she wipes her good arm across her eyes. How long has she been asleep? Or was she unconscious? She drags her fingers across the back of her head through matted hair, a warm drizzle of stickiness trickles down her neck. Dark drops on her fingers: blood. What happened? The Parco. The painting! Desperate, she digs around her, crying out: the school bag is gone. Her mind searches desperately for some kind of hand hold, but finds none. She was on Signora Morgenfeld's doorstep. Isabel reaches across the mental blankness for the box in the housemaid's hands, but to no avail. Nothing after arriving at the villa and speaking to the housemaid makes any sense. Perhaps Gritti had followed her there? But he vanished from the squero so quickly. Still, he could have sent someone after her. He was a gangster and a thief, that much she knows. *Thief.* The word has lost its meaning. She weeps in anguish, incredulous, inconsolable. She is the thief and no one is coming to save her.

Antonia was always the one to have answers and a plan, a way out. Isabel misses her friend in a way she didn't think possible. When she closes her eyes Antonia is running a comb down the length of Isabel's unkempt hair, cursing the knots even as she praises its thickness and strength. They are sitting on a stool at the back of her café and the steam is rising from a cup of black coffee on the counter. It grows like a weed is Isabel's standard response to any compliment about her hair but she feels the heat rise in her cheeks and the rims of her ears just the same. Insults are somehow easier to take, she can fight them off, rail at her accuser, avenge the hurt. Antonia pays her no mind and deftly twists her wild tresses into two perfect braids.

Isabel opens her eyes and there is only wet earth and stone, the mushroomy scent of rot and mold and somewhere below water is dripping like the dot dot dot ellipse at the end of an unfinished sentence. Twisting painfully she digs at the wall next to her as if she can tunnel her way out. But when she snaps off the tip of a fingernail against a jagged facet of stone, she screams out, wrings her hand in pain. She should never have listened to Niccolo's absurd ideas. But she was curious. Bored. Greedy, too, if she's being honest. Why had she been so stupid as to trust Niccolo? If she hadn't, she'd be safe in bed right now with the day's late homework as her only worry. She envies that girl, the one lounging in bed bored with life. All along Niccolo must have been following her for this very reason: that time he broke into their flat, that time at school in the courtyard before Teresa showed up. Isabel's dissatisfaction, her far-fetched dreams for the future, all of it made her stand out: she was an easy mark. He probably only pretended to read Sartre. And now she cannot even remember his face, there is a round black stain where his mouth should be, like an oil pit.

The tears fall in frustration, and Isabel makes a strange sound deep in her throat as the thin shaft of light fades into shadow. She holds her breath, her shoulders heaving, knowing that it's pointless to wish everything would stop: this day, the Squero, Gritti, the ridiculous painting. When she exhales, nothing has changed. Nothing except a rising confusion. Without all the usual cues, the thrush singing outside the kitchen window, the morning light and its gradual shifting to full throated afternoon, she cannot begin to guess how long she's been stuck in this hole. Nonna must be at home right now checking her wristwatch for the umpteenth time, tapping a slippered foot with impatience as she finishes the washing up. Isabel feels a sharp and guilty pang of sympathy for the old woman, a remorse and fear too. Nonna is always left waiting.

Isabel tries to recall her father's face from the photograph with Nonna and Albert, his white shirt and cardigan, but Leo's face too has disappeared, a white blur where the familiar features used to be: the long slender curve of his nose, the hard curl of his chin. It used to bore her, life at home but compared to this purgatory, Nonna's flat, always such a prison with her penchant for order and predictability, seems like freedom itself.

A sudden flicker of movement from overhead distracts her and then she hears it, the slow procession, like the hushed whirring of a bat descending an inch at a time through the gloom. Her stomach turns over in dread as acute as her hunger. A cold sweat, the terrible cramping in her legs and back because she can barely straighten any part of her and the dark bat continues to descend, by this point is almost within reach. A shot of pain jolts through her knee when the heavy bucket drops down, she cries out; the rope on its handle still taut.

"Hello? Who's there? Hello!" Her knee is pounding but there is no room to reach down and rub it, so she rummages feebly inside the bucket and finds the smooth curve of a glass bottle. Miraculous. She brings the jug to parched lips and guzzles, the water streams down her chin and forms an instant puddle at her feet. Such is her thirst that even the suspicion that the water may be poisoned is not enough to prevent her from drinking. She sets the empty jug back down in the bucket and grips the splintered edge. There's something else inside. With great care, she lifts the paper parcel and ravenous, tears off the wrapping. Trembling fingers run along the coarse flaky sides of a loaf of bread and the smooth shiny skin of an apple. She stuffs down mouthfuls, can hardly chew fast enough, it's the most divine food she has ever eaten, and bit by bit the blood flow returns to her legs and the strength to her arms.

"Please! Anyone! Is anyone there?"

Her voice is sturdier this time, resolute echoes that float upwards and then stop. Silence. But the shaft of light overhead grows brighter, a flashlight's radiance shining down the hole. In the bright beam of light the last item at the bottom of the bucket is illuminated: a piece of paper. Isabel unfolds it and, squinting at the shaky block letters, reads "Use the Rope." Obediently, with equal parts hope and dread, she unties the rope from the bucket and with her good arm fastens it around her waist, tucking the rope under her lifeless arm and squeezing it against her side. The knot is as good as she knows how to make, the one Antonia taught her, the kind sailors use to fasten the masts. She cranes her head: the ascent looks steep, but up is the only way out. Don't look down.

She nods breathlessly, whispers the prayer they used to say in temple on Shabbat, Oh, please dear God, let someone hear it this time, Nonna's God, Sister Angelica's, anyone's. Then, without any idea who or what she will meet at the top, she tugs back. Ready. Slowly, tentatively at first then gradually more pendulous, she sways mechanically back and forth. The narrow walls batter her hips and elbows, and the rope burns like ice against the bare skin of her waist but fear overrides the pain. With both hands holding on and the strong upward pull guiding her, she fixes her feet on the slimy wall and takes one slow step then another, climbing ever closer toward the glowing light.

CHAPTER TEN

Davoglio had been there. In the camp. He had been in the camp with the rest of them. "I swallowed whole the crusts of bread, choked down the guilt," he says, eyeing the envelope on the telephone table. "Oh, the Biennale! A wonderful event. But please, signora, approach with caution. I wouldn't trust your collection with Signor Agresta, if that's who it's from." he shakes his head. "I don't have to tell you whose side he was on in '38."

His story is amazing. He was there. Just amazing enough to be true. When Lila couldn't control her retching over the side of the rotting wooden bunk, when Miriam had writhed with fever and yet somehow survived, Davoglio had been there too. Although, thanks to the light color of his hair and eyes, they didn't believe he was Jewish, not really, and he was given special favors: he was even allowed to work in the commandant's office. When the stolen artwork began to come through they let him run his fingers along the mahogany frames, the Monets, Manets, and Titians. He helped them inventory every painting, every sculpture, and was awarded extra rations. As the rest of them withered with typhus and dysentery, Davoglio thrived, grew a little richer he said, merely by the proximity to such spectacular art. He counted and tagged each priceless object. If he could someday have a hand in returning the stolen treasure to the Jewish collectors, he could finally see a point to living. He made a careful plan for survival: eat whatever they give you, do as they say, remember in the future there will be a way out, his path to renewal, to helping his fellow Jews. He was not a religious person but as he worked he took to praying, did what he was told, put one foot forward at a time. Of course there was a downside. He could never look away from all that suffering and had nightmares about his Jewish mother, deported a full week earlier than he was, still in her night dress and slippers.

By the time they move to the parlor, Lila has decided not to place any trust in this Signor Agresta, and flushes at the curator's every exclamation. A young man who cared for his mother always tugged at her heart. For his part, Signor Davoglio graciously feeds her answers to her many questions. Where did he sleep? On the floor of the commandant's office. With a blanket! What did he eat? Bread mostly, sometimes a hunk of cheese. He fooled them all. And he made it out. With his gold cufflinks and sharp jacket, the well-turned out academic was, indeed, a Jew! He had shared their fate. He was one of them. Lila cannot stop smiling; but she must look a mess! She runs her fingers through her hair like a teenager, like a groupie.

Davoglio picks up a small wooden sculpture of a shepherd boy playing a harp and begins telling Lila about the piece. Italian. Sixteenth Century. In the certainty of his attention, the order and gravitas he brings to the hodge-podge of curios on the shelves is a salve, a balm for frayed nerves. Beyond knowing the provenance of each piece, Signor Davoglio is adept at puzzling out the underlying story the small bric-a-bracs told of a bygone era. Clearly, like Lila, he has earned his wisdom through trial, and when he stops to admire the small oriental mask and the knitted kuba cloth beneath it from Albert's trip to Africa, she cannot banish one simple thought: she has found her curator.

They talk in the parlor for what seems like hours over cups of tepid jasmine tea and soon the grandfather clock chimes once more. Signor Davoglio rises, shaking his head at Lila's offer of another cup: he has overstayed his welcome. He must get on with his appointments. They linger at the front door, and he extracts a promise that she will call with her answer and soon. Lila nods, closes the door, breathless.

He had been there too.

After he is gone, she practically floats around the room in her flowery house dress and apron, lighter on her feet, her feather duster tickling the edges of all the small and previously overlooked objects which are magnified beyond their previous stale ubiquity. As she dusts, she hums tunelessly, Davoglio's regard following her at every turn.

The next day a sleep-deprived Lila pauses at the open door of Isabel's bedroom: her granddaughter's bed hasn't been slept in. She had missed dinner and must have never come home at all: her room is far too orderly and her school bag is gone. Lila is trying not to panic when the phone rings. It's the school secretary inquiring about the girl's absence and why Lila hadn't left any word.

"But you say she hasn't showed up?" Lila twists the telephone cord around her hand so tightly the web of blue veins on her skin bulge. It's all her fault for getting too caught up with Signor Davoglio and the collection. But it was an intoxicating hour. Her face burns with shame.

"Surely your granddaughter must have mentioned why she didn't attend school yesterday." Lila knows more than she's saying, the school secretary's tone implies. Just sickening! The superiority of the people at this school.

"As I said, signora, Isabel doesn't tell me much these days."

"I see." The woman clears her throat. "Well it's not surprising, we—,"

"Should have called sooner." Lila swallows her impatience, counts silently to ten. The truth is she has no memory of talking to Isabel at all during the last couple of days. Maybe longer. The girl had come and gone like the vaporetti, only docking long enough to pick up supplies before heading out once more.

"I'm sorry Signora Lesser. But we have called you. Many times. Haven't you received any messages?"

Lila cannot help but notice the woman's needling tone.

"We've called the house and sent letters."

Messages. Of course. Isabel must have been taking the calls and intercepting the mail. Deceptive child! More like her father everyday, God help them. Lila thanks the woman, for what she hasn't the faintest idea (for doing a bureaucrat's job? for not taking care of her granddaughter?) and hangs up the phone. She massages her throbbing temples, the pulse of blood, a blinking neon warning sign, and cautions against panic. No sense in it. One must take stock of the situation in a reasonable way. Be scientific in the approach. So. Back to square one. Searching the girl's bedroom and going through the pockets of her spring coats yielded no more than two wrapped hard candies and a broken cigarette. Lila poured the small handful of tobacco into the bin, shaking her head. If that's the only infraction, it's the least of things and she can live with it. God knows she has dealt with far worse. Of course, there would be repercussions and consequences. Lila makes a mental note. They would have a talk about that later.

The telephone receiver jumps in the cradle. Lila pounces on it.

"Hello?"

"Lila! I'm glad I caught you."

"Oh, Miriam. It's you."

"Well thank you very much."

"Oh, I'm sorry dear. I hoped it was—never mind."

"Well I'm calling because, you'll have to forgive me Lila but I couldn't wait a second longer." There's a pause and throat clearing at the other end. "Have you thought more about him?"

"Who?"

"Who? Davoglio of course!"

Miriam is aglow about the curator, cannot sing his praises enough, and isn't it wonderful he has agreed to help with the paintings and doesn't Lila agree? Miriam insists on an answer, but Lila's sigh is tectonic, the movement of plates, whole civilizations have risen and fallen in the wake of such a sigh, at the other end her friend cannot restrain a little gasp. "Lila, what is it—has something happened?"

"It's nothing Mim. Really —" But her thoughts are a jumble. The clock in the foyer chimes the hour, and she gasps. The appointment at the bank! How had she forgotten? "Oh no. Look, Mim, I have to go."

"What do you mean go? I thought we were—"

Lila hangs up the phone with her friend still talking and races down the hall to get dressed.

At the top of that long climb upward, at the mouth of the long tunnel and just inches from freedom, Isabel is grabbed by unknown hands. She has time only to smell hot breath on her face, stale and strong with tobacco, as the sack is pulled over her head. She suffers quietly, riddled with fear as these same hands prod her along, one unsure step after another through black space. A musty smell like dead leaves in winter, worms turning over earth and the threat of rain invades her nostrils, as though they are standing at the edge of a wood. Under her feet is the crunching of twigs, and she smells soft peat, grass, and the scent of honeysuckle heavy with droplets of water. The moisture soaks through her thin sweater when she brushes past. They are moving forward, she is out and alive, even if she is limping along with one shod foot and the other bare, and her underpants sopping wet from when she could no longer control herself in that cramped space and warm wetness pooled beneath her. The smell of her own pee shames her, and she wants to curl up, go to sleep and wake up in an entirely different world.

Instead she licks her parched lips with a dry tongue and remains vigilant. Hover outside of your body like a fly; she tells herself. To survive is to suffer, Nonna would say, and Isabel banishes all dark thoughts from her head, finds the substance and strength once more in her back, her limbs. Each step means she is one inch closer to everything: food, water, shelter, relief, a reason why; or perhaps to nothing at all beyond more pain, more waiting, an end to suffering. Fearing the last possibility most of all, she settles on the former, calls upon Nonna's instruction, never project the future, only protect it.

I will, Isabel whispers as the force at her shoulder turns her left while another hand pushes the top of her head through a narrow space: a doorframe, perhaps the entrance to a cave. Underneath her one bare foot the feel of smooth tile and enveloping her is a luxurious warmth: a crackling fire. They are inside a house. Mixed with the delightful scent of wood burning is the odor of meat cooking. Her stomach turns over in anticipation. The hand on her shoulder compels her to sit down on the tiled floor.

"Stay there. And be quiet!"

She finds the corner of the wall and leans back, shivering with exhaustion. The voice is gruff and male, but she cannot say it's Gritti's. She cannot think beyond hunger and thirst and the ensuing warmth replacing hours of wet cold, and when her sobs of relief erupt with a shaking force, no one is more surprised than she is.

"Enough!"

And with that one word, she covers her mouth with both her hands and falls silent, swallowing free will and with it, any hope of escape.

CHAPTER ELEVEN

Isabel's legs have long since gone pins and needles beneath her. She crouches in dark space, enduring long stretches of unmeasured time without a chair to sit in. In the gloom isNonna's chiding finger, Antonia's pleading eyes. An entire universe of what she could have done differently. This is what happens when you close your ears to good advice. Her face in her hands, the bitter taste in her mouth, her head pounds to a dull thudding drum beat while her bones ache like never before. She struggles to keep faith: to imagine that somehow this strange nightmare will resolve itself. Her broken arm scrapes against the wall, and she winces in pain. In punishment. But she is resolute, and she conjures up the better dream, the one she concocted in the tunnel, the one where she is running barefoot to the end of the clover-covered meadow and the soft, wet sand edges the sunlit water. She is nearly to the warm, gently-lapping waves when a hand slaps her face and stings her fully awake.

"Eat!" A man commands, his voice deep with a slight accent. German.

A match is struck and the familiar after-smell of sulphur is a small comfort, if only for a second. Now she can see that the room is windowless and small with walls grimy from smoke and age, and everything a bit sooty and out of focus in candlelight. Directly in front of her is a small card table on which a bowl has been placed, steam rising from its center. She breathes it in deeply: the succulent smell of chicken, a balm for the senses. She grabs the spoon with her one working arm; the other remains curled at her side like a porcelain doll's limb. In her haste to eat, she burns her mouth and tongue, but she doesn't care; the hot soup activates every cell of her body, and she brings the bowl to her lips and slurps down the rest. She is suddenly past any ability to taste, past any sense of savoring. The last bite is a bit of something mushy, a potato, a carrot, and she gulps this down too.

The man serving her is another shock: he wears a large-beaked Venetian mask with the face of a crow and from behind the bird's face makes a clicking sound with his tongue. "Didn't your mother ever teach you how to eat properly?"

"My mother's dead." The first words out of her mouth in what feels like forever have a different ring: truth.

"Well." He fans himself with a hand. "So's mine, but I still know my manners." He takes the empty bowl and disappears through a narrow doorway. For the moment he is gone and she can breathe. She moves her legs and tries to stand, but instead falls over in a sad little heap, her feet still numb and tingling. Before she can give it a second go, the man returns. He approaches the corner where she leans like a useless shop mannequin, trembling, she is grateful to the wall for propping her up. They are the only two here, alone at the end of the world. And she wants to live, to make it to the next moment and then the next in spite of the fear. He is inches from her face with the nose of his crow's mask grazing her forehead; he sniffs the air. "Perhaps it's true what they say about Jews." The masked face shakes disapprovingly.

"Do you have any water?"

He gives her no answer. No doubt the mask hides a wide bemused grin. "Please. I'm so thirsty. How long have I been here —,"

"Drink." He hands her the bottle. "You have been here two

days. Does it seem longer?" He takes a step back: his pants are well made, tailored but like the walls, shabby and from another era. "First things first: do you like chocolate?"

Isabel gulps. Her throat is dry, and his question inconceivable.

"I, myself, prefer marzipan. Almonds, you know." He clears his throat. "Second things, but most importantly, your wealthy grandmother values her little girl, yes? She will give everything she has to get you back safely. You think all the money I get will buy me some marzipan?"

He talks about chocolate and marzipan with the same gravity as he discusses his crime. Isabel nods of course, but the mention of her grandmother is a cruel reminder of how she's found herself at this end-of-the-world place talking to God knows who, Gritti's man or someone else, in any case, he knows more about her family than he first let on, about Nonna, Albert Lesser, about the paintings. He brags about bits of his plan and Isabel's stomach twists as though all the organs in her body are too crowded together, one on top of the other, the stomach pressing on the liver, the liver on the spleen and all of them pushing upwards against her heart.

"Your life for the paintings, that's the only way this can go," he says, grinning like a lunatic behind the mask, the gleam from the eyeholes giving him away. "Anything less is unacceptable. Rest assured, miss, that all the arrangements are already underway, have been for days." But he falls silent again when she asks what day it is and then begs for an answer, demanding to know when he will let her go. No. All questions are dismissed. "But not to worry," he says, "if everyone cooperates all will be well." All contingencies are planned for, notes have been taken and lists have been made. He is a great believer in making lists, but needless to say, he is also a realist, and the outcome is far from certain. He lowers his voice to a growl above a whisper. "It's best to make your peace."

With what? She wants to ask but doesn't dare. Perspiration seeps through her blouse and goose bumps rise on her legs.

He ladles out the rest of the soup, now tepid, and the strangling sensation around her torso is not unlike the thick leafy vines that encircle tree trunks to the point of suffocation. The bowl is set down and with a shaky hand she brings the soup to her lips, gulps down the rest like tap water. Still, she cannot quiet her mind. In the book of her life they will write that once there lived in the Ghetto a stupid girl, naive and selfish, a thief who stole from her own family. As if the Jews hadn't suffered enough, they will say in the campo, and Nonna will sit shiva for yet another dead child. The spoon hovers shakily in mid air. She cannot gulp down the soup past the lump in her throat. If she survives, she will do differently. Better. She will think of others first. Offer her seat on the vaporetto. Let the old women cut her in line at the grocery. Read to the blind who visit Saint Dominica's on Saturdays. And never, ever steal again. Not even a breadcrumb off the counter at Goldberg's. She will become someone Nonna will be proud of. She vows this and more as the strength recedes from her arms and her head grows heavy. As the room begins to shrink in size, she slides down drowsily against the wall, and the man in the crow's mask straightens her collar. It's as if she is his little doll for the taking. Docile. Lifeless. She has this wish: never to see his real face. To be blessed enough never again to see him in life. She smells the tobacco and cooking grease off his hands, and slowly, surely the walls begin to spin. The soup comes up in a horrible, wrenching hot torrent: bits of potato and carrot stick in her throat and open mouth and then litter the dirt at her feet.

The man in the mask leaps up and out of the way. "Poor girl," the lips in the crow's mask say. "Poison is never easy on the body."

The sound of water dripping into a pot wakes her. Drip. Drip. Drip. Slowly and with much effort, her eyes open. Water from a leak in the ceiling drizzles in an unending stream into the old soup pot on the floor, but a searing pain in her belly forces her eyes shut again. Ugh. She cannot rid herself of it, the putrid smell of bile, her clothing wet from throwing up, and the room is still spinning.

Outside the door muffled voices discuss something in strident tones: one voice is a deep baritone, the other somewhat higher, conciliatory, a boy. They trade comments, go back and forth for a few rounds before the door flies open, someone is pushed into the room, and the door slams shut again. At first her vision is clouded but then she sees him, the tall thin boy with a ripped shirt and muddied trousers. He staggers forward, his beautiful blond hair matted from bits of debris, as if he'd been rolling on the ground fighting. He is from another time, another life and she has never been so happy to see anyone.

"I'm so sorry," Niccolo says. His voice is different, older. His nose is bloodied and his lip is a swollen garden slug. She gasps at the sight of him, tries to stand, willing her legs to support her but ends up on her knees. He kneels beside her holding her face in both hands, and the warmth of him is a down blanket that forces her eyelids to grow heavy. Perhaps they could sleep together in this place for a little while, a few minutes only, they could talk later. He shakes her gently, tries to lift her up but her head has become the head of an immovable marble bust, cool and untroubled. When a sudden fit of coughing wracks her chest, Niccolo grabs onto her hand and doesn't let go.

Lifting her eyelids one at a time, he peers closely at her with concern. "You've been drugged." His breath is a warm breeze. She forgets where they are, then remembers. They are in the darkened theater, and the film is about to begin, the good part when they kissed.

He strokes her cheek as she blinks blearily up at him. "Where were you? I waited." She studies his bloodied face. "Did he do that to you?"

"It's nothing." Niccolo turns his head away. "Apparently I wasn't a very welcome guest." He points back toward the door. "He has your painting. From that rich lady."

Rich lady. She tries to think back, but it all seems so long ago. That's right, at the villa. And the maid who answered the door. "You were there?"

"I had to make sure you were alright."

It makes no sense. He was there and said nothing, did nothing to stop all of this. "Why would you send me there alone?" She shakes her head, incredulous.

"Isabel, please. You've got it all wrong. I didn't send you. I would never. He's my father's worst enemy."

"The man in the mask is your father's enemy?"

"He knows about the art now, I mean the whole collection, Isabel, and I don't think I need to tell you that he isn't a patient man."

A loud thud at the door stops them both, and Niccolo quickly sets a piece of paper on her lap and fishes around in his pants pocket before pulling out a pen. "Look, there's no time. You have to let your nonna know that he's got you. He's willing to do an exchange. This is urgent. This guy is crazy. He won't give up until he has what he wants."

The pounding on the door increases, the pen in her open hand. She doesn't grip it. She will not make this decision. She must think. She must be deliberate. There must be a way out. Drip. Drip. Drip. A small piece of plaster flutters slowly to the floor like a dead moth.

"Listen." He takes her face in his hand. "He'll kill me. And then he'll..." He trails off, strokes her cheek lightly. The scent of the theater still lingers on his shirt, and the Rossellini continues to flicker in waves of light and shadow across the screen. "We can still get out of here," he says. "Together." But he is that stranger at the end of the movie. The one in the shadows. His eyes are dark with intention, and everything in his voice and face and body, the force of his will is compelling, magnetic. She wonders if she wants nothing more than to lie back in his arms. That's what she wanted at first. To let him control whatever happens next like that night in the darkened theater when she squirmed in the velvet seat and his fingers traveled past her skirt, under the wool tights and down into her underwear, and her skin began to burn, the skin she never dared touch herself. As his tongue probed the far reaches of her mouth everything in his body and in his every movement said girls are supposed to give in, and she felt a bit stupid, thinking he must be right. She could not bring herself to speak to him about it after. Not then. She sits up weakly and watches the room settle back onto its moorings.

"What's it going to be Isabel?" He smiles, caresses her hand. A little too firmly.

None of this is right. None of this has gone as he promised. He remains a stranger, someone who takes what he wants. From the very first minute she first found him in the flat, that's all he's done. Nonna's apple. The paintings. Her own body.

She pulls away and the sheet of paper flutters away and the pen falls to the floor. "I'm not going anywhere. Not with you."

Finally. A full breath in. A full breath out. His protests are useless. Her mind is made up. At that, the door to the room groans open and the man in the crow's mask swiftly crosses the room.

"Bravo, bravo." The man claps his hands together, once, twice. "Looks to me like you've lost your touch, Casanova."

"Just a minute more, sir." Niccolo shivers in the crosshairs of the man's attention. "She's coming around, I swear she is."

Isabel gasps. They know each other well. Niccolo called him 'sir.'

The man in the crow's mask holds up a silencing hand, then throws his arm wide and sends Niccolo reeling backward against the wall. He crumples to the floor. "As usual, you've no one to blame but yourself." The distance between Niccolo and the man is a mere three steps and the cracking sound Isabel hears next is like the breaking of a chicken's wing. Decisive. Permanent. The room fills with violent sound; Niccolo's anguished cry is louder and more urgent than the fireboat sirens on the Grand Canal. But the man steps over the writhing boy like rubbish in the road.

"Does that help with your decision, miss?"

She says nothing, not even when Niccolo raises his head, his face flooding with a kind of new disbelief. For once, she feels no shame.

"I see." The man in the mask casts around the room for something, and when he turns to face her, the blade of the hunting knife gleams in the dark. "Believe it or not, I don't like blood, miss. Not one little bit. It's messy. It stinks. But you give me little choice."

"I can't—,"

"But you can." The man waves the pen like a maestro's baton. "One word from you will seal the deal, miss. One little word." He picks her up by the lapels of her sweater like a sack of laundry and drags her to the table where the piece of paper has been set out once more. "Write!" He lets her go and she folds onto the floor like an old bed sheet off the clothesline.

"My arm is broken," she whimpers.

The man shrugs, taps hard on the paper. "Use your other hand. I recommend it. For a change of perspective." He points to a quivering Niccolo, gone silent in the corner. "Look at him. He's not complaining."

"But Nonna won't recognize the handwriting. She'll never believe it's me."

"Problems. Problems. Well, luckily I am fixed on the solution. We'll just have to add a little something else to convince her." He disappears momentarily. She cannot see where he has gone, but as the blade slices the air, the bellow of Niccolo's scream is like the faraway tremulous cries Lila whispered about sometimes with Miriam when she thought no one else could hear. Isabel keeps very still as if the tiniest motion could alter her fate. Another quick slice of the blade combs down the row of pearly buttons and the school cardigan is torn from her body. The remnants of her blouse only partially cover her exposed chest. Like a proud fisherman the man holds up his prized catch for all to see. She smells it before she sees it, the curving rivulet of blood running down his arm, and Niccolo's severed finger is exactly like the fat stub of one of Signor Gritti's cigars.

"This one little charm and that," the man points at the SDS logo on the sweater, "is all the proof we'll need." He taps the paper. "Now write."

The vaporetto to the bank cannot arrive soon enough. Lila bustles past the pack of tourists to board. She has been so muddle headed. On the phone with Miriam she rapped her knuckles on the telephone table, unable to concentrate on a single word her friend was saying. It was too much to talk with Isabel gone who knows where. Of course it was nothing and the girl would be back any second, she was probably at home now trying to figure out what else to pilfer and lie about. Lila didn't like to think of herself as paranoid so much as pragmatic, a deeply observant person. A person who moved cautiously through a world where reality is based on careful observation and deduction. A psychological sleuth of sorts. Yes. That's what she was. A better kind of Sherlock Holmes because of her woman's intuition.

In her hastily assembled outfit, blue navy skirt and sweater set, she races down the dock and hangs a right at Calle Drio l'Archivio huffing and puffing up the main stairs that seem far longer and steeper than they have any right to be. Through the revolving doors of the savings and loan she takes her place at the end of the queue. Deep breath in. Slow breath out. She straightens her chignon, tries to purge herself of the negative and be grateful that the sun is shining. She taps her foot, rubs the ache in her lower back. Finally: her turn. Lila places her heavy purse down on the counter and smiles. The clerk wears horn rimmed glasses and a deadpan expression: clearly, a battle-hardened bureaucrat, and before Lila can state the purpose of her visit, the teller window is slammed shut and a little sign appears on the glass window:

"Closed for lunch."

Lunch? Finally Lila has the money to pay her debt; the problem could be solved once and for all! She pounds a fist on the counter and winces in pain. She had meant to take care of it sooner, she would have, but one thing or another always came first. The collection, this curator person, and now, worst of all, Isabel's strange disappearance. It's her late husband's fault for being so stingy, so controlling with the estate even in death. Such an idiot, she was. Such a fool to fall for the great Albert Lesser. Well. This was her punishment. Surely.

She speaks the last word out loud and at that, the guard at the door throws a glance of disapproval; Lila stands up straighter. No sense in letting them think she's crazier than they already do. It hasn't escaped her: the looks of passersby as she rushed down Venetian streets, the parting of crowds at the plump Jewish woman coming through. Defeated, she marches back out through the revolving doors.

Outside, the small of her back against a cool marble column, Lila rummages in her purse for a stick of gum and finds her wallet, her house keys, an old fraying receipt from the bakery and at the very bottom, an unopened padded envelope. She had forgotten all about it. Signora Volterra handed it to her the day before yesterday. The concierge ambushed Lila as she usually did at the post boxes with that insufferable wide-eyed expression of hers, the one that said, "you should talk to me, I know a secret or two." And she did. The woman knew all the comings and goings in the building, and in the campo at large. Who was stealing from their husband's billfold and who was flirting with the groundskeeper in the piazza. Lila meant to open the envelope right there and but like all of the tenants in the building, she was eager to avoid another protracted conversation. Now she tears the top of the envelope and pulls out a note, first reading Isabel's shaky and uncertain scrawl. She can only get through *Nonna please help me* before glancing down to the strange block letters at the very end of the page. A seagull's taunts ring out overhead and Lila stops short, sliding down the column to the ground like a puppet whose strings have been let go.

All the way to Miriam's, Lila's teeth still are chattering. She dare not think. She dare not breathe. She must not do anything other than push her body through space. Finally with Miriam's building standing before her, Lila exhales.

"I didn't expect you until later!" Miriam stands stiffly in the doorway, broom in hand. "Lila? What's happened?"

She wants to explain, tell Mim everything, but the words, far from rushing out, remain stuck in her throat. It had happened once before actually. Once. Right after Leo died and Lila saw him, his vacant eyes staring at the falling snow. Never blinking, not even when the flakes accumulated in his lashes. She was silent then, mute for days. Weeks maybe. She would have never spoken again, but she had the baby to care for, Leo's baby, who was sickly and so needy and alone. Little Isabel. Lila begins rocking back and forth on the doorstep, unable to stop. She stares at the tiled doorway, wringing her hands.

"That's enough now. You're scaring me." Miriam grabs Lila's arm and drags her inside to the parlor where she sits her down in an overstuffed armchair, the velvet fabric coarse against Lila's sweaty hands. "So?" Miriam fixes her with an expectant look. "Spit it out."

If only Lila could spit it out, the trajectory such news would make across the tiled Venetian rooftops, across miles of land and water all the way to Poland, that other poisonous place, over long miles it would fly. Her granddaughter tied to a chair somewhere, Lila grips the velvet armrests, is too much poison to swallow.

She hands Miriam the note and stuffs the envelope back in her purse.

Miriam lips move as she reads quickly out loud. We have the girl. Your art collection for her life. Her mouth falls open, silenced too.

Lila's thoughts fly, blind as bats this way and that, Isabel injured and bleeding who knows where, until one word, the only word that matters comes forth.

"Ransom."

"Ransom." Miriam repeats with disbelief.

Lila wouldn't believe it herself if she didn't feel the truth of it in her bones. These people, whoever they are, want the paintings. Albert's paintings, and, if it's up to Lila, they can have them. Isabel rotting away in a dank cellar somewhere while the rest of them run around like chickens. Nothing is worth her granddaughter's life. The collection means nothing now, how could it? A bunch of hardened oil droppings on stiff, musty canvas board, no more. And Albert, a selfish bastard to the end, a lying cheating coward awarded a relatively quick death leaving the rest of them to deal with the details.

Lila points a trembling finger toward the door. "Get them." Her voice is a croak. She takes the note out of Miriam's hands.

"Get who?" Miriam mumbles fearfully.

The question is a needless one. Because it's not a who. It never was. The shadow looming over their lives, making them a vulnerable target for criminals. It's a what. They should have lived more simply. Albert. Lila and Leo. The whole Lesser family. They should never have made themselves vulnerable to thieves and murderers. And now it's too late. They have run out of time.

"Get who, dear?" Miriam kneels beside Lila, the slender curve of her face outlined in sunlight as the room grows chilly and silent as winter.

Lila rises from the chair. "The collection."

On the phone with Signor Davoglio, Miriam is persuasive. There is a gravitas and a conviction in what they must do that is unfamiliar, yet totally necessary.

"He's on his way over," Miriam says, hanging up the phone, and gratitude and guilt surge in equal parts in Lila's chest.

Not long afterwards there are two hard raps from the foyer, but Lila can't seem to move. It is Miriam who rushes to the door.

Muffled voices at the front door: the musicality of a masculine tenor and an overly deferential soprano. Lila forces herself to stand and joins Miriam in the parlor. Signor Davoglio languishes at the threshold, his house keys still in his hand. He fidgets uncertainly with his tie for a moment, his eyes filled with concern.

"So good of you to come, Signor Davoglio, under these circumstances. Really, so good of you. May I take your jacket?" Miriam hovers at his side like the maitre 'd of a fine restaurant.

A bit too much fawning for Lila's taste but Miriam seems to be following a script of some sort, after all she knows her way around these people, art patrons, curators.

Davoglio declines. He will keep his jacket on. "Horrible news. Really. The worst news."

"Please. Do sit down." Miriam motions to a wing chair, the one she bought at auction last fall and would never shut up about. How ridiculous, thinking of that at a time like this.

Signor Davoglio nods at Lila, an affirmation, his recognition is a warm wave lapping at her feet. "Please. Tell me. How can I be of help?"

Miriam does the talking: they need help with transporting the art, Alvise will give them access to the vault at the shop. Lila notes how the curator's eyes widen with surprise at the mention of the vault. Besides Lila, only Miriam and Alvise know of its existence. Not even Isabel has a clue. But Alvise is as trustworthy a boy as they come. Miriam deftly fends off the curator's suggestion to involve the police. Too dangerous for Isabel, she says. Lila's thoughts exactly. Everyone in the campo knows the Italian police are not to be trusted.

"Still, your shop is such a public space. Is it wise to keep the collection there?" Davoglio smoothes the lap of his trousers, his sartorial instincts at the fore even when discussing practical matters.

Thank God for Miriam who knows what to say. She assures him that yes, it is wise. Where else to house the paintings but in a stationer's shop where no one would ever suspect? Lila had paid a good deal of money for the reinforced steel at a time when she had money to spend. Davoglio appears hesitant, but he is generous with his time, eager to be of service, and after a moment's reflection, he assures them that if Lila approves, he can have the art transported through trusted colleagues.

Lila's eyes well up; she can't imagine what she's done to deserve such benevolence.

"Isn't that right, Lila?" Miriam looks at Lila expectantly. "I was just saying that we could not be in better hands."

Yes. Lila nods, they are beyond grateful. The man came straightaway. Certainly he may have his agenda, nor could she blame him for wanting to curate the collection, but at a time of crisis a person's true qualities shine through. Her voice, when she finds it again, is no more than a raspy whisper.

"Signor Davoglio, you are a miracle. I am truly indebted."

At the stationer's shop, Miriam wrestles with the lock for a quick second but the key won't budge. It's pointless. She has never had any hand strength. "Are you sure it's the right key, Lila?"

"Of course I'm sure!" There is no other key, and besides Lila always keeps the shop key clipped inside her purse on a separate keychain, the one with the little sterling boat fob. "Here. Let me try."

"They changed the lock." Signor D'Agostino looks up from where he is standing, munching on an apple in his navy grocer's smock like a man who skipped breakfast. "Two men came by this morning," he says.

Lila spins around. "What men?"

"Oh, one guy in a double-breasted suit and the other was that locksmith fellow from Giuseppe's down the street. DeAngelis? Yes, that's it. He had the door open in under three minutes." The grocer points to his cheap Timex, grinning. "I timed him. They took out an awful lot of stuff, crates and such."

"That's impossible." Lila trembles, indignant. They couldn't have gotten to the paintings. No one else has the vault combination.

D'Agostino shrugs. "I'd have called but I don't have your home number." The apple cores fly into the gutter and land in the runoff. D'Agostino trudges back to his grocery store leaving Lila to pound on the shop door in frustration.

"Lila! You'll hurt yourself!" Miriam hovers nervously. "Look there's a letter." Miriam pulls up the envelope stuck in the seam of the door and rips it open. "It's from the bank. They said because of your debt they were forced to file a lien against the collection. Why are they still talking about a debt? Didn't I give you the money for all of that nonsense?"

You did, but I'm an unlucky person, Lila wants to say, and the teller went to lunch instead of depositing the check. She crumbles to the curb, the contents of her purse spilling out: her billfold, a handful of coins, two tubes of lipstick and a comb. A wave of fatigue creeps across her like a bank of fog. That snowy day in the yard, her son lying still at her feet, she was tired then, too. The array of personal items fanned out on the ground look as though they belong to someone else. Without the paintings, she has nothing to show but another huge failure. First as a mother and now as a grandmother. God in his universe got it wrong. All wrong. She turns to say the thing she meant to say long ago, that it should have been her, her and never Ilse who died in the camp.

But Miriam is pacing slowly, an expression forming on her face that Lila hasn't seen in years, hardened lines around the mouth and chin, something well beyond complacency, something more akin to determination, and the kind of sturdy jaw that tenses when voicing an objection. "Do you have a phone number for your assistant?"

"Alvise? Why do you ask?"

"Because there may just be another way in. Come on. The least that silly grocer can do is let us use his phone."

Stooping to pick up the contents of Lila's purse, Miriam helps her friend to her feet, and linking arms, they hurry across the street.

CHAPTER
TWELVE

Miriam's plan is supposed to be simple: Alvise would, with the good Davoglio's help, break in through the back window. They needed to assess the damage for themselves and this was the fastest way. First he would need to file through the bars, loosen them and remove them. Smash the glass like dizzy criminals stealing from themselves. Fortunately, Alvise is willing to give it a go, and, although tall, he is still slight enough to fit through the narrow shop window while Miriam stands watch in front of the store. Davoglio is late.

"I'm stuck." The boy's intones nasally.

"Well, don't moan about it." She simply needs to see for herself, surely D'Agostino was wrong, surely the men from the bank couldn't have taken everything.

But Alvise is taking far too long. They should already be well past this part, in her mind they already are and he is inside the shop tackling the vault combination lock, which, for the uninitiated, could be sticky. After several interminable minutes the boy is still kicking around inside the shop and by the time Davoglio arrives looking trimmer and more well turned out than before with pink-gold cufflinks fastened to starched shirt cuffs and

French cologne that trails him like a tail, Lila can no longer manage any show of even-temper.

"What's going on in there?"

The boy mumbles an incoherent few words through the glass shards.

"How can I be of help, signora?" Signor Davoglio touches her gently on the shoulder.

Lila shakes her head. "It's so good of you to come signor."

"Truly."

Miriam carefully peels off a glove. Even on a hot June day, she wears them. Cotton. Always. And always kept pristine white like a woman without any children. Smart woman. Lila would never have had any kids either if not for Albert insisting that they try. It was a mitzvah to have a child after all, he said; finally they would have an heir. Even if he was right, what did he know? He didn't have the burden of care, the worry. Kids get taken or they leave and never return. That's what kids do.

"Is the safe open? Alvise!"

"Yes signora."

Lila braces. "What do you see? The paintings should be in stacks at the sides of the vault and back. Well?"

"Come signora, you must see it for yourself."

He waves them around to the front of the shop where he unlocks the door. The shop has a vacant feel with the shades drawn and the shelves overstocked for the clients that never come. Lila follows Alvise to the back with Davoglio and Miriam trailing behind. There, with the vault door wide open is an empty black space, a cavernous space where the collection used to be. On the floor is a small package wrapped in brown paper.

"I don't understand. They've taken everything. How could they do this without the combination?" Lila is incredulous.

Davoglio examines the vault door. "They used a tool, must have. It's been pried open." He picks up the small package. "There's something in here." He pulls out a rectangular wrapped object no wider than a large twig and rips off the tissue paper. It falls from his hands, black with blood, an otherwise perfect little finger that lands with a surprisingly solid sound at their feet.

Lila sweeps both arms across the nearest display table at the front of the shop. Stacks of paper scatter and drift to the floor. Markers and pens follow hard in the snowy wake. Miriam dodges a red marker careening toward her as Lila wails, waves her arms at the cobwebs hanging from the old shop light fixture overhead. "They cut her, Miriam! They maimed my Isabel!" She falls against one of the shelves, howling with shock and grief.

Davoglio gestures for quiet with the phone receiver and presses it once more against his ear. "Hello? No, I cannot hold. This is urgent — there's been a crime. A kidnapping. I need to speak to a detective—" His words are drowned out. The crashing of the display shelves and a full inventory's weight scatters papers, leaking pens, and clips of all sizes across the shop floor. "Signora!" Davoglio hangs up the phone in astonishment.

Wading through the debris with her ink-stained skirt hiked to her knees, she is only sure of one thing: she must destroy everything that has brought her to this point. Every last piece. The papers Miriam and Alvise have been attempting to collect flutter to the floor in the wake of Lila's rage. Good. Let it all go. All of it. Every last unimportant piece.

The little shop bell rings faintly and a police officer enters, trailed by the wide-eyed D'Agostino holding his hat in his hands like a contrite parishioner. Lila straightens up and, just in time, stops herself from flinging a box of paper clips. She must charm the carabinieri, get them on her side.

"I told you something was off." The grocer nods at the disheveled Lila.

"Are you Signora Lesser?"

"I am."

"I am the neighborhood patrol, signorina."

"Officer, it's good that you've come. There's been a crime. Please I need to report— " Lila waves her shaky hands in the air.

"Please signorina. No need for hysteria. We can discuss this reasonably."

"Yes. Then I'd like to report a kidnapping."

"A kidnapping? That's absurd. We don't get kidnappings in this neighborhood."

Before she can stop herself the unopened box of paper in her inky hands flies full force at the front door with a kind of strength she hasn't felt in years. In flight it becomes a torpedo, a glorious cannonball speeding toward its target and lands with a crunch inches from the patrol officer's boots. A spray of thick stock pastel paper. At that the carabinieri rushes her full force against the wall, and, deflated, Lila slides down slowly, a runny egg cracked wide open.

"Signora!" Alvise runs to her side.

"What have you done? She's hurt!" Miriam kneels down next to her friend.

"I am clearly acting in self defense. This woman assaulted me with a weapon." The officer looks to D'Agostino who nods his agreement. "For your nose, signora." He hands her his handkerchief.

Lila's white blouse is covered with dark ruby drops of blood. She presses the cloth against her face and tries to stand up, but Davoglio and Miriam insist in unison she must remain still, that something could be broken. There's the taste of blood on her teeth and tongue and the doom in the air of broken things that can never be fixed.

"Put pressure here." Miriam pinches her own nose. "And tilt your head back, like this." Lila gazes at her friend blankly and does nothing.

"They repossessed her art collection." Davoglio gestures to the bank letter on the counter. "A violent abduction or worse. That's what we have here, officer." With a raised voice and somewhat theatrical gestures, he shows the severed finger to the officer.

At the sight of the finger, the man steps back, askance. "That looks like a crime may have taken place, but abductions are not in my remit. You should call the dispatch and report it. The rest is between you and your bank, signora."

"Of course, Officer, we will report it right away." Davoglio says, his tone obsequious.

"Until you do, we don't know what we don't know. There is organized crime everywhere these days." The officer turns toward Lila. "If you are the owner of this art as you claim to be, I suggest you produce the bill of sale right away, signora, or any documentation that proves ownership. This is just my advice. And that's all I'll say on the subject." He straightens his cap, muttering something about private individuals owning great works of art that by rights should belong to the state.

Outside little rain pellets tap against the shop windows; if only Lila were able to laugh or cry, or be shredded like bits of paper that blow away in the wind. Isabel was out there somewhere, injured and alone, the paintings gone and with them any hope of a bargaining chip.

"You're very lucky I was passing by, Signora Lesser," the officer intones. "And very fortunate to have a concerned neighbor like Signor D'Amorino here."

"D'Agostino." The grocer tries in vain to kick free the sheet of ink-stained paper attached to the bottom of his shoe.

"But be that as it may." The officer points to the pair of handcuffs on the utility belt of his smart, recently-pressed uniform. "I'm afraid we're not finished. You, Signora Lesser, are under arrest."

"Under arrest?" Miriam's typically dulcet voice is practically a scream. "For what?"

"For assault of course. You will come with me, signora. Without any more fuss. If it is your collection like you say, you can prove it at the station. For the finger, well, that's homicide. Third floor."

CHAPTER THIRTEEN

Not more than a day later, they have taken Isabel out, the purplish sky reads evening time and they have finally freed her from that hole. But then the drugged dreams descend again and she is at the mercy of dark hands and watery depths. As she comes to, from somewhere not too far off comes the crunching of rubber tires on gravel. Gusts of wind buffet her cheek, a window rattles. Closer still, hoarse voices mutter and raucous bursts of male laughter break through the din. Isabel blinks slowly, her dreams evaporating and the light of day shifting moment by moment, until she awakens fully. Except for the searing pain running down her arm, her rib and back, she would sit up but heavy wooden crates press down hard against her shoulder, and the thrumming in her right arm increases. She cranes to see past the crates blocking her line of sight, but she cannot move. Just then a bump in the road jostles the whole cargo and she realizes with mild surprise that she is wedged tightly in the bed of a truck. The next bump sends another, far sharper stab of pain down her arm. She cries out.

"Hey, what's going on back there?"

The curtain that separates the cab from the cargo stirs, and the crow's face pops out like the cuckoo bird chiming the hour, and then just as quickly disappears.

That bird of death, its hideous face, she should be used to it by now, but she gasps like the first time she saw him, each breath an effort. She grits her teeth. In and out of consciousness, she has become someone else, something else, a pitiful animal that cares only about lessening suffering, an end to torment. The truck rounds a corner and one of the heavy crates bears down with its full weight and a wooden board cracks. Fresh pain instantly overwhelms her: a large splinter of the crate has pierced her skin and is now lodged firmly in her side. Pinned, she watches with a strange passivity the wooden shard jutting out from below her ribs, the blood seeping through her blouse and running down her leg.

For a moment or two, Isabel continues to gaze dully at the strange object projecting awkwardly from her body. Finally, she grabs hold of the sizeable splinter and pulls hard. But the wood is wedged deep and puts up a certain tugging resistance that sets her teeth on edge. She tries and fails, she tries once more, but no matter how she pulls the shard doesn't budge, and she wails in desperate frustration. The driver doesn't hear her cries, no one does. She closes her eyes as the truck careens around another corner, and with her remaining strength, she pulls one last time. The shard suddenly releases its grasp on her flesh and slides out. Isabel tosses the bloody thing aside without looking at it and presses a hand against the wound, exhaling slowly, a little older for the struggle. Laughter continues to echo from the front of the truck.

The bleeding from beneath her ribs goes on unabated.

"I'm hurt!"

She calls out, louder this time.

"Please! Someone!" Isabel begs, but there is no response. Her eyes flutter and fall and then stay closed. I'm sorry, Nonna, she thinks. So very sorry.

The truck abruptly comes to a stop. The engine is turned off, and two hard raps on the passenger side jolt Isabel fully awake. She has no exact idea how much time has passed but it must be the next day and morning time. Her entire body feels as if its separate parts no longer work, individually or in unison. Both her hands are sticky with blood. The truck's hatch is now opened and golden sunlight floods the cargo hold. Outside, silhouetted by the setting sun, two strange men stare down at her, one with a crowbar and the other a smile. The one with the crowbar is short and stocky and wears coveralls. Soon a third man joins them, and all three shake hands warmly.

"Enchanté Monsieur Gritti!" The man in the crow's mask greets the one with the crowbar.

"Et bonjour Monsieur Corbeau!" Gritti's voice is booming while the third man mumbles something unintelligible in a French accent from behind him.

Isabel looks from one man to another, each face more foreign than the next, and the men stare back at her with frozen grins, as if she is a wild animal caught in their trap.

The scent of petrol, the rush of traffic, taxis honking and the pungent smell of tobacco fills the air. A camion whooshes past spraying her mouth with dirt and exhaust. She is outside now, the men nowhere in sight. She waits. Waiting is now her special power, bearing pain comes in second. She would laugh if it didn't hurt so much. This must be it, the opposite of boredom. It had been Isabel's constant complaint at home, boredom, banality, the overly familiar. The windows on Rio Terra San Leonardo that always rattled the same way, the wind in Venice that had the same stale taste, the stray and mangy cats that always rubbed her legs in the doorways. Front and back, back and front, meowing for bits of bread. Bitter, crushing, dry-mouthed boredom. Now, of course, she would take a sweet crumb of that scene and never ask for another thing.

Footsteps round the corner.

"What have you done to this one?" She could be one of the relics under glass in Santa Croce, the way Signor Gritti is peering at her. Isabel's empty stomach turns over and the nausea rises.

"Me? Not a thing." Corbeau lights a cigarette. "This prima donna gets carsick riding in the back, that's all." He exhales a rope of smoke through a rigid smile. The rough-looking third man stands behind him.

"And what's with that thing you're wearing?" Gritti pantomimes in front of his own face to the masked man, grubby fingers elongating his stubby little nose into Pinocchio's.

"The mask?" Corbeau clucks his tongue. "Let me tell you, you can't be too careful. You of all people should know. Venice is crawling with little old ladies, and ears in every open window." A pang of homesickness replaces the nausea and Nonna waiting at home, scared and worried is all Isabel can think of. These men are nothing, evil; her life is a whim to them. She gags at the thought of what they will do.

"Yes. Yes. But we're not in Venice, are we? And it's not Mardi Gras. Maybe it's time to take it off." Gritti drags on his cigar. The third man, who now has the crowbar, speaks softly in French in Gritti's ear and he nods. "What's the plan then?"

"Her. She's the plan." Corbeau grins. "She's my insurance."

"Oh?"

"As long as we have her, we're safe. The carabinieri won't risk a human life for a few stolen pictures. It's too political."

"Political?" Gritti's laugh is a congested smoker's, low and gravelly, and he soon succumbs to a bout of coughing and throat clearing.

"Take my word, rich Jews like these won't skimp to have their little darling home again. With their money and influence, they can have the police at their beck and call. I'm buying us time. Lots of it. And just think, it's good news! She'll be a boon to your friend's little enterprise." Corbeau gestures to the Frenchman who exhales a putain and drops the crowbar on the ground.

Gritti glances over at the Frenchman and clears his throat again. "My friend would feel more comfortable if you...if you were a bit more transparent." He points at the crow's mask. "You understand."

"Of course." Corbeau spins around and when he faces them once again there is nothing of the rogue kidnapper about him. Instead a human face stares back, one with clear hazel eyes, a patrician nose and solid jaw; it's a face that would be just as comfortable in a classroom or seated in a wing-backed leather chair, a professor, a banker, a man with coiffed hair and a well-turned out wife. "Happy?" He stares down his two accomplices with a slight frown.

"Delighted." Gritti gestures to the Frenchman who scoops up his tool again, climbs into the back of the truck and begins prying open the nearest crate.

"Ooh," Gritti gasps at last when the wrapping is removed and the canvas revealed. Even the Frenchman cannot help but smile, ever so faintly.

"I give you: 'Christ Carrying the Cross,'" Corbeau beams. "Don't let them tell you it's a Giorgione. This, my friends, is our countryman. Titian. This one will set us up for life, my friend."

Gritti chuckles to himself. "Really, Corbeau, you've outdone yourself."

Even with a numb and dangling left arm and her bloody blouse stuck to her ribs, Isabel takes in a sharp breath at the wordless, thrilling beauty. It's plain as day, that there, in the greased-stain hands of the Frenchman, is part of her inheritance. Stashed among the other covered crates in the truck, Corbeau has both of the paintings Signora Morgenfeld had taken such pains to save and only just given her, Christ Carrying the Cross and Madonna and Child, their serene power somehow unaffected by the darker energy of the grimy men clutching them.

The ambient noise is foreign and shrill, and the air is colder and smells strange to an Italian girl accustomed to the Mediterranean. Isabel scans the distance, then shudders as if a ghost has passed through too quickly to haunt her. The exit sign off the highway reads Paris 15 km. Paris. After all this time! She shakes her head ruefully.

"What's wrong with her?" Gritti drags on his cigar.

"Carsick." Corbeau laughs, and they begin gathering up the canvases.

Isabel glances down. The bleeding has stopped; she notices with some relief. A bit of luck. Someday, she thinks, she will tell the story of a stupid selfish girl who got everything she ever wanted. In her telling, she will draw out the dangerous parts and linger on the absurd in the way she likes to in her essays for composition class. It will be a funny story, and when Antonia bursts into laughter and slams down her cup, espresso spraying the counter, Isabel will laugh too, tears streaming down her face. They will laugh and laugh, like two old friends who have lived through the bad times and survived to tell the tale. And Isabel will be older then, vastly older, with the wisdom of someone who has suffered enough to know the beauty of waitress aprons and school uniforms and the lined, careworn face of an old woman painstakingly choosing the challah for the evening meal.

They have given her tea, hot red tea, cups of it all morning and her tongue is as dry as leather, her teeth metallic. But she tries all the same, to sit up straight like a proper lady in the hotel drawing room, in the ivory wool Chanel suit, very French, her pinky extended like in the movies. She crosses her legs, prevents the satin-lined wool jacket hovering around her shoulders from sliding off. She could never fit her arm, now in a cast, through the sleeve. Soaking in a hot bath has done a little to shift her thoughts but a scab has since formed under her ribs where she was cut, and while things remain dire, she has a bit of bread in her stomach and the edges of a plan of escape forming in her mind. She obsessed about it all morning as she got dressed, her legs bruised and scratched but Corbeau said silk stockings would do wonders, and Corbeau was right. They glitter like the rays of sun on the Champs Élysées, the taxi driver said when he dropped them off on the boulevard outside the hotel. Corbeau had pulled her from the back seat like an unwieldy valise, and the driver couldn't help but admire the shape of her calf and the high-heeled pump when she extended her leg through the car door. Perfection, Antonia said eons ago in the dressing room of a little boutique. Another lifetime. In this one, all eyes are currently on her. She pretends to sip her tea.

"Radiant." Gritti whispers to the barman. "She's a honey trap, that one."

Corbeau nods, obviously pleased. He hasn't spoken a word to her and has not yet even introduced himself. Not properly. They are staying in a rundown pension across the city, where the halls are crowded with women of all ages in various stages of undress. Avoiding any eye contact, a young girl not much older than Isabel, had washed her with a soapy hot cloth in a little moldy toilet with a cold-water sink, and then later dressed her wounds. After a shivering Isabel was towel dried, her broken arm was encased in plaster by a strange doctor with oiled hair who spoke in a Slavic tongue. She was then corseted and powdered, her eyes lined black, her mouth and cheeks enhanced with a soft pink hue, her hair swept up in a French twist with little ringlets left at the back and finally fitted into the tailored Chanel. She barely had the chance to acknowledge the fabric, rich ivory-colored wool, as soft and nubby as a baby's blanket. She glanced in the mirror at the furious activity around her: surely these girls preening and fussing shared the same predicament and were also stolen from somewhere far away. She must follow their lead, and through the powdering, hair pulling, brushing and twisting of curls, she sat completely still. The cloud of perfume misted liberally on her hair, shoulders, neck and back was not strong enough to obscure the lingering medicinal -smell of the liniment drifting off her wounded arm. They gestured toward the mirror, but she closed her eyes at the alien reflection in the glass. Their work complete, they marched her downstairs and drove off with her in the cab to the hotel across town. Hotel Lutèce. They presented her in the lobby, a fait accompli, to her captor. Ever since, Corbeau hasn't stopped staring.

Isabel tries not to squirm beneath his unnerving gaze. She is seated on the gold couch, trying to act the part of someone more composed and experienced. Someone hands her a tea cup and she takes a cautious sip of hot tea.

"Priceless," Corbeau says. He's said that already once before, his blue eyes greedy, calculating an enviable sum. "Monsieur Vauvenargues. Welcome."

Corbeau ushers the man to the high backed armchair. Monsieur Vauvenargues, for his part, sits stiffly in the chair, crossing and uncrossing his legs. His socks are fine silk, periwinkle blue and expensive. His navy suit is immaculate, his dress shirt starched. He wears a bow tie and has the air of a dandy from the fin du siècle. He removes a small flat silver case from his jacket pocket, it's engraved, illegible. He opens the case and fidgets with the cigarillos inside but then puts it back in his pocket without removing one. How odd. The only way out is through, Isabel thinks. She tries to sit up and then takes another sip of the tepid red tea.

"Would you like a light, Monsieur?"

The tall man says nothing, drums his fingers on the armrest.

"A drink perhaps?" Corbeau gestures to the tumbler of scotch on the bar.

"I haven't got all day, monsieur. Shall we get to it?"

"Of course, monsieur. Sandrine here is at your disposal."

Isabel's stomach tightens at the name they've given her. But then a heaviness begins to pull at Isabel's eyelids and the soporific combustion of perfume and liniment lulls her into a dreamy state. She sips again at her tea. If Nonna somehow found her now, she would never recognize her, not in this place, not dressed like this.

She would be shocked, painfully so, at what has been done to her granddaughter: all her very worst fears finally come to pass.

"Sandrine, is it? How lovely." Monsieur Vauvenargues smiles up at her expectantly.

It's a cold splash of water. When he says her "name" and then his awkward smile, both. Everyone is as they were, the girls hovering in the doorway, Corbeau at the other end of the sofa and the new gentleman grinning at her like a Cheshire cat. Isabel tries to smile back but cringes so hard it hurts her bruised ribs.

Corbeau leans over to shake the tall man's hand; instead he gives him the room key.

"What's wrong with her arm?" The tall man pockets the key in his vest.

"It's nothing. A scratch. She fell in the tub."

Apparently satisfied, the tall man nods and rises quickly. A sharp look from Corbeau compels Isabel to do the same, and she stands with some effort on unsteady high heels. She follows him uneasily to the staircase.

"Speed up, my dear, or we'll be here forever."

The tall man pinches her elbow from behind and dutifully she begins to climb the stairs one by one, trying not to think of the destination, until Corbeau calls after them in a thick, insinuating tone.

"Room one thirteen. Top of the stairs."

But it's no use. As soon as the number is spoken, the thing is rushing to mind, Room 113: the bed against the narrow window, the fluorescent light buzzing overhead when the cord is pulled, the whining creak of the coils when she is pushed down hard onto the mattress. And the smell: musty from moldy curtains that keep out the sun. She can see and smell and feel it all like it's happened already. She holds onto the banister tightly, beneath her new stiletto heels the carpeted staircase is soft as marshmallows and each stair is more dizzying than the last. Again, a jab at her elbow from Vauvenargues; she climbs without looking back until they reach the long expanse of dark hallway and stop short at the first door. Vauvenargues turns the key in the lock and waves Isabel ahead. Slowly, she enters, as though caution is still called for, as though caution could save her from anything now.

The room is nothing like she imagines. Where there was one narrow window in her imagining, in reality there are three wide ones forming a bay window with a red velvet banquette. The walls are plastered with flowered paper, daffodils and irises, and a framed vista of the French seaside hangs on the wall above the bed, which is meticulously made with thick pillows propped on pale blue sheets. Isabel brushes the airy texture against her fingers. Silk. The effect of pale yellows, twilight blues and nocturnal purples is that of an impressionist painting and is every inch as opulent. In fact, each object is placed with a mind toward beauty and effortless enjoyment: the flutes are crystal instead of thin glass, thick bath towels wait thoughtfully in a stack on the ottoman and laid out on the mahogany desk is a pad of paper monogrammed with hotel's initials HL. The light doesn't buzz at all when Vauvenargues switches it on but rather bathes the room in a warm glow.

Vauvenargues smiles, revealing a handsome mouth of straight white teeth. He is not at all out of place in such a room, whereas Isabel, even in the Chanel suit, is incongruous.

He takes off the hat and hangs it on the coat rack next to the door.

"What is your real name?"

His question is direct as an archer's arrow, and she is caught off guard. She pauses to consider, her hip leaning awkwardly against the bed. They called her something, didn't they, a pretty French name belonging to a girl who wears sweaters and pedal pushers way more fashionable than anything Isabel has in her closet. It's no use. Whatever name Corbeau gave her has gone completely out of her head. "It's..." She falters.

"I appreciate authenticity. Even in the girls I see. So if your name is really Sandrine, we'll leave it at that."

"It is. Yes." She tries to smile. Her memory is a sieve, recent events falling out the bottom; the room is blurry around the edges, and the dull headache isn't helping.

"Shall we?"

Vauvenargues sits on the taut silk sheets without adding a wrinkle to the surface and pats on the mattress for her to join him. When she sits down, she is close enough to see the color of his eyes, dark brown, the silver-gray dots of late afternoon beard on his chin, his skin slightly loose at the jaw line, wrinkles at the eyes. Should that be a consolation? That he is an older man, perhaps a grandfather himself? It isn't. But his cologne is citrusy and slight, the scent envelops her. She sits up straighter. She must be the thing he wants. Whatever that is. But like a silly primary school girl, all she can manage is to stare down at her hands in her lap.

"How old are you, mademoiselle?" Vauvenargues' raised eyebrows speak of unmet expectations. "Your accent—is that Italian?"

She blushes, apologetic. Fragments of reality must not creep in. She must be better than that. Sinking down into the plush mattress, she begins to remove the Chanel suit jacket but when it catches on her casted arm, she winces like a baby.

"Here. Let me." Vauvenargues gently takes off the jacket and a warm breath of air from the open window ripples through her thin blouse. "So this famous bathtub injury. Does it hurt?"

She shakes her head.

"Oh, but you are so petite. I realize you girls like to be so skinny these days but may I ask: when was the last time you ate?"

She doesn't know how to answer. Normal activities involving food, meals, dining...that was all was years ago it seems because time is an illogical, nonlinear thing, expanding and contracting when you least expect it. But yes, some time ago she did eat, there was a dark little room and a bowl of something lukewarm. She blinks away tears.

"Come now." Vauvenargues dabs at her cheeks with his handkerchief like a man who, despite his kindness, can think of at least one other better thing to do. "We will have them bring something up." He lifts the phone receiver, a gaudy design from the nineteenth century she might have admired if not for the anguish of her empty belly. He dials. The phone rings once, then twice, then finally three times before anyone answers.

Hunger is an equalizing thing, rendering the whims of reality in stark black and white: sleep and death, food and breath. She will not give in to the heaviness, the call of sleep, but the sight of the lavish bed doesn't help. The second bite of baguette is warm and delectable. She wills her drooping eyelids open.

"Is it good?"

Isabel nods, takes another mouthful of bread as Vauvenargues watches her wipe the crumbs from her lips. When he brushes a ringlet of hair from her cheek, she recoils but then he takes the empty plate from her, loosens his tie and sits at the bed's edge as though it's the most natural of things, and begins easing her towards him. She goes cold. There's a sheen of sweat beneath her blouse as one, two, three buttons of the sheer blouse are undone in quick succession and then, rung by rung, the vice-like corset is unclasped with a surgeon's patience. She wills herself not to resist, it will go easier if she doesn't resist, and lets out a breath but it's everything she can do to quell the rising panic. He nods his approval and removes the tight corset until she is left with only the bra, borrowed lace that the other girls loaned her, and the skirt, still loose at the waist, only kept in place when the blouse is tucked in.

"There's a good girl," he says, cupping her breast with a cold soft hand; a shudder runs across her bare shoulders. He is an older man, well dressed and repulsive. He has paid for the service and she must do nothing. But it goes against every impulse. She would bolt, run far from this place if she could. Her worst fear is to see the naked body beneath the fine clothes. As if reading her thoughts, he removes his suit jacket and shirt, laying them down on the corner of the bed, perfectly flat and folded like a valet. His bare chest is hairless and pale as a banker's, thin sloping shoulders, ill-defined arms, sagging skin, a sunken chest and an extra padding of flesh on his belly where the croissants and profiteroles go. It's hard to believe the difference, actually, the cut of his suit, the line of him when dressed. Antonia was right: fashion works miracles. But in hindsight Antonia was right about many things.

"Lie down."

She is compelled by his voice, a low monotone. He straddles her prone body, begins to unzip the fly of his trousers and grunts a little with the effort. She tries to focus elsewhere: not on the Sister's stolen crucifix, or Nonna's missing apple, not on the cocktail dress in the window that Antonia shoved in her bag, or the priceless paintings once meant to be her birthright, all those bright, beautiful, innocent objects that had brought her, in her stubborn greediness to this very point. Instead, she thinks about the coolness of the sheets against her arms and back, the reassuring solidity of the mattress. Submission is nothing, she tells herself, it is simply a nodding off, a letting go. Her eyes flutter closed, and plastered against the encroaching blackness are the wallpaper flowers, daffodils, irises, tulips, all wafting overhead like gorgeous, riotous spring.

Isabel sits up in bed with a start, the flowers still spinning around the room.

"And so she returns." Vauvenargues is standing at the foot of the bed, completely dressed. A slight frown at the corners of his mouth.

"What happened? Did we—"

"Please." He holds up a hand to silence her. "I like the girls as much as the next fellow, but I'm not a monster, and you, well you strike me as...shall we say a bit new to the game. And I'm not the teacher type, mademoiselle. Am I right to say that you have not done this before?"

She springs out of the bed before she can answer, barely makes it to the toilet in time, the steady stream of urine flowing like a waterfall. Her little secret, that she is a minor, a foreigner, and inexperienced at that, well..., no amount of designer clothes and well applied mascara could conceal it. She sighs with more relief than she has felt in days, years. When she returns, Vauvenargues silently looks on as she stoops to pick up her blouse. Next to it on the carpet is a business card. It must have fallen from his suit pocket. "Serge Vauvenargues, Specialist, Gallery Owner, Italian Renaissance Art."

Goosebumps sprout on her bare skin. Because such a moment is, and, must by definition be, divine. An opportunity. An invitation. Someone somewhere must have put this man here. Isabel buttons her blouse slowly, the smell of lavender soap wafting from her wet hands, her head lighter, but clear, why else would this man present himself today? Whatever it is, she must keep her wits. She straightens her fallen French twist with the hairpin.

"I apologize Monsieur...it must have been the red tea. I'm sure it was in fact."

"Pardon?"

"They gave me red tea to drink."

"Of course they did. Say what you want, I have principles. That's why I didn't touch you." His face falls. "I tell these idiots every time, do not give my girls anything! No mickeys, no medicinal teas, no potions of any kind. But do they listen?" Vauvenargues shakes his head in disappointment.

Her blouse is buttoned and tucked in, but her legs are still bare, the stockings somewhere on the floor, and the little woolen skirt wrinkled from lying down. Dressed once more, she puts her heels on bare feet. They are less unwieldy than before, and she sinks into them solidly, suddenly convinced she could walk for miles if that's what was needed.

"I didn't tell the truth before, when you asked for my real name..."

"Oh?" His hands run impatiently along the brim of his hat.

"It's Lesser. Isabel Lesser."

The man sits back down at the edge of the bed, his eyes clouded over with memory. "Lesser," he repeats, as if it were the refrain of an old song from years ago.

CHAPTER FOURTEEN

Lila shakes her head miserably and cranes her head out of the kitchen window, stripes of late day sun crossing her bare arms as she reaches to separate the lace curtains. That the idiot carabinieri made her sit next to thugs, drunkards, and unwashed criminals for a full three and a half hours before allowing Miriam to bail her out and issuing her a summons to appear before the magistrate within two weeks' time wasn't the worst of it. What troubles Lila, even after tears and embraces and promises from Miriam that they will find dear Isabel, no, what bothers her truly is that after numerous calls and finally getting someone on the line, the bank had the audacity to deny repossessing the collection; they lied outright, flatly denied it. Even after she assured them she has their letter asserting as much–she neglected to mention that the letter has been missing since the incident. Still. As if an entire catalog of Italian Renaissance Art held in a steel vault could simply vanish. No one knew the combination. Not even Miriam. And Alvise with his stammering contrition, his sheepishness and self-effacing head tilt would never have been capable of such a thing.

In any event, 'repossess' is the bank's term, not Lila's. It was never a possession of the state to begin with, and they had no rights to it, not that that had ever stopped them before. And without the collection she cannot negotiate Isabel's release–the bank had stolen it before the kidnappers could. Stolen it and denied the crime. She wants to weep but the tears won't come. Just recriminations. Shameful recriminations. She should have been a better nonna. She glances at Miriam pacing the few feet of kitchen floor. And a better friend. a far better mother. Poor Leo. He deserved better. They all did. Her head is pounding; she smoothes her chignon.

"In any case, Signor Davoglio will be able to help us." Miriam wrings her hands. Lila is not so sure. With the collection no longer at his disposal, the curator has been less available than previously. Miriam insisting that he was continuing to work on his contacts at the bank, all sounds a bit thin. Hearing it repeated is no help at all but Lila cannot keep herself from asking.

"Do you really think he'll call, Mim?"

"Of course, Lila, it's only been a few hours. As soon as he knows anything. I'm sure he will."

Nonetheless, Lila had been silent on the vaporetto ride home, silent too as Miriam removed the kettle from the flame, and now can barely look her friend in the eye as she hovers at the kitchen table with the teapot. None of it matters anymore, not the paintings, not the stupid exhibition, not whether to show the bloody artwork or leave it in crates. That decision has been taken away and to her surprise, she feels an odd sense of gratitude where only obligation used to be. She straightens the linen napkin that Miriam has seen fit to set the table with for some reason, as if ironed linen could smooth all fears away, as if dainty teacups on little rose-lined plates could save the day. She would laugh if she could, a bitter nauseated laugh, but she always abhorred that quality in others, the true cynicism of those who have lost all hope. All that matters now is getting Isabel back in one piece. The severed finger flashes to mind, and Lila shudders. Miriam lifts the teapot to pour her another cup of tea.

"I've had enough, thank you Mim."

Miriam places the teapot back on the cozy and sits back down, dejected. "What do we do, Lila? I mean, what do we do now?"

Lila drums her fingers on the linoleum tabletop, in quick succession. One. Two. Three. Four. She hides her head in her hands, squinting, trying to remember.

She throws the crumpled napkin on the table. It lands in a heap next to the teacup.

"Lila, what is it?"

"There was something Isabel said once. We were sitting there." Lila points to the dining room. "She mentioned someone. A new friend. Anna Maria or Antonia-someone." She shakes her head. "But maybe it's nothing. Nothing that matters anyway."

"No, that's good, Lila! That's good." Miriam's face brightens. "Do you have a phone number?" She marches toward the telephone table in the foyer.

"No," Lila calls after her, buttoning her cardigan, "But I think I just may know where she works."

They have barely caught a glimpse of the girl: tall, lean, pigtails swinging as she exits the café hauling a bag of trash to the outside bin.

"Go ahead!" Miriam nudges Lila again. "Here's your chance!"

Lila wipes the perspiration from her brow, certain one second that this must be the girl, Isabel's friend, and then thoroughly convinced the next that they haven't even found the right café. A purplish swath of clouds wipes out the sun. Rain is the last thing they need. They are unprepared, no umbrella, no contingency. Regardless, this girl fits the bits and pieces of description that Lila has remembered from Isabel's occasional ramblings, and although this girl is older than Lila would have thought and dresses in a café workers apron and uniform, a real citizen with a job, and not the sort of friend Lila would have imagined for her granddaughter, there are no other options.

"Excuse me!" Her words are louder and more strident than Lila intends, and the girl jumps a little in her sandals, the bag of trash falls to the floor and breaks open.

"Oh! Look what you made me do!"

She crouches down, and begins collecting bits of debris with her bare hands: orange peels, egg shells, a silver spoon someone has thrown out by mistake which she slips into the pocket of her apron before continuing to gather up the messy assortment.

"Are you Antonia?"

The girl straightens up with a surly look, her hands covered in coffee grounds which leave long brown streaks across the white apron when she tries to wipe them off. "Who wants to know?"

"I'm Lila Lesser." Miriam smiles and purposely links her arm through Lila's. "And this is my friend Miriam. I believe you know my granddaughter Isabel?"

The café is empty. They have been sitting idly at the counter for a few minutes waiting for fresh coffee to be made, Lila clutching and un-clutching her handkerchief and Miriam playing with a tassel on her shawl.

"Please, isn't there something you can tell us?" Lila is at her wit's end, after this, she has run out of ideas.

"Like I said, I haven't heard from Isabel in days. I was getting worried myself." Antonia unleashes a long pour of hot steaming coffee and nearly upends the little cup. "Sorry! I'll get you a fresh one."

"I don't need any —," But the girl has already slipped into the back room.

"Lila, why not tell her everything? Just this once?" Miriam nudges her with an elbow.

"I know what I'm doing, Mim."

The girl returns with a clean cup and pours fresh coffee for them both. Lila nods in thanks but doesn't touch a drop.

"We were hoping you might at least have some idea of where she could be."

Antonia gazes at them somewhat suspiciously for a second, then shrugs. "What do I know? I'm always here, working most days. She's a kid in high school. Maybe she doesn't want to be found, you know? At that age, I was the same. I once stayed away for a week. My father didn't miss me until he had to work overtime."

"I see. Well." Lila shivers, not wanting to say the words out loud. "It's just that, well, we received...something."

"A gruesome thing!" Miriam cries out, and Lila puts a calming hand on her friend's shoulder.

"And we have reason to believe someone has taken her, and she's badly hurt...," Lila trails off, choking on the rest.

"They cut off her finger!" Miriam blurts this out, and then looks horrified by what she's said.

When Antonia turns to face them, her face is quite changed. "Isabel," she says in a shaken voice, "is my best friend." She stands up and unties the grimy apron. "Look, I can't promise anything. But maybe I know someone. It might be worth a shot."

Bolstered by this change of heart, Lila and Miriam wait nervously out front while the café shades are drawn and the front door is locked. Together, now, the three women hurry toward the canal.

Lila's legs ache from trying to keep up; the girl with the braids walks too quickly, long strides like the arc of a gondolier's oar cutting the water. By the time they arrive, Lila is huffing and puffing as Miriam hangs on to the banister of the great stone staircase as if for dear life. The local hospital looks as austere as ever and, as always, remains a place Lila detests and has tried her very best to avoid, only the once when Leo broke his arm, and the other when Isabel had a terrible pneumonia. The hospital is their second stop. Because Antonia thinks there may be a certain boy who knows something, they first paid a visit to a dilapidated house in the Dorsoduro where a neighbor yelled at them in Venetian dialect about an ambulance waking up the neighborhood the other night.

Lila rests a moment at the top of the stairs, having finally caught up to Miriam who waves her on: Antonia is already through the revolving door.

The squeaking wheels of an empty gurney follow them closely along the shined linoleum of the main hallway. They stop midway down the long, brightly lit hall. Room 102 is what the receptionist said in the lobby.

"Niccolo?" Antonia peeks her head in the door, crowding the doorway.

Straining to see beyond her, Lila catches a momentary glimpse. By the far window the sun streams in on a young man lying quite still. A wide stripe of light on a frail ghost of a person hooked up to a tube. Before Lila can make any sense of it, Antonia leans against the doorframe completely obscuring her view. Lila nudges her to make room.

"Yes? Are you family?" A nurse stands at a patient's bedside; the young man sleeps, some tubes attached to his arm from a drip at the side of the bed.

"We're friends." Antonia pushes the door open wider while remaining at a respectable distance.

The nurse finishes checking the boy's pulse and gingerly lays his hand back down; she smoothes the sheets and fluffs the pillow before taking a step back. Seated next to the bed is a woman dressed in a black dress and shawl, the knitting needles in her hands the only animated thing about her, these and the bright blue ball of yarn that spins at her feet.

"Oh..." Lila steps into the room. "We didn't realize someone was here."

"Is it alright with you, signora?" The nurse waits for an answer but the woman continues knitting in silence.

"Forgive us for intruding, signora." Miriam is always on point. "We hoped to pay our respects."

"What happened to him?" Antonia points to the boy's hand covered in gauze and propped on a pillow. Her own hand falls and grazes the bed rail.

"A terrible accident. Just terrible. Isn't that so, Signora Gritti?" The nurse adjusts some knobs and the soft purr and lap of the breathing apparatus at the bedside grows louder. His chest rises and falls with the artificial rhythm of the machine. In repose the boy's face is classically Roman, but the skin is sallow, the cheeks sunken and bruised.

"Is he sleeping?" Antonia asks the question before Lila can.

"No, signorina. He is in a coma. And you must not stay too long." The nurse frowns a bit and then closes the door softly on her way out.

"Poor Niccolo." Antonia holds onto the bed rail tightly, as if it were the balustrade of a ship setting out to sea.

The knitting needles in the woman's hands freeze, and when she examines them her piercing blue eyes are a shade darker than the yarn. "You know my son? You know my Niccolo?"

"No," says Lila, in a grim tone. "But he apparently knows my granddaughter."

"So they are friends?"

"Yes, signora." Antonia jumps in quickly. "They are very good friends." Antonia turns and gives Lila a look.

The woman picks up the knitting once more, quick, deft gestures that take greater skill than thought.

"So, that's why we've come, you see." Lila falters and begins again.

The signora leans forward in her chair. "Well, here he is. Take a look. That's all you can do. You see the state of him." Her voice breaks and she leans back quickly resuming her knitting.

"Yes," Lila says. "A terrible thing, signora. We're here because something has happened to my granddaughter Isabel." She clears her throat, "Niccolo's friend, you see. She's gone missing along with some paintings from a family collection."

"But that's not why—," Antonia glances at Lila worriedly.

"Perhaps your son has mentioned something about my Isabel?" Lila ignores the girl's signals and takes a step closer to the signora.

"What can he mention?" The woman's voice rises and falls, the Venetian dialect, the inflection one Lila could never master. "He is a boy, a good boy who loves his family."

"Of course he does, signora." Antonia leans in a bit closer. "We only want to ask him some questions. Anything he may know could help. We could leave him a note. For when he wakes up."

"I know this will be difficult, signora. As a mother myself...please." Lila hands her the small package, taped back together. "There is a note inside."

The signora drops the knitting in her lap. "What is this?" She casts a suspicious look at Lila. "What have you brought me?"

"Please, signora. Take a look. We have no one else to ask." Lila covers her mouth with her hand.

The signora carefully opens the little parcel and pulls out the note, which she reads quickly before unwrapping the tissue paper. The severed finger exudes a greenish cast, and for a moment, the signora stares at it like a reminder of something long misplaced. When she rises from the chair, her hands are curled into fists and as the knitting falls from her lap, the ball of yarn unravels across the floor. The note in one hand, her boy's severed finger in the other, the woman crosses herself over and again like the priests and their parade of heavy wooden crucifixes swaying across the San Marco piazza. "My God, my God!" Her cries mix with the toll of the church bell outside.

"Whoever hurt your boy wanted me to believe this was my Isabel's finger and not your son's."

"I don't know what you're saying. I don't know what you're talking about." The woman's hand closes around the finger as though it were a family talisman. "What kind of horrible people are you?" She takes a sudden and determined step in Lila's direction, but before she can accomplish her goal the smallest noise, like the thud of plastic against metal cuts through the room; they all stop and turn.

There in the bed Niccolo's eyes are open, bloodshot but open, and the tubes attached to the IV in his twitching arm bump with life against the bed's aluminum side rail. The woman in black falls to her knees. With her eyes squeezed shut, she mumbles prayers into clasped hands, and in the next instant, she is back on her feet, showering the boy with kisses as the other women move closer to the bed, their wavering shadows silhouetted against the stripe of sunlight on the wall.

She repeats the boy's name, thanking God between each breath; even when his eyes close once more, the woman won't let go. "Nurse!" The woman pats one hand against her chest, and drops the amputated finger, which noiselessly rolls under the bed.

"Truly, a miracle." Miriam says more to Lila than anyone else.

When the woman turns to face them next, there is a steady calm in her face. "I told him...I told my husband, that man is not to be trusted. He should never work for you. He's an animal, I said. Don't hang around with the likes of him! But did he listen? No, because he never listens. There's no living from the fish in the sea, he said. There's no bread for the table, he said. Can you imagine? And then him bringing home expensive wine, Chateaux Margaux of all things! More than his family, more than his own son, it's only the money he cares for!" Her blue eyes are brimming with tears.

"So you'll help us?" Miriam offers her hand and the woman takes it. "Please signora."

"And we can help you. Maybe we can help each other?" Antonia stands by Miriam's side.

"No!" The woman instantly releases Miriam's hand. "I know what you want to do. But I swear to you on my son's life. I will not allow it. There will be no police!" The shawl falls off her petite frame, and somehow without it, she has taken on a larger looking appearance, her posture straighter, her narrow shoulders determined like a runner at the start of a race.

"Trust the police? Why would we do that?" Antonia looks amazed.

"No police." Lila nods. "That I can promise."

They wait, the sunlight retreating, long shadows rolling across the bed as a tall boat in the canal outside passes by.

"He has a truck," the signora stoops to gather the unraveled yarn at their feet, "a little truck for deliveries outside the Veneto."

"Does he?"

"He never tells me anything. But I have ears and I have eyes." She sits back down, but ignores the needles and yarn in her lap. "I overheard him saying something to that horrible man about Paris. And now he and his truck are gone."

Paris. Lila stifles her tears and nods her thanks. Paris. A tiny path emerging in a thorny and overgrown wood. The three women head toward the door just as the nurse returns with a tray. Lila lingers a last moment in the open doorway.

"You have helped us immensely, signora. I will not forget."

They hit a bump in the road that jostles them side to side; Lila squirms in her seat.

"Never fear, Signora Lesser. As I said, I'm an excellent driver." Antonia rolls down the window of their rented car as Lila hunkers down, her hand clutching the armrest.

Whatever is left will be something to be thankful for. Ten fingers. Ten toes. Just like when she was born, Isabel will still be whole, and beyond that Lila cannot imagine. She must not expect or hope for anything else. First the homecoming: a hot bath, some supper, baked potato — Isabel always liked that. As a little girl she'd eat the whole potato, even the brown skin. And then, at last, a night in her own bed with Lila sleeping on the floor or curled up in the rocking chair, a sleepy-eyed sentinel in the bedroom corner, who, upon being granted a second chance, would never fail so spectacularly again.

Lila rolls down her window for a blast of warm air. Antonia, for all of her bluster about it, is a surprisingly good driver. Lila herself has never driven a car, or a boat for that matter, although Albert owned both. Living in Venice, she never had a need for a driver's license and anyway, with her nearsightedness she had no business behind the wheel. Her watch says almost noon. They have already come a few hundred miles, driving through the night and stopping for a nap shortly before sunrise and then back on the road, each passing sign another breadcrumb in a long serpentine path toward Paris.

If she is a good driver, Antonia isn't much of a talker, and the two of them have spent hours cramped side by side on the truck's miserable vinyl car seat in near silence. Lila learns only a few basic things, that Antonia runs her father's trattoria on the outskirts of the campo and likes her job, too, but what she and Isabel possibly have in common remains a mystery. Nonetheless, the straightforwardness of the girl, the spine of her at a harrowing time like this, none of this is lost on Lila and she has come to understand in some small part why the two girls are friends. A friend drives long miles and keeps promises. She thinks of Miriam who is staying at the flat in case anyone calls.

Many static-y radio stations later, endless chatter in Italian, then German, Dutch and finally French about something, politics probably, and all of it punctuated by the occasional pop song, they reach the outskirts of the city. Antonia tries to sit up straighter in the driver's seat, but Paris is more awake than either the driver or her passenger. The car idles up to the curb of a crowded boulevard, and the engine is turned off. They step out onto the sidewalk. Firm ground, at last! The wind feels good on Lila's bare legs, too hot for stockings, the fashionable of Paris will have to forgive her, for once, she doesn't care. She stands on the uneven cobblestone with her summer dress blowing against her legs and the bitter smell of petrol in the breeze. Antonia leans against the hood of the truck and smokes her cigarette. Priorities. So different for the young. Rather than scold the girl for indulging, it's still a nasty habit after all, Lila asks for a drag. The curl of smoke down her throat and in her nostrils is burning and sweet, the scent of other days, some better, certainly younger. She takes another puff with the assured air of a reformed die-hard smoker and hands the cigarette back to Antonia. To think, this is Paris, and this, her first visit would be under such abysmal circumstances. In better times, Albert had talked about them taking a trip to the French capital, a trip that like so many of his other promises would fall through the glaring cracks of their marriage. For her there would be no bateau mouche drifting along the Seine, no view at the top of the Eiffel Tower, no sauntering hand in hand like tourists along the Champs Elysees, not even the requisite gift: expensive perfume handed to her over a four-course dinner in a little linen box.

"Well. We're here. Now what?" Antonia laughs at the irony, a youthful bell of a laugh. Lila envies her that. She once had a laugh like that too.

"Surely someone here knows something. Or has seen something" Lila strikes a hopeful note to appease the girl. But she would be kidding herself if she didn't admit that the last few sleepless nights have been among the worst of her life and that her only prayer is that they find her granddaughter alive and in one piece. Still, they have gotten this far and she must not let herself be destroyed by worry. She must remain sharp and in her best form if they are to find a way out of this mess.

At the corner tabac, a small throng of readers peruses the pages of Le Figaro: well-dressed patrons who have already lunched and smoked, they scan a headline or two before heading off toward the iron-gated square of well-tended green across the way. Antonia checks the pack of cigarettes for another and, finding none, crumples the package and throws it in the gutter, a clear breach of etiquette that Lila chooses to ignore.

"I suppose that's it then." Lila glances at her watch. "You need more cigarettes, and we...," she rummages in her purse for her handkerchief, "we need a city map."

She dabs her upper lip and forehead before heading up the street like a Parisian woman who knows her way around, a pedestrian who has the right of way. And why not? Might as well act like you know the place, scowl and be scowled at. She feels the eyes, look there! they seem to say, look at the old foreigner and her granddaughter. If only they knew. The stagnant air, more humid than in Venice, sticks to the skin like a shameful insinuation, and there is barely enough room to pass the throngs on the sidewalk. Antonia lags behind.

"Stay close!" Lila sighs in frustration. Truth be told, she hates the heat, hates not having a real plan, not knowing their way around. A gang of rough-looking boys amble past, boys with matted hair and stained T-shirts, their deadened eyes lock onto Lila's for a fraction of a second before the sudden force at her side forces the vertical line of sidewalk, shops, and passersby horizontal. In the second it takes Lila to tumble to the ground, Antonia is at her side.

"Are you alright, Signora Lesser?"

Her hands stinging, Lila feels inside the pockets of her summer dress, her heart pounding like a hammer, her arms strangely lighter. "My purse! They've taken my purse!"

Like a shot, Antonia takes off after them, snaking her way easily through crowds of shoppers and passive onlookers leaving Lila calling after, her back against a lamppost, her chest heaving for breath at the few snatches of conversation overhead, the Frenchwomen's rising and falling inflection of surprise, the men holding them tighter, and everyone staring and fussing but offering nothing in the way of help. Finally Lila gets to her feet, no small effort, and smoothes her dress. She's tempted to laugh uncontrollably or cry like the feeble old woman she most certainly has become. She gulps back tears, reflexively goes for the handkerchief in her purse but the purse is gone, and then all of it repeats, the boys running past, Antonia flying after them and, defeated, she sinks back down on the ground. A cold shadow falls over her shoulders.

Vauvenargues hangs up the phone, wearing that same distracted look that's been haunting his face since Isabel told him her real name.

"They want me back downstairs, don't they?"

"They don't." He pours a glass of water from the pitcher on the side table. "It's all arranged. I have you for the day."

Isabel fidgets with the button of the Chanel suit jacket. It's too hot for such finery. She gazes beyond Vauvenargues at the door.

"If you're thinking of bolting, you won't get very far. Please—," Vauvenargues holds out a hand and takes the jacket after she's finished peeling it off. "It's best if we stay together."

"Forgive me for asking, Monsieur, but what does it matter? I mean, really?"

"It matters, dear girl, because of you. I never knew Leo had a child. Albert never knew." His voice softens. "Your grandfather is a friend."

She squints at him. "You knew my grandfather?"

He nods. "And what kind of friend would I be if I let his granddaughter wander Paris alone? Albert and I...attended private school together in Geneva. We've remained friends ever since."

"That's not possible, Monsieur." Isabel's voice rises a good octave. In her fidgety hand is the Chanel jacket button trailing loose thread, which she immediately puts in her skirt pocket. She should be used to it by now. This man, like all the others, is a fraud; this is some kind of hoax, he's a gangster, surely, a well-dressed con man. "Albert's dead." She blurts out. "He died in the camps."

"Well, many people did, it's true, but your grandfather was lucky, luckier than most. I was happy for him that he could get out of Europe. I'm not Jewish myself, but Albert had worries the rest of us never understood. I'm getting ahead of myself." He clasps his hands together and begins again. "Right before the war broke out Albert booked passage on a steamer bound for New York City; the famous photographs of Ellis Island you've seen in the papers? That was Albert."

Isabel sinks down on the bed. The rest of what Vauvenargues has to say, escape, New York, a new life of freedom, disappears like an onslaught of music, the rush of an orchestra to take up the theme when the violins, the flutes, all join in the great surge toward something bold, truthful. He finally takes a pause to hand her a glass of water from the bathroom sink, which she holds like a stage prop, never drinking.

"But that's impossible, Monsieur. There was a memorial, a will, an estate. Nonna said he left her everything."

"I guess in a way he did. In the divorce."

Isabel laughs, an incredulous burst. "You cannot divorce a dead man, Monsieur. Even if it were true, why return to Venice? Surely my grandmother would have gone home to Warsaw."

"As if Poland was any better? You must understand, home countries are a luxury for gentiles, my dear, not for the Jews." He glances at his watch. "Look, I may as well tell you, because it's important: Albert fell in love. '—Une grande histoire d'amour,—' as we say. I told him, I said be careful. It's not a problem unless it's found out. But your grandfather has always been a seeker, impetuous, hot-tempered. I understood all that. Even admired him for it. It's what prompted the end of his marriage, you see, because your nonna was livid, rightfully so I suppose, but when they divorced, to have this new wonderful life he wanted, he gave it all away, the money, the collection, all of it. Far too much if you ask me." He straightens his tie, his cheeks flushed.

She almost wants to believe him, that this is it, the piece that perfectly explains all the silences around the dinner table, all the ellipses in the family history. But there's something about it that still rings false.

"I've said too much. I'm a talker. Believe me, Albert always chided me for it." He throws her a beseeching look. "But the point is...who among us hasn't had a dalliance or two?"

Dalliance. The word, antiquated and obsolete, is better suited for poetry books, for Verlaine and Rimbaud. "Albert was a married man," she says again slowly as if talking to a simpleton.

"He was." He nods solemnly. "What was his wife's name? Liza—,"

"Lila. Lila Lesser." Nonna's name is the steadying church bell from the tall tower that sounds from miles away for all to hear.

"Indeed. Well!" He fidgets with his hands. "Albert's granddaughter!" He tilts his head as though admiring a portrait hanging in a gallery. "In Paris of all places!"

Isabel rises unsteadily to her feet, her head suddenly pounding. "But definitely not by choice, Monsieur, I was kidnapped."

"Dear God!" He motions for her to sit down at the little table, but she remains standing. "I'm not saying these gentlemen are solid citizens, but kidnapping a young girl?"

"Believe me, these men are not to be trusted." She turns toward the door.

"Please wait, stay a little longer. You must be starving."

"I'm not."

But her stomach rumbles while he rattles off a long lunch order on the phone, and reluctantly she takes a seat. His eyes are trained on her as they wait, and she can feel it depleting, the little energy she has left. When the food arrives, an array of dishes wheeled in on a squeaky cart, the rail-thin bellboy closes his fingers around the few francs Vauvenargues hands him, while Isabel eats ravenously without fully tasting. Between mouthfuls of steak and potato and sips of wine, something kind in his eyes compels her and she tells Vauvenargues a bit more, the blind, bottomless well, the man in the crow's mask, the dark bumpy journey in the truck, until gradually she has told him everything, even her stealing with Antonia and later conspiring with Niccolo. And when finally, she gets to the part about Signora Morgenfeld's help with saving Albert's paintings, she struggles to say the heiress' name out loud because it's Nonna's face she sees, Nonna's face swollen and tearstained. Isabel sets down the fork next to the half-eaten flank of steak, the potatoes swimming in the pink juice.

"Amazing." Vauvenargues shakes his head in disbelief. "It's another of Albert's miracles, that you somehow found your way here. And to me."

She still hardly knows what to think: he's either an incredibly good actor and con man, or an angel sent from the gods she doesn't believe in.

"Please. Let me help you. It's the least I can do." Vauvenargues glances at his watch again, before grabbing his hat and suit jacket off the hook. "There's something you need to see. Quickly, before our hosts change their minds."

By the time they arrive at his apartment, Vauvenargues has become more mysterious than the straightforward man she met back at the hotel, turning around every other moment in the back seat of the taxi to look in the rearview. The apartment block is white stone, of the Haussmann-style Isabel has long admired in photographs. He is on the sixth floor, and when she huffs up the last flight and he finally unlocks the front door, the musty scent of a distant era rushes to greet them. The tall French windows are unshuttered and thrown open, and as Isabel sinks into the stiff-backed settee, gray afternoon light floods the room, enough to make her squint.

"Forgive the mess. I just need a moment." The nearby urgency of a fire siren drowns out his rummaging through the drawers of a sideboard. On a doily-covered surface stand porcelain miniatures: elephants and donkeys, a whole forgotten ménagerie. As his methodical search becomes more frantic, papers, file folders, dusty scrapbooks and curios wrapped in tissue soon tower around the figurines in lopsided stacks.

"Oh, here we go." He removes a photograph from a frame and

slips it in his pocket, then holds up a finger to silence her when she hasn't said a word, and finally disappears down a dark hallway. There's the click of a light switching on and the clink of china following after, the running of water like a stream. Her eyelids flutter with fatigue, but he returns right away with a tall drink of water, which he hands her, and she drinks down in one gulp, before he takes a seat on the armchair across from her and crosses his legs. The gesture, and the low height of the chair, deflates him a little.

"My mother's flat. I can't seem to part with it." There's a catch in his throat, the kind that comes from too often repeating explanations that never satisfy. He uncrosses his legs, fidgets with his wristwatch, his face changing by degrees in the light from gray to dusky yellow, middle-aged man to years younger. "Here it is then." He hands her the photograph with surprising reluctance.

The photo, a grainy black and white on yellowing paper, is of two young men standing against the backdrop of a night club marquee, their mouths pressed against each other in a lovers' embrace, a blur of pedestrians flitting this way and that on the sidewalk around them.

"Who is this?" Her spine stiffens against the velvet upholstery.

"This is all that's left. The only picture of Albert and me." He glances up nervously.

"I don't understand."

He gazes at something just over her head. "Some people are like that, you know. They like women and men. Either or both." He sighs a little with impatience. "Surely you've heard of this?"

But she hasn't. Not really. Certainly in books she has read about such things but she's never seen them in real life. Antonia would know, of course. Isabel brings the picture closer. In the photograph the man kissing a youthful, dashing Vauvenargues looks nothing like the Albert Isabel seen in Nonna's photos, Albert the unsmiling businessman or Albert the serious family man, pant legs rolled at the seaside. There's nothing about him to suggest a resemblance to her grandfather other than the pinky ring on his finger, she's seen it before in nonna's jewelry box, a topaz set in platinum, and here it is again, his hand clasping Vauvenargues's shoulder. If Albert was a solid sort of handsome in the older photos, in this one he is radiant.

"Albert was on the paranoid side of cautious and insisted that I burn the other pictures. He was right of course. We only made it through at all because of his connections. Thank God for Isadora, who was kind enough to accompany us everywhere after that first storied introduction at the Palazzo. Instant friends, you could say. And there we were, the Isadora Morgenfeld by our side at every restaurant, cinema, and always at the nightclub. Isadora was the one who took the picture. She was more than a little infatuated with him; nearly everyone was. She even bought him passage on that ship." He smiles as though reminiscing with a friend but when their eyes meet, his smile quickly dissolves. "I'm not surprised in the least that she tried to help you, too."

The outside light has shifted from gray to a strange pale yellow, highlighting the veil of dust that sits on every object in the apartment. Isabel's casted arm twitches with pins and needles, she would tear off the plaster if she could, but instead she remains still as the porcelain ménagerie of animals on the sideboard. "So you loved him?"

"It should have stayed a secret, and if I hadn't phoned Albert to warn him about the yellow stars being handed out, your nonna would never have caught on. I was just so worried for him. I told him it was only a matter of time before the pink stars found us."

He stands up and moves to the window, and in profile she can see the younger man he used to be: the man in love with her grandfather, holding hands in the Piazza San Marco under the cover of night, making plans for a secret future together.

"And Nonna and Leo? Why didn't they leave with him?"

"Albert begged your nonna to get on the ship but she refused. She didn't want any gifts from that heiress. That's what she called her, like Isadora was the cause of all their problems. I think your nonna truly believed they would survive it, she and the boy."

There's no looking past the cloud of sadness and regret in the dim light, on the dusty surfaces, in his gaze as it settles in anguish on hers. He is everything she couldn't see before: feminine, masculine, both; the slender angle of his profile, his cheeks wet, the slight curve of his neck in the white dress shirt, the starched collar a bit too big. "I suppose in a way they did survive. I mean, here you are." He tries to smile.

Isabel hands him back the photo in silence, fully awake for the first time in months. Stranger stories are the ones that are more often true, and often the stranger they are, the more truthful. Finally, it all fits. Finally, there is something to hold and to see, an old photo that reveals and explains, where before there was only a blank canvas, covered over with secrets and lies.

He places his hand on her shoulder. "Now, let's get you on your way. But first, a phone call. Your nonna must be out of her mind with worry."

A brusque banging on the door has Isabel jumping to her feet and Vauvenargues spinning around. "Oh, no." He grabs her by the good arm and leads her through the kitchen to a back staircase landing. Here he opens his wallet and presses a few crumpled bills into her hand along with his business card. "Get yourself to Gare du Nord and wait for me there. There's a man, a certain Monsieur Vaugirard, at the Central Kiosk who will help you. Tell him you're my friend." The banging at the front door grows louder. "Now go!" She descends the staircase quickly, taking the steps in twos and threes, never looking back.

Many dense city blocks before her, Isabel walks resolutely through the swirling cacophony of cars and taxis, the pack of pedestrians at every crosswalk jockeying for a sliver of standing space on the narrow stones. Each time the traffic light turns from red to green she charges on, but by the time she reaches Place de La Concorde, she can no longer pretend it isn't there, the one slow moving sedan that's been tailing her almost the moment she left. Just as she reaches the square's massive open space, she breaks into a run down an alleyway. Turning left and right past dustbins overflowing with all manner of debris, through a nauseating cloud of rotting food, she darts this way and that in a labyrinth of back streets, pubs, and grungy one-star tourist hotels. At the next corner, she glances back: the sedan is right behind her. They reach the end of a dead end street at the same time, and the car door swings open.

From behind the wheel Gritti hoists the hem of his trousers, revealing the glimmering blade cuffed to his ankle. "Get in," he demands.

"No," she pants, her heart pounding.

Gritti leaps out of the car and grabs her by the arm, shoving her violently into the back seat. She is barely seated when the car speeds off.

CHAPTER
FIFTEEN

"Are you alright?" A tall woman in a linen suit and flats leans over. An English speaker, thank goodness; Lila nods, suddenly a bit timid. The woman offers a gloved hand and Lila slowly gets to her feet, keen for the crowds to disperse, the drama to be done with.

"No. Yes, I mean I'm fine. It's just this heat..." Lila fans herself with her hand, which she notices to her dismay is scratched and bleeding. She wipes it quickly on her skirt.

"I know! This is Paris in summer I'm afraid." The woman holds her parasol over them; it's a great relief, accommodating like the branches of a small shade tree. "There's a café just over there. Come. We'll get you a glass of water."

Lila nods gratefully. "Do you think they would let me use the phone? My purse was stolen —"

"Dear God." The woman shakes her head. "It gets worse every year, the treatment of tourists in this city. Of course they will. I'll show you the way."

"S'il vous plaît, madame."

The barman at the café sets the phone down on the counter, and Lila closes the phone book, offering up her best merci as he scowls.

"Hello?" Miriam answers on the first ring.

"Miriam, thank God! I need—"

"Lila!" A breathless string of information follows. Miriam has news: she has finally gotten hold of Davoglio. He's been extraordinarily busy, of course, with clients and he was on his way out the door but not before assuring her that he is committing to doing whatever he can to help and that, if necessary, he has a connection or two in Paris, who may be able to offer some guidance. And there's something else. A fraction of a moment passes as Miriam prepares for this next revelation, and Lila barely has the patience for it but before she can express her displeasure, out it finally comes.

"I called her back."

"Called who?"

"Signora Gritti. Niccolo's mother. It didn't sit with me, something she said. So I called her back and we spoke. You'll be glad to know the boy has been released from the hospital. He's on the mend. Anyway I told her, I said, I didn't mean to brag but Chateau Margaux is a wine in scarce supply, a rare offering served only at the finest of venues, it's not some trifling Beaujolais you might find at the market, and did she think it was possible it could have been some other wine. And do you know what she said?"

The barman taps his fingers on the counter, still frowning.

"Look, get to the point, Mim, I don't have much time."

"Of course dear. Apparently she didn't trust us at first but afterwards thought better of it. Her Niccolo spoke kindly of Isabel apparently, and as a mother herself she didn't have the heart to see another young person suffer."

"How noble of her."

"Lila, she said that his little delivery truck is actually a van! A navy blue van with a hand painted sign on the side panel."

"I'm sorry Madame, but other patrons wish to use the phone." The barman gestures gruffly for the receiver. Lila glances behind her: there is no queue, hardly any patrons either in fact other than the British woman and a couple huddled in the corner.

Lila grimaces. "What does the sign say? Did she tell you that?"

"Yes! La Vie en Rose Booksellers. Booksellers, Lila! As if this Gritti person knows how to read."

"Oh, that's good Mim. That's very good." Lila is giddy with the possibilities. "I'll need you to wire me some money to continue the search." She gives Miriam the name of a Parisian bank she had spied. "Those horrible street thieves took everything."

"What street thieves?"

"It's nothing. I'll tell you all about it later. Kisses!"

Lila hangs up the receiver, goosebumps rising on her arms even in this heat, and the tiniest shred of hope alive once more. The barman impatiently returns the phone to its place of inertia on the back shelf next to squat bottles of whiskey and Armagnac.

When Lila returns to the table, the British woman is sipping a café crème.

"Thank you for waiting. You've been so kind."

"Nonsense. It's the least I can do. Some cities are friendlier to their strangers; unfortunately for us, Paris is not one of them."

"Do you desire something else, Madame?" The barman appears at the table, linen towel draped over his arm as though such preciousness has a point in a run-of-the-mill café.

"A sparkling water, monsieur." Lila sits up in the chair.

The barman says something to the British woman who responds in flawless French herself. Lila cannot help but be impressed. Such expats are always astonishing, their ease with their host country's tongue, their ability to surf the whimsy of foreign customs when, even after thirty years, Lila barely feels at home in the Piazza San Marco. The barman leaves them never acknowledging Lila's order.

"Any luck with your call?"

"I'm not sure. Maybe." Lila pauses. "Does La Vie en Rose mean anything to you? Aside from Piaf of course."

The barman returns with Lila's sparkling water, and she cannot help but feel a small victory at having been acknowledged, finally. The British woman asks him a question, Lila's question (she can infer that much), and without missing a beat, the barman snaps his fingers and tosses off the answer, pointing in the direction of the door.

"Monsieur says there's a bookshop by that name in the second arrondissement."

"Bonjour!" The barman exudes a glum welcome at the arrival of the newest customer.

"There you are!" Antonia arrives breathless and red-cheeked as a poppy. "This, I believe, is yours, Madame." She ceremoniously places Lila's purse on the table.

"How did you—?"

"All I can say is thank God for those tiny pebbles! They're everywhere in that park and my throwing arm is not too shabby. Caught the first guy in the temple and he dropped the purse like a hot potato before running off with his little friends."

"Your traveling companion?" The British woman sets her cup down in the saucer, and rising, leaves a few coins on the table. "You take good care of our friend here, young lady."

"I will, madame." Antonia stands up taller.

"Thank you again for...everything." They wave goodbye without having ever exchanged names, Lila realizes as she opens her purse and is relieved to find her wallet intact, all the bills accounted for and everything just as it was before being tucked under a boy's filthy armpit.

They have left the rented car parked where it was: the train will be faster. Standing on the metro platform, they wait with the throng of tourists. Still, Lila reflexively clutches her purse a little tighter as she stares at Antonia in astonishment. At such a young age, to be so sure of herself, so poised. Bright, quick as a sparrow and strong. And to pursue a gang of boys and return victorious, Lila's wallet in hand. Lila shakes her head. But as bright as she is, how foolish to run off like that. Impulsive. Headstrong. Careless. It's the age nowadays, she supposes, what the girls do. The train screeches up to them and the doors slide open. They quickly press through the crowd and find one improbably empty seat, which Antonia immediately yields to Lila. Respectful of her elders besides, she'll give her that.

Lila squeezes next to a man hunched over his cane, the grumblings of her stomach drowned out by squeaking wheels on dirty tracks. They haven't eaten all day. Or have they? She decides they haven't, in fact, can't remember the last time she put a morsel of food in her mouth. She salivates at the thought. They're only going one stop to the Louvre, a museum she had long dreamed of visiting in another life. At the center of the spiraling arrondissements in the city, they emerge from the long, wet stairs of the metro to pass patisserie after patisserie, their rows of millefeuille pastries and the bishop-shaped religieuses inviting more than just a casual glance.

"Don't know about you but I could eat a horse." Antonia presses her forehead against the shop window.

"No time." Lila hustles her along, past the next shop, a variety store and the next, a boucherie where skinny ducks hang from hooks. Something has been nagging at Lila.

Earlier, Antonia had casually mentioned that Isabel and Niccolo had gone to the movies not long before Isabel's disappearance, but the pinched look that fell over the girl's face when she said it, like there was something else, something she didn't want to say.

"What did you mean they went to the movies?" They have been circling the Place des Victoires for the last ten minutes unsuccessfully.

"Just that. They went. Saw some Italian film."

"Are they...sweethearts?" Lila immediately regrets the question. Not the question exactly but the language. It's old fashioned. Of course the kids probably don't say that anymore and who knows what they say, although it wouldn't surprise Lila in the least, the two of them holed up in a dark theater doing things Isabel knows better than doing. Lila shakes her head as if trying to wipe this image from her mind.

Antonia folds her arms across her chest. Clearly she's said the last on the subject. "I don't see any van, do you?"

"There." At the intersection, Lila points at the shop with the blue awning: La Vie en Rose scrawled in French cursive.

They cross the street, and indeed, there is no blue van, nothing but a silver Vespa and a shiny red Citroen crammed in the one parking space out front. A little bell tinkles as they open the shop door and Lila cringes, the audio memory of her own shop bell too close even at such great a distance.

"Bonjour, madame, mademoiselle!"

The shopkeeper is a slight, bearded man with curious, kindly eyes behind thick glasses. Certainly not the sort to abduct a child. But what better disguise than a kind expression? She clears her throat.

"We are looking for a nice hotel, something a bit posh. Do you know of something like that in the quartier, monsieur?"

"I'm sorry, madame. As you can see this is not a tourist kiosk." He gestures to the shelves of books around them and then looks slightly guilty. "It gets a bit confusing, I'm sure. Perhaps I can draw you a little map."

The bell on the door jangles again and a middle-aged woman sings out her bonjour before disappearing down the first overcrowded aisle of books. A horizontal stripe of blue flashes through the display window: a van pulling up to the curb out front. The thud of a car door slamming precedes the bell on the door.

"Sylvain, enfin! Ça va?" The shopkeeper greets the driver who puts down his heavy box to shake hands. "You, monsieur, are late!" He raises an eyebrow but speaks through a smile.

Sylvain is tall and gangly, the shadow of a day-old beard on his cheeks. A heavy waft of strong filterless cigarettes trails him, the same scent Lila had smelled with disdain on Isabel's school sweater once or twice while doing the wash. She wrinkles her nose.

"Perhaps your friend, monsieur, perhaps he knows of a place?" Lila intones as much nonchalance as possible. "A posh hotel, but not too posh if you take my meaning. We have a budget to consider after all."

"Madame, as I've said, the tourist kiosk at city hall is far more equipped than we are to answer your question."

"I may know of a place." The tall man speaks softly, but Lila catches every word. "Do you, monsieur?" She braces.

"I suppose that depends. Are you looking for something this evening?" He turns to face them. A thin serpentine scar runs the length of his jaw line.

"Indeed, we are." Antonia puts an arm around Lila's shoulder. "My grandmother and me."

"Sylvain! What are you up to?" The bookseller shakes his head, smiling. "Still drumming up business for that little cousin of yours?"

Sylvain disappears behind the counter with the heavy box and returns empty handed. He smiles at Lila and Antonia.

"I can take you if you want. I'm heading there now."

They are riding in the blue van along a narrow street, folded into the back seat somehow, the two of them, Antonia and Lila, Antonia's long legs and all, knees almost grazing her chin, with a little stack of sealed boxes piled next to them. Sylvain puffs his filterless out the open window, leans on the horn, swearing, at the next light. By the time they arrive, after so many sharp senseless turns one after another, they might have gone to the moon and back. At the next stop Sylvain wrestles with the hand brake and turns off the engine. They emerge into the cooling evening air, and Lila's legs nearly buckle beneath her.

"Steady there!" Antonia catches Lila by the arm.

"Hotel Lutèce, Mesdames." Sylvain invites them to follow him up the red-carpeted stairs of the main entrance. A brief whirl through the heavy glass doors and then nothing but soft carpet: wine red covering every inch of the lobby. The color, like French manners, is a bit over wrought. Lila glances around for the driver but he has already vanished.

A woman in a crisp suit greets them cheerfully from behind the counter in the lobby, a narrow little corner with velvet papered walls and damask curtains as suffocating as relatives clustered around a sick bed. Lila stumbles a few steps forward.

"Is Madame alright?" The young woman behind the counter conveys an earnestness that is unusual for Paris. Lila's attempt to return the smile fails badly, her teeth clenched against the dull thudding behind her eyes.

Antonia steps forward. "My grandmother's fine. Just famished. Can we reserve a room please and have our meals sent up?

The young woman takes their dog-eared passports and fills out their registration before sending them up the main staircase with a room key and a few suggestions for making their stay more pleasant.

When Lila wakes up, she blinks uncertainly at her wristwatch: a full two hours have passed somehow. The mattress is stiff and smells of detergent, the bed still made, satin cover and propped pillows untouched. She lifts her head slightly: her summer dress remains un-rumpled, and stranger still, someone has removed her shoes.

Antonia settles the service cart next to the table in the corner. "You're just in time." She removes the cover off a dish and a great gasp of steam escapes. "Lovely. And still hot too."

Legs still a bit wobbly, her vision off center, Lila joins her at the table. "Is it morning?" She spreads the linen napkin in her lap.

Antonia raises her eyebrows. "Half past three in the afternoon. You must have been exhausted."

Lila nods, incredulous. She uncovers the dish, inhales the pungent scent. The things that pass for fancy cuisine here: a wedge of rare beef stewing in a puddle of its own blood, potatoes gratinée, limp carrots drowning in butter, and of course the ubiquitous wineglass which Antonia fills against any objections. Too light headed still, she avoids the wine and instead takes a bite of meat and then another and another in quick succession before moving on to the potatoes.

"Do you really think she's here, of all places, in a four star hotel?" Lila pushes the empty plate away, her vision finally clearing, her bare feet digging into the pile of plush carpet.

Antonia shrugs and downs the last gulp of wine. "She has to be. Where else would they bring a girl like her?"

"What do you mean 'a girl like her'?" Lila scowls at the possible implications.

"Isabel is posh. You must have noticed. With her books and her poetry. Anyway," Antonia gives her an evaluative look, "don't worry so much. She'll know how to handle herself. Besides..." Antonia quickly rushes on, "I paid the front desk girl a visit while you were having your beauty sleep. She's as friendly as they come. We're missing cocktail hour by the way. You should see them, the men in their fancy suits and ties chomping on expensive cigars in the lobby bar. She complimented me on my height, you know how petite the French are, oh and she said I had a perfect complexion. Can you imagine, me? With all these freckles? God, I love the French. So, I got up the nerve to ask if they were hiring."

"Hiring! For what?"

"Hostesses or housemaids or whatever they call it here. I work in hospitality, as you know, and this could be our way in."

Lila teeters next to the bed and then plops back down on the mattress, off kilter. "I don't know what's wrong with me."

"Nothing a little more sleep won't fix." Antonia places a fluffed pillow beneath Lila's head. "There. You rest. I need to take care of a few things."

"What few things? Where are you going? And where are my shoes—"

"They're in the corner." Antonia points to Lila's oxfords lined up next to the door. "And don't worry, you won't need them. I'll be back in a jiff."

But ticking minutes in bed pass into a bloated hour of tossing and imagining the worst. Lila sits up: she's no use to anyone like this. The flowers on the walls dip and dive like summer flies; she tries to catch one in her hand and, grimacing, catches a whiff of her underarm: it's been ages since she's had a bath. The air has finally cooled down enough, and there's nothing better for a headache; reluctantly she trudges toward the bathroom. The hot water runs, drowning out the eye-pounding metronome in her head as thick bubbles from a little glass bottle of syrupy liquid fill the tub. Plunging in, the water line tickling her chin, her thoughts wander the length of highway miles and wide boulevards and then finally circle the chandelier overhead, with the moths. After a long hot soak, she carefully rises from the tub and wraps herself in a towel. The room is dark, the only glimpse of light is the summer sunset, pink and gold seeping through the blinds. The phone rings, and Lila jolts.

"Madame Lesser?"

"Yes?"

"Your granddaughter asked me to convey a message. She is out for a walk and will be back shortly. It's a beautiful evening, Madame."

"I see. Well, yes it is, thank you. Since I have you on the line I'd like to place a long distance call please." She rattles off the number.

Ten rings later, an answer, finally. "Hello? Hello Miriam? Can you hear me?"

"Lila! Thank God." Miriam pounces on her from the end of the line, barely able to contain her relief. "I couldn't just let the situation stand, I had to follow up with them."

"Follow up with whom, Miriam?"

"Lila, can you hear me? Why, with the bank, of course."

Lila tries to respond but Miriam is relentless.

"I hope you can hear me. About the paintings? They're not budging, Lila. They're saying they need proof, proof that the collection is yours before they can release it. And I know that you don't have the title to the collection. But we both know someone who very well may. Please Lila, Signora Morgenfeld, for all the trouble she caused, was the only person who saved the collection—"

"Absolutely not. It's out of the— "

"A grudge is a luxury, Lila. Do you hear me? A luxury. It's only a matter of a phone call which I can do right now. Of course the heiress must still have the paperwork, the provenance of each work, everything we need to prove it belongs to you. This is our best hope. I swear on my life it is."

"Of course there are other alternatives, I could..." But Lila struggles for ideas. "How can I accept any help from that —,"

"The clock is ticking, Lila!" Miriam breaks in, her voice sizzling with uncharacteristic anger. "Think of Isabel."

Lila slams down the phone, shaking, and the bath towel falls to her feet. Outside the sun is setting, and the goosebumps rise on her naked skin. Other alternatives. She unzips the suitcase and pulls out clean undergarments, a slightly wrinkled blue blouse and folded skirt. Her hand on the bedpost, she steps into the black skirt and fastens the button at the waist. The blouse fits a bit looser around the chest and arms: so much the better. Shoulders back in the bathroom mirror, her eyes settling on something invisible just behind the quivering face staring back, she applies a thin layer of pale pink lipstick, steadying herself for battle.

CHAPTER SIXTEEN

Isabel stares at her arm. It works as well as ever but the skin looks flaky and pale without the cast and when she makes a fist, her unused muscles feel sore and tender. Everything that had come before remains a blur, the car picking her up, Gritti hustling her like unwieldy luggage through the hotel side door and then up a disused staircase down a narrow corridor to a crowded room. Then the crisp zing of the grinding saw in the old doctor's shaky hands, the other girls looking on, as it presses against her cast, the deepening low growl like buzzards circling, the saw digging deeper. She closed her eyes at first; she didn't want to see the cast come off for fear of what would still be left beneath it, bare bones or bloody skin or nothing at all but black space where a limb used to be, but there it was again, her old arm, a bit worn, not quite good as new, but still there and moving. She perks up; even now, as she gazes in the vanity mirror at a young woman whose hair has been oiled and smoothed, the cheeks smeared with rouge and the lips stained with red lipstick, the eyelids daubed a garish light blue, she can hear it still, the low growl of the buzzards.

"Hold still." The girl fixing her hair into a French twist sighs audibly. "It's way too thick. How can they expect—,"

"Is she ready?" A brunette with a fashionably short fringe peeks her head in the doorway. "The boss is asking."

The hairstylist gives Isabel an appraising look. "As ready as she's going to be."

A tucking of loose strands and a final blast of hair spray aimed at the lopsided bun projects an aura of metallic-tasting mist about Isabel's head, and the empty can is jettisoned to the floor. The scent burns her nose and throat and forces a violent room-clearing sneeze; when finally she reopens her eyes, there's been a change in personnel. Standing in the open doorway like a castle sentry is Signor Gritti, a new captive at his side.

"Oh!" Isabel gasps at the sudden appearance of the tall girl standing next to Gritti. Her impulse is to smile and to run and kiss that kind, familiar face, that same kind familiar face she's been wishing for so long to see and exactly the one she realizes, with stomach-dropping certainty, should never be here at all.

"You, out." The hairdresser quickly obliges Gritti's order, leaving her combs and brushes behind. "You two know each other?"

"Never seen her before, Monsieur." A vein visibly throbs in Antonia's forehead.

Still, Gritti inspects her as he would a fresh catch off his boat. "Found this one in the lobby dressed like a housekeeper." He looks at Isabel. "What do you think, do we need a housekeeper?"

The question hangs in the space between them. Isabel concentrates her gaze instead on her new manicure, French, white perfectly rounded crescent moon tips on each fingernail. She was forced to sit for it while before the most recent ordeal of hair-styling, moments ago, hours ago, she can barely conceive of time. Ticking minutes, hours, watches, clocks and appointments are luxuries for other people. She only remembers, wait, sit, eat, say hello to the nice gentlemen. Whatever comes next in the bed with these well-tailored men under French perfumed sheets she can barely recall, a little more jostling than sleep, that's all, a bit of prodding, poking, the noise of a grunt or a moan, while she sings a song to herself, silently in her head so as not to hear the noises of these strange men, a Hebrew song Nonna used to sing. And anyway, the manicure is a blessing, pretty nails to focus on, instead of her dear friend because perhaps if she doesn't look, Antonia will be magically transported back to her beloved cafe in the campo. Because no one else should have to bear the consequences of her foolishness, least of all Antonia, a good, kind person, a genuine friend. Widening her eyes to keep the tears from forming, Isabel can't help but glance up at Antonia who remains trapped in Gritti's grip. As if a silly childish notion could really work. This is how the pieces fall, stupid selfish girl.

"So, are we hiring a housekeeper?"

"A housekeeper? I don't think so, monsieur."

"You don't think so, monsieur." Stubby fingers tighten around Antonia's arm, and she squints in discomfort.

"I mean no. No, we are not."

"Well. Are we hiring a hostess then?"

"Yes. I mean, I don't know, monsieur. Please if you could just, you're hurting her—"

"You don't know?" Gritti yanks Antonia's arm back, and the girl's escaping squeak is only half stifled.

Once Isabel had come upon a wounded sparrow in the campo making exactly the same pitiful chirp. She watched helplessly as the tiny bird struggled on the sidewalk, the shudder of its broken wing finally coming to rest. Then just as now, Isabel had ground her teeth together, keeping silent, never once looking away. But this time is different. This time she's the one who caused the damage, and such luxuries as complaint and self-pity are reserved for someone else, someone better. She pins her gaze on Gritti, willing him to release his grip on Antonia's arm, but even her most hostile stare does nothing to deter him, and his arm remains locked around her friend. An abrupt knock shatters her concentration, and the door swings wide open.

"Corbeau! I was just about to bring this one to you." Gritti's grip loosens and Antonia wrests herself away from him, rubbing her arm vigorously.

Corbeau's freshly shaved face crinkles in disapproval. He is dressed in a three-piece suit, a silk red handkerchief peeking out from the lapel pocket, in his hand the amber lion's head of a carved walking stick. "And what's all this?"

"Just cleaning up, that's all."

"And who was it this time? Who made the mess?" Corbeau appraises Antonia with a forced smile.

"Found this one trying to pass herself off as a domestic. And that one," he points accusingly at Isabel, "well it's obvious, isn't it? Tell the truth — you two signorinas know each other, don't you?" He stares them down but both girls remain silent.

"Well." Corbeau's cologne is nauseatingly sweet. A few taps of the walking stick toward her and he has edged up closer to Isabel. "First running away and causing us all to worry and now... well I don't have the time. Some of us have a job to do. That's you, mademoiselle." He pokes a finger at Isabel, and she recoils. "Your next client is here, Sandrine."

The alias is as sibilant as an uncoiling snake's hiss. Isabel jumps quickly to her feet, glancing at Antonia who remains staring downward in a kind of wooden trance. "As you wish, monsieur." There's little choice but to see the next gentleman in the expensively tailored suit, to greet him with a seductive air in the doorway. Isabel holds off a shudder, she must not think of it, it's the only way through. Perhaps he will be a kind man, a man she can reason with. With a little luck, she could steal a minute to phone Vauvenargues. She pats at her skirt where she had pocketed the business card.

"Good. Off we go then. Well," Corbeau appraises Antonia, "she's seen better days, hasn't she?" He opens the door, catching a woman mid-knock in the threshold.

"Oh! I was looking for the—," Lila's best false smile fades. "Signor Davoglio? What on earth are you—" A long straight swipe like a rower's paddle catches her at the side of the head, and, like a ragdoll dropped from a child's hand, she crumples to the floor.

"I told you, I said, don't get too greedy."

Gritti paces in front of them, gestures wildly at Corbeau, grumbling something about always having to clean up his mess while Isabel and Antonia clutch each other like the last person each will ever see, their hands intertwined. The vision will not go away: Nonna at the door out of nowhere and then lying here, inexplicably, a ruby trickle edging down her brow. Impossible. It has to be because none of it is real. Nonna would never have come to Paris, never. Surely she's at home peeling potatoes or in the parlor carefully watering the potted geranium on the sill, only a few drops or else it will die, but then Antonia's nails dig down hard into her hand, and Nonna lies where she's fallen, crumpled in the doorway and nothing is impossible. Nothing will be impossible ever again.

"And always me left picking up the pieces!" A palpable sentence rises out of Gritti's mumbling.

Davoglio leans the walking stick against a table. "Again, my friend, you're not paying attention. This works out perfectly, you see. Now we have them both. This one," he gestures to Lila on the floor, "has the deed. And once we have that we don't need her anymore. Don't you see? We have the paintings and the granddaughter."

"We better hope so." Gritti glances at Isabel.

"Good." Davoglio grabs the walking stick.

"And the old lady?"

"Well, like you said, there's a bit of clean up. Get the deed from her first, then get it done, will you?"

"Right. You! Out!" At Gritti's bark they jump to attention, Isabel grabbing onto Antonia's arm. Her legs are pins and needles, her mind a hollow cave. A wave of cold air hits them as they follow

Corbeau out the door, Isabel swallowing the tears lodged in her throat as she whispers to her silent friend not to look back.

By the time Lila comes to the pink summer sky outside has dwindled and an early evening violet filters in through half-shaded windows. In the darkened corner a man facing the washbasin produces a prolonged trickling. When he turns around he's still pulling up his fly. "It's pretty crap, this."

"What?"

His coveralls are paint-stained and his face sweaty, unshaven. The accent is Italian, unmistakably Venetian. He squints at her through cloudy moonstone eyes like a workman taking the dimensions of a room.

"I'm saying, a posh hotel in Paris not having a toilet in the room, that's crap."

Lila has no idea how to respond, his words make no sense to her even if the accent is familiar. And something is wrong beyond all of this. She gropes around on the floor beneath the wet folds of her skirt.

"No, dear, you haven't pissed yourself."

The light is turned on, and on the table a pitcher lies on its side. The dripping water has pooled into a little puddle at Lila's feet, and the sticky wet patch on her forehead pulses, the pain dull and constant. She rocks her feet automatically from side to side to feel a bit of the life come back into them. A hot red line sears down the middle of her back when she stops, and suddenly everything returns: the hotel, the long bath, tossing sleeplessly in bed, Antonia stepping out of the room and never coming back.

"Where is Isabel? Where is my granddaughter?"

The workman shrugs and drags hard on his cigarette. The embers glow like a warning light.

After a moment, he flicks the lit stub onto the rug and steps on the smoldering ash before it catches fire. "You were there at the hospital with another Jew lady. My wife told me she saw you there."

Lila's brain whirls painfully. Niccolo's mother, the woman at the boy's bedside who gave up her husband to save her son. Or so she said. Well, so much for the allegiance of mothers.

"My wife said you would come. She has a sixth sense for these things. Watch out for that old Jew lady, she told me, she's coming for you." Gritti now hovers over a squirming Lila, his hunter's knife gleaming.

"I only came for my granddaughter." With a suddenness that is unexpected, the cool prick of his blade pierces her neck; she gasps. Not once in all these years did she ever imagine that she would breathe her last in Paris. After all this time, she'd become convinced it would be Venice where she finally let go, in the campo in her bed after a full life, long-lived, the city where she had a husband and a child, property and a name. Not Paris! That city where her husband met his favorite lover for the very first time. The pointed edge of the knife burns against her skin, but Lila tries not to squirm.

She struggles to speak. "If you have any sense, you'll realize you won't succeed this way. Davoglio's a thief — he'll only rob you blind!"

Gritti laughs. "You're one to talk, stealing from the lot of us all these years."

"My husband was an Italian, signor! You are stealing the paintings out from under my family!"

"You can't steal what belongs to you in the first place, can you? Your husband was nothing but a Jew, and he got what was coming. Those paintings were never yours." Gritti pulls her by the arm to a standing position.

"You're a fool if you think Davoglio won't take it all for himself." Lila struggles to stay upright. "He's making off with the lot of them as we speak. And yet you trust him! Even after what he did to your boy!"

"What?" Gritti grabs her by the shoulders and pushes her against the wall. "What are you saying about my boy?"

Lila looks him in the eye and shakes her head. "Your wonderful friend Davoglio chopped off your son's finger and left him for dead; that's what your friend did. Do you really think a man like that would ever share the spoils?"

A bluish cast invades Gritti's face, and he tightens his grip. "So no one is as smart as you, right?" A disparaging sound gurgles deep in his throat. "Now move!"

"Listen! Signor!" Lila frantically improvises at the doorway. "If anything happens to me, you will never know what I haven't told anyone. About the other paintings, I mean. That secret will die with me."

Gritti pauses and then gestures to the chair with the knife, and Lila sits down. The lie takes shape in the violet air of the stuffy room; and when it's all spun out, she almost believes it herself. There are three other paintings, she says, two Titians and a Tintoretto, Italian Renaissance all. She describes at length the colorful scenes in each, the youthful and innocent maidens, the swarthy soldiers weary from battle, gold-leaf halos hovering above angels' heads. Gritti, listening intently, finally puts the knife away and joins her at the table, pours her a tall glass of water, which she drains in one gulp. He needs more information, more reassurances. She delivers all of that, more.

"Think of it," she continues. "You and your wife and son will have complete financial security. That's what you wanted! All I require is the safe return of my Isabel and her friend. Once we are all safe and returned home, I will tell you where the paintings are, you have my absolute word, signor, but only when the girls are with me and you let us leave in one piece."

"Is that right? So, you're all cozy back home but what about me, where's my insurance?" He stands up suddenly, and begins pacing the length of the table.

"The hiding place is in Venice, signor. If we all make it home, I can show you exactly where."

As Lila continues to speak, she is shocked to see a man creeping silently into the room behind Gritti. A familiar man with a face that Lila hoped never again to see in life, a face she had last seen in a crumpled photograph thrown into the bottom of a drawer, almost, but never quite forgotten.

Gritti leans forward slightly to make another comment, but just as he opens his mouth, his eyes widen, his head jerks back, and he crumples to the floor.

"Are you alright?" The familiar face is now on the same level with hers. A tall man in a gentleman's fine suit and tie kneels next to her holding her hands in his.

Lila can only blink.

"Can you stand up?"

"Is he dead?"

"With any luck, yes. Now quickly! I have an idea where they've gone."

CHAPTER SEVENTEEN

The taxi careens around the next corner, and the driver turns up the music, the Algerian flag on the rearview mirror swaying.

"How on earth did you find me?" Lila's whisper can barely be heard over the ululations of lively North African radio.

Vauvenargues glances at the rearview window every few seconds, ignoring her question. They continue on in stony silence.

"How much longer will this take?"

"No souci, madame! You will arrive in a petite moment," the driver says, taking the next traffic light just as it turns red.

"How on earth did you find me, Vauvenargues? Tell me!"

He stares at her for a full second, his face improbably smooth and unmarked, his long hair meticulously tousled, his hazel eyes as clear as in his youth. "Imagine my surprise when in she walked! Your Isabel. I guessed you couldn't be far behind. Or rather, I hoped..."

"Where are we going?"

"We're almost there."

Not two streets later, they screech to an abrupt stop. Lila clutches the handle, and the door flies open, the few bills she throws through the driver's side window land in his lap.

"This way." Vauvenargues has taken the lead across the square with Lila shadowing close behind. The June sky rolls crimson and blue above, the clouds are ripe with rain, and the top button of her coat has come undone. When the rain begins to fall around them in big clumsy drops, Vauvenargues holds his jacket over her head. "It's not much further."

But by the time they arrive a young woman at the entrance is locking up.

Lila clutches at the young attendant's arm. "Please, mademoiselle. You don't understand: my granddaughter may still be in there." The attendant shakes her head, the key jangling from her belt. It's not possible. Not possible. Opening a simple door with a simple lock. Lila changes tack, softens her tone. "Please," she begs. "A young girl's life is at stake. A girl not much younger than you!" Not possible, the attendant says, shrugging.

Lila turns away in defeat, Vauvenargues still at her side.

The corridor is winding and dark, lit only by the small bouncing flame of the candle. Finally they are led to the place where the narrow hall widens into an artery, and they stop. The flame on the candle suddenly winks out and Isabel gives a gasp. For a moment all is darkness, then the crackle of a match drowns out Isabel's intake of breath, and the candle in Davoglio's hand once more illuminates several passages branching out in front of them. The light is trained upon the walls, and what had seemed to be stone is revealed as something else: around them are stacks of human skulls, femurs, slender arm bones and jagged spines and all catalogued neatly like hats in a millinery's shop.

Isabel grips her friend's arm. "But how did you find me?" she whispers.

"Niccolo's mother," Antonia whispers back.

Isabel's eyes widen in the dark. "What? How did you...?"

"He took me to his house...once."

"Why? What for?"

"I never meant to, Isabel. You know me. I couldn't care less." Antonia's whisper tickles the back of Isabel's neck. "It was all his idea."

"I don't understand. You mean he kissed you? Or more?" Isabel shakes her head, as if to banish the image that is now lodged firmly in her head. It doesn't matter, it doesn't matter, she tries to tell herself. "It doesn't matter," she repeats out loud, but speaking the words only confirms the lie. She should never have asked. It was just a niggling feeling, that's all. But one she couldn't shake. "But wait, was it after our date at the movies?" She turns and gives her friend an imploring look.

"Please, I never would have—"

"Was it?"

Antonia says nothing.

Niccolo had made a pass. Or worse. And it was after...after he had spent those hours in the dark with Isabel. Her stomach twists. It was a lifetime ago, and yet the sting of his betrayal feels brand new, and all the more abject in the darkness of winding corridors.

"Please, Isabel, if I'd known, I never would have—"

They have now reached the end of the passage, and at its final stop is a low closed door, which Davoglio unlocks with a skeleton key. From the gloom he pulls two smallish, square wrapped packages, the very same ones Signora Morgenfeld had been so kind to entrust to Isabel in her garden. Voices suddenly rumble and echo from somewhere in the far distance. With a sudden movement, Davoglio thrusts the whimpering Antonia into the darkness beyond the open door.

"Two packages come out and one goes in." He locks the door against the muffled, terrified cries.

"Antonia!" Isabel can't help but scream. "Antonia!" She yells her friend's name again and again and pulls at the handle on the door until Davoglio grabs her around the waist and shoves her back down the hallway. "Don't be an idiot," he hisses.

Antonia. But Isabel can do nothing. The name bounces off the passage walls for seeming hours as they retrace their steps, Isabel hears the echoes as Davoglio continues to shove her forward each time she stumbles, each time she slows down, and as they feel their way against walls made of jutting bone, the last reverberations are finally extinguished. Long after the candle has gone out, a rectangle of bright light appears: the entrance.

At La Vie en Rose, Vauvenargues paces nervously in front of the bookshop. The shade on the door is drawn. Lila knocks once and listens again.

"It's the lunch hour, Lila. Let's just wait."

"I'm waiting. I'm waiting." She waves him off exasperatedly. He has been relentless since her last attempted phone call with Miriam who never picked up, rushing her from the hotel to the taxi to the bookstore, guiding her smoothly and kindly along. He can't have changed that much. Perhaps he has, though, grown up a bit. It's possible. Before she can knock once more, the door opens a crack.

"Can I help you?" The bookseller stares at them blankly.

"Oh! Bonjour, monsieur, we were here earlier? A young woman and I, we came to ask about a hotel. Your driver was kind enough to help us."

"Oh, yes, that's right. Come in."

They hover in the doorway uncertainly. The shop inside is shaded and still. They follow the clerk to the counter, passing the towering, overstocked aisles that somehow seem changed from before, where once there had been sunlight and movement, a strange lethargy has since settled.

"We thought you might be able to... help us, you see." Vauvenargues falters, his tone rising where a question would.

"Are you in the book trade, monsieur?" The bookseller cocks his head.

"I'm actually looking for a particular book...a book about art, you see."

"Italian art," Lila offers, catching on to Vauvenargues' ruse.

"Yes, about the artist Titian in particular."

"Titian, you say? There hasn't been much trade in Italian Renaissance art for years." He disappears through a door at the back of the shop. Lila is clearly dismayed but Vauvenargues shrugs.

"Where is he going?" She can't stop fidgeting with her purse. She takes a deep breath. Vauvenargues waits in silence.

The man reappears behind the counter in minutes.

"I'm afraid, monsieur, there are simply too many boxes to count." He folds his arms against his chest.

"Might we have a look?" Vauvenargues nudges Lila.

"If you like. Come —it's just through here. Mind your step, the hallway is narrow."

In single file they head down the narrow passage to a closed door, which the bookseller opens slowly. A light switches on, and in the center of the room a man sits on a folding chair, not a box in sight, only a strong smell of damp and must.

The bookseller turns around to leave, closing the door behind him.

"Signora Lesser. You came." The seated man wears worker's coveralls and greets them like long lost friends, a stain of dried blood on his forehead. "And Vauvenargues, too. Perfect."

"Do you know this man?" Lila glances at Vauvenargues.

Vauvenargues, deflated now, his air of bravado all but evaporated, takes a step back and hangs his head. Vauvenargues, the liar. The cheat. It's the two of them, Albert and him, at the party all over again. And she, yet again, is the naïve one, the stupidly gullible one. To think he had offered his help and here is in cahoots with this thief.

A shamed Vauvenargues gives Lila a crestfallen look. "Lila... I did try to help. You know I did. But I owe them too much money. What choice did I have?"

Gritti laughs and shakes his head at Lila. "You trusted this pigeon?" He laughs harder, triggering a short burst of coughing that finally ends when a cigarette is lit. He inhales deeply. "There is something else. A detail. Signor Davoglio insisted on it."

"Signor Davoglio?"

"Yes, signora. He's asked for the deed to the collection. To make it official."

Gritti blows a stream of smoke at Lila who has been holding onto the counter's edge to stop the spinning, a confusion of book aisles, dark hallways, windowless rooms, folding chairs. Of course, the deed. Miriam was right to try the heiress. If only she had picked up the phone. For a vertiginous moment they are alone in the room, Lila and Gritti, the others long gone, the paintings gone, the bodies all buried. Gritti smiles.

"Where is my granddaughter?" Lila gathers her composure, clarity descending with an arrow's focus. Besides the door they entered, she thinks, there must be another, a back door heading to an alley.

The howling of sirens comes from the front of the store, the sound stretches long then slows and chirps. Soon loud footsteps down the passageway and the door flies open.

"You, move!"

Signor Davoglio, his voice quite changed, his usually impeccable suit grungy and creased, pushes the young woman in front of him and she stumbles a few steps forward. Lila cannot stop it, the sob caught in her throat at the sight of her granddaughter, skin and bones, her arm in a makeshift sling: Isabel, somehow here and alive.

Davoglio nods at Isabel. "Sit! Ah, Gritti. Good. You have things in hand. My apologies for not arriving sooner. Fortunately even in midday Paris traffic, you can always count on the police for a ride, eh Gritti? Half of them on the payroll and the rest repeat clients. Here, take these, will you?" He hands the wrapped packages over. "Set them down there. There's a good man." He swipes his hands together twice as if wiping away dust.

Isabel slumps in the folding chair. She is tinier than ever, frail-looking. An ill-fitting cocktail dress hangs off her shoulders and hips, and strange and slightly garish makeup covers her features. She would almost be unrecognizable if they passed in the street.

Davoglio unbuttons the bottom button of his jacket. "Do we have the deed?"

"I was just asking the very same thing of Signora Lesser myself."

"Of course she wouldn't have it here." Vauvenargues chimes in. "It must be in Venice."

"Shut him up please Gritti, will you?"

Gritti squeezes fat fingers around Vauvenargues' neck, muffling his pleas, and causing his legs to bend and scrape like sticks against the floor. When at last he lets go, Vauvenargues drops breathlessly to the floor and quickly scuttles into the corner, still gasping.

"Please! Gentlemen! There's no need." Lila summons her courage. "I will get it for you. Can you say more about this deed?" She feigns ignorance, buying time.

"The collection has a deed," Davoglio says as though speaking to a child, "and the deed can be transferred. Officially, of course, by you, madame."

Lila nods, her best attempt to reassure. With all the details of securing the paintings and storing them at cool enough temperatures, there are other matters, matters she has long neglected. Until Miriam told her the heiress had the deed all along, Lila had never been aware of its existence. It is the moment she has always dreaded, her lack of interest in Albert's business affairs and the bureaucracy of the gallery coming back to haunt her. Albert must have kept documents, provenance, proof of ownership, that sort of thing. He talked about it endlessly but over the years she barely listened. There would come a time, she always chided herself, when she would need to know. She digs her fingernails into the clammy palms of her closed fists.

Davoglio grabs her by the arm and pushes her closer to Isabel;

the girl raises her head and tries to mouth something, a word, a protest but no sound comes out.

"Look at the sight of her," Davoglio says. "She isn't well, signora. She has had a fever. And her poor little friend. Now that was a real shame."

"Please, signor. Let me." Gritti moves closer.

Davoglio's fingers tighten around Lila's arm. "The lady says she has no deed. So, we'll just have to help her produce one, won't we."

A stout arm encircles Davoglio, holding him tight. "I'll have to insist, signor. This," Gritti whispers, brandishing a gleaming knife, "is for my son. For the finger you took." He plunges the blade deep into Davoglio's chest. The wounded man wavers briefly in the space it takes for realization to catch up with action, before sinking to his knees, a trickle of blood running from his mouth, the arrogant knowing look in his eyes slowly replaced by blankness.

CHAPTER EIGHTEEN

At each turn, each bump in the road, Lila sways this way and that, her hands tied in the back seat, the never-ending hum of highway vibrating beneath them, her eyes fixed on Isabel, slumped over in a feverish sleep. Thin scraggly tree branches line the autoroute and shimmer as they pass, casting long shadows across her granddaughter's face.

Without warning: a sudden stop, and just as quickly as she'd been trussed, the rope is cut from her hands, and she is shoved out into the street. A gravelly voice mutters, 24 hours before the van screeches away. In front of Lila, the pale painted brick of her building, her home. She is home. Everything is the same and yet everything, every single thing is different.

The weight of years pushes her up each stair, Davoglio's newly dead eyes, her mother's face in the yard in Hrubieszow, shooing that guileless stray dog who came around; he wagged off every slight, every harsh unkind word, that mutt.

She reaches the final stair and final stair, and the front door is slightly ajar. She enters the darkened apartment.

In the parlor, the empty frame that once held the Titian hangs sideways on the wall. Her writing desk in the bedroom is torn apart: drawers overturned, letters scattered, the invoice to the power municipality never sent, Albert's old address book face up on the carpet. In the middle of scattered sheets and twisted blankets, a pile of cheap jewelry has been dumped on the bed, the little gold locket with a tiny broken clock inside, a sapphire ring set with missing zirconia. She picks up the phone to dial the number, a number she would never allow herself to dial, but has always held in mind; she is scarcely aware of the throbbing at her wrists and ankles, the skin rubbed bare from the rope.

"Hello," says a proper voice at the second ring.

Lila holds her breath for a fraction of a second. "Isadora Morgenfeld, please."

It's all arranged. Lila fastens the little blue straw hat in the hallway mirror and tucks a stray lock of hair behind her ear. She reaches for her keys before she remembers. They're in her purse, the purse in Paris. She starts when the phone rings and picks it up quickly. The woman probably wants to send a car around. "I'm leaving just now."

"Calle della Rosa, Castello 2234. Come alone." The gruff voice says and the line goes dead.

The drawing room is silent except for the ticking. On the credenza, a small Venetian table clock, overwrought and gilded in gold leaf, tells the time. Not yet two. Twenty-four hours, he'd said. There is still time. Lila tries to sit up, but her ribs hurt and her head feels heavier than the gaudy marble bust in the entryway. A small painting, a bit tame for the Signora's usual tastes, a landscape of boats moored in a harbor hangs on the drawing room wall.

"Sugar?" Isadora Morgenfeld is poised on the divan with a kind of practiced stillness that only those rarified people of means have mastered; in front of her is a tea service etched in pink English roses. They have been sitting in silence for what can only be minutes, but seems far longer.

"No sugar, thank you." Lila shifts in her seat, such formalities are strange, but she is intent on keeping her expression pleasant, her mind focused.

"You'll forgive me," Signora Morgenfeld says. "This is all so unexpected. I have wanted to speak to you for so long." She pauses to sip but then puts the teacup back in its saucer. "As far as the deed to the collection, I have only the copy. I told your friend Miriam as much on the phone. I'm afraid that won't be enough for the bank to release it."

Lila leans forward, determined. "Then we'll need to ask him, won't we?"

"Are you certain?"

Lila nods, waving away Leonora's offer of more tea. Her cup has gone tepid, the tea untouched. "I've never been more certain of anything."

Signora Morgenfeld sighs. "Alright then. If you're sure."

The phone is carried in with a long cord trailing behind. The dialing of the number slows down time further still. A drip, not a pour. The tea is cold. The little table shakes a little when Lila's knee brushes the edge. Some words are exchanged, a few pleasantries across the wires and all of the Atlantic before the Signora motions her.

The receiver in Lila's hand feels light, a feather, nothing like the burden she imagined it to be. "Hello, Albert," she says, just as she had hundreds, perhaps thousands of times before.

"Hello, Lila."

The voice on the other end is more familiar than any she's heard in the intervening years, and as clear as if he were in the other room reading the paper but simply couldn't be bothered to look up. As if he'd arrived home from the gallery at the end of a tiring day and would now make his typical complaints about dinner. The same old meal, the lateness of the hour, her shortcomings as a cook. The cold sweat on her skin is the memory of their last real exchange. He was leaving her again. He said it as many times but never made good. This time was different. The soldiers came the next month and not long afterwards the freight trains.

Her heart skips once but she quickly recovers.

"How is New York?"

"New York is New York, Lila. But let's get straight to it. How much do you need?" He is matter of fact, as ever himself.

Lila braces. "It's not money. It's the deed, Albert. The deed to the collection." A long uncomfortable silence ensures. "Albert, you still there?"

"Yes, I'm here Lila. And is she alright? Isabel, is it?"

"Yes, Isabel, of course. That's just it, we don't know–," Lila's voice cracks.

"How did this whole thing... It's unthinkable, Lila, that you never told me about my own granddaughter! Not to mention that when I left you in charge of the collection I was very clear..." He trails off, sounding older and more feeble than she remembers.

"Will you help us?"

"I have my treatment tomorrow. I'm not well. I have a nurse, you should know. And it'll take a few days at least to sort the papers."

"We don't have a week, Albert! She could be dead by then."

Signora Morgenfeld motions for the phone and speaks quietly into the receiver, while Lila attempts to calm her heart's wild beating. After a moment the phone is hung up, and the Signora assures her all will be well.

"This is his granddaughter, Lila. He can be a selfish prig at times, but this is Isabel we're talking about."

Lila shrugs. He never cared for anyone. Not really. Lila wants to say it but doesn't. Instead she shakes the signora's hand as Leonora shows her to the door and offers a faux smile of gratitude, her heels on the stone like a forlorn character in the last frame of a film. But there is still something, she thinks. Lila quickens her pace; there is still something to be done.

Number 2234 is not a house but an open space, a yard with boats and gondolas in disrepair. A workman in paint-spattered overalls is hoisting a skiff onto its side and then re-stacking it against the wall like a book on a shelf. Lila has come alone as directed, refusing Signora Morgenfeld's offer to send police after her. There could be no mistakes. These men meant business.

Tucked behind a pillar at the front gate, Lila scans the yard: there's only the one man. No sign of Gritti. She strains to listen to muffled voices over the intermittent sound of a buzz saw, and then inching closer toward the gate she passes through, slowly, steadily. Each decision is weighed, each risk cast aside. The sound of the buzz saw becomes louder, more crisp, and when she crawls along a bit further, the sudden appearance of two dusty boots tucked into a pair of sawdust-covered pants blocks her path.

"You're a long way from home, aren't you?" A workman peers at her, in his hand a dull hammer.

Isabel blinks her eyes. A whole section of time is blank. Isn't this Paris? The landmarks outside say otherwise as the van careens around corners and floats through stops: where there had been the Seine, there is now the Grand Canal, where they once pushed through the crowds in the expanse of Place de la Concorde, they instead sail along the narrow periphery of a bustling city. In stops and starts, the van lurches and stalls and then restarts. Through the open window, the gondoliers sing love songs to tourists, snatches of Italian and English float upwards.

Isabel strains to see but her broken arm has gone numb, a

sharp ribbon of pain travels from her shoulder down the contour of her back, but the certainty of one thing remains: Nonna was here. Distinctly. She was. But if that were true, it is no longer. How long ago had that been? Nothing but the van's cargo, stacks of boxes, and some flat packages ride along with her. Finally, the vehicle comes to a complete stop, and she lurches with the cargo against the metal wall.

"Come on. Out." Gritti holds the door open.

"Are we here?"

It's pointless asking. She knows better. All of it is in her bones, the smell of the sea, the baking of bread, seagulls squawk, fish brine at the edges. They must be somewhere near the city center. As she is pushed down the gravel path, gondolas lying this way and that as they cross through the yard, the realization of home anchors her once more to place, and she is fed, a renewed energy creeping into her fevered blood and bones.

It's been too long now. But Isabel can still hear it from inside the tool shed, the sound of a saw. She staggers up and tries the door. A futile sob sticks in her throat: she will not give up. Not with Antonia locked away somewhere under the Paris streets. Isabel pictures her friend's stubborn chin and defiant sea-blue eyes. Antonia would never give up. A key crunches in the lock and the latch turns.

"You. Follow me."

The strange man looks as surprised to see her as she is to be here. They head down a narrow hall and out into the sunshine. The light is blinding, otherworldly, and she squints and wants to shut her eyes, to go back to before, to the burial of dreams and blackness, which had somehow been more reassuring than this brilliant light of day. When her vision clears, a shorter burly man leans against the wall eating a sandwich.

"Here she is." The man pushes her down until she is kneeling at his boss's feet.

Gritti takes his time, swallows his last bite of sandwich before tossing a crust in her lap, a morsel Isabel gobbles up greedily.

"Eats like a stray dog, that one," the man who brought her says.

"She bites like one, too. So watch yourself." Gritti picks his teeth with a dirty finger.

"Now what?"

"We wait." Gritti squats down to look Isabel in the eye, mustard in the corners of his mouth. "Is your nonna a prompt person?" His combination of cigarette smoke, onions, and stale sweat has become familiar.

"I don't know." And for once she doesn't. She can hardly picture Nonna in any emergency, let alone a situation like this.

Gritti laughs, the oval of his face becoming rounder, without contour. But then there's a whistle and he turns around.

"You expecting someone?" The other man nods toward the front of the yard.

"Take her back inside." Gritti seethes.

When the man pulls Isabel by the shoulder, she grabs at a fistful of earth in her attempts to remain, her bare legs flailing on the gravel.

"Papa?"

She freezes. No time at all and a lifetime have passed, but the voice is still the same, even if almost everything else is entirely different. But it is him: tall, gangly, movie star hair; the boy she once knew. Or thought she knew. Standing there as if all is forgiven. His hand is bandaged with only the little white fingertips visible. He glances at her and looks away.

Lila makes her way toward them with great care. And there on the ground is a bit of good fortune: Isabel, at Gritti's feet, while the boy, Niccolo, looks on. But good fortune or not, she has no strength to counter them, no weapon of any kind. What fury could an old woman in a spring coat unleash? Plenty. It's Miriam's voice. Hurry, Lila. Hurry, please.

She inches closer and, clinging to the polished edge of a gondola in the stacks, is close enough to make out the words.

"She's done nothing, " the boy says, red in the face. He grabs his father's arm.

"Get out of my way!" Gritti bellows.

He takes a wide swing and clocks the boy squarely in the face. Niccolo reels back two steps before lunging. As the two men tussle, the slack-jawed man looks on. The father and son spin and twist, raining glancing blows, until Gritti lands a hard one and Niccolo falls to the ground, blood streaming from his nose.

"Wasn't I clear enough?" Gritti kicks dirt at his boy, still dazed on the ground. "Take her back inside, I said!"

As his handyman leans down to grab Isabel, Lila's hands do something her mind cannot. They formulate a plan. She pushes against the suspended stack with every bit of strength she has left until they all hear it, the great cracking sound as gondola after gondola comes crashing down. When the cacophony of splintering wood ceases, she takes a breath.

Signor Gritti lies on his back under the wreckage, still as a log, only his work boots visible, the three others cowering from a few feet away.

"Papa!" Niccolo staggers to his father's side.

For Lila kneeling on the dusty earth, it's the slightness of Isabel in her arms, the delicate bones, the warmth of her skin.

Nonna, Isabel says between sobs. You came back, you came back. She says it over and over.

Lila and Miriam had spent hours on the phone with the gendarmerie in Paris, shaken off multiple refusals until they were granted access: first the captain, then the sergeant and finally the commissioner in charge. Apparently, the police had never gone around, not even after they had been called numerous times by a certain M. Vauvenargues, but a tour guide hearing strange noises down an unused passageway did finally alert the manager who alerted the municipality who called the police. They found the poor girl only inches from fatal dehydration and took her immediately, sirens blaring, to a local hospital.

"I still can't believe it." Miriam stirs her tea distractedly, but the sugar cubes are still in the saucer.

"I've been talking a full minute and you're barely there, Mim!"

"I'm sorry Lila." Miriam sets her spoon down on the napkin. "It's Carlo. I haven't heard from him in two days."

"And?"

"Two days, Lila. We never go a day without speaking."

"So he has business."

"He would have told me."

"I don't know...perhaps the gallery... Miriam, I need to make a call. I'm arranging a train ticket for Antonia. She's well enough now. She's arriving tomorrow.

"That's wonderful. And Isabel?"

"Still in her room," Lila rises from the table, worriedly.

"And the paintings?" Miriam calls after her.

Lila dials the phone in the hallway. The police recovered the two Gritti had, and, now that she has the deed she intends to bequeath the lot to the Metropolitan Museum.

"Carlo has contacts if you need—"

Lila shushes her and hangs up the phone to redial. Just then the phone rings, a bright startling jangle.

"Yes, this is she. What? What do you mean?" After a moment's silence, she finally says, "I see." She hangs up, her face ashen.

Lila what is it?

"Miriam, you'll need to stay calm.

"What is it?"

"It's about Carlo."

The whispers of Nonna and Miriam from the kitchen, the whoosh of swallows darting over the canals outside her bedroom window, these are the constant sounds. Isabel turns over in bed away from the glare.

She's heard them talking: saying she hasn't spoken a word, that she's left her tea cold in the teacup, and lain in bed for days fully clothed, refusing to change or bathe or even eat the hot food Nonna leaves at her bedside table. Plates appear; plates are taken away, all the meals untouched. It's strange to think of, truly, a bit unreal, this silence surrounding her, because nothing but words have been resounding in her head, full conversations, the tiniest of details even, a woman's face on the metro, the pebbles in her sandal at the Jardin de Tuileries, dark stacks of glowing bones, one memory after another, all of them echoing loudly, too loudly, except for the fact that, evidently, no one else can hear.

In the water taxi, Isabel holds tight to Nonna's hand and stares down at her lap. The buttons on her good blue sweater are little pearls. She has no memory of putting it on or of how her arm ended up in the white sling. Nonna said it had been reset in two places. They sit in silence, Nonna on one side and Miriam on the other, jostling her a little as the boat hums along the roiling black water.

Once docked at the quay, they begin the solemn walk along the canal bank. The glass doors into the lobby of the police station are leaden and the tapping of their shoes against the polished floor is an especially repetitive and hypnotic sound, but when Nonna squeezes her hand, Isabel tries to rally.

With his pinched mouth and freshly groomed mustache the carabinieri behind the desk has the appearance of swallowing words rather than speaking them.

"This way, signora. He's expecting you."

At their entrance, the commissioner stands up automatically, a soldier at attention.

"Please."

He points to the chairs where Lila and Miriam, barely breathing, sit down. A third chair is brought in by a harried clerk, and the gentle pressure at Isabel's shoulders force her knees to yield slightly and sit down too.

The placard on the desk reads "Commissioner Tommaso." The dark-eyed man folds his hands and leans forward.

"Which of you is Signora Lesser?"

Lila raises her free hand, keeping hold of Isabel's with the other.

"As I told you on the phone, we are still in the process of ascertaining all the facts, Signora Lesser. But what I can say is that there has been a campaign."

"A camp–,"

He silences Lila with a hand. "A long-orchestrated campaign, signora, months in the making, by a group of individuals both here in Italy and in France; some of whom it seems you are already acquainted with."

"Yes, we are," Lila wriggles uneasily. "We told the police on the phone, Officer, that it was Gritti. Gritti and that Davoglio person. Those are your culprits."

"You did tell us, Signora. But it's been long in the works, our investigation, and the French police have been cooperative. But we had to wait until these men really struck to be sure. Now we can say with certainty—"

"You've had to wait—? Do you mean you were aware all this time that someone has been targeting my family?"

He pauses. "How do you know Carlo Spinelli?"

"Carlo?" Miriam perks up. "Through the opera foundation of course. He's a patron and a successful businessman. He also happens to be my fiancé."

The door opens and an officer ducks in with some papers and delivers an inaudible message in the commissioner's ear. He leaves the papers behind on the desk. In the commissioner's hand a photograph of a man in a smart suit stares back at them; he has a sallow, oblong face and a thin mustache.

Isabel's mouth opens slightly. It's him. The same face flashes against the wallpaper of the Paris hotel, the girls coming and going down the narrow hall when she passed them by, the borrowed silk stockings sagging loosely against her legs.

"Miss?" The commissioner hands Isabel the photograph. "Do you recognize this person?"

Isabel clears her throat. "Yes," she says, her voice soft but certain.

Miriam's eyes widen.

"You do?" Lila frowns in confusion.

"Yes," Isabel says a bit louder this time. "I know that man."

The color drains completely from Miriam's cheeks.

"What this place needs is a proper scrubbing."

For the second time that morning, Miriam drags a wet soapy rag across otherwise shiny surfaces in the kitchen, the stove, the countertop, her unrolled sleeves soaked with sloshing water as little bubbles fly up into the shaft of sunlight.

"Not Carlo," Miriam says, scrubbing even more furiously, "not my Carlo."

Nonna stands in the kitchen still wearing her dressing gown, her arms crossed. "I only just cleaned in here, Mim."

Isabel ducks in at the doorway.

Nonna turns to look at her granddaughter. "Where are you going?"

"To the station. Antonia's train arrives at 10."

"But I said I would go...are you sure you're feeling well enough?"

"I am."

After these last few revelatory and claustrophobic days, Isabel has been only too antsy to get out of the house, and in the end, she leaves the two women to their parallel tasks: Miriam cleaning furiously and Nonna trying valiantly not to stop her. It's amazing, Isabel thinks, just how patient Nonna has been throughout; almost as if the steel core of her, held tight and rigid for so long, might actually be softening.

Down the street, a renewed energy in her step, Isabel's thoughts are fixed on something else: getting to the station on time. She won't believe Antonia is back among the living until she sees her in the flesh. The train, however, is uncharacteristically late. Up and down the station walkway she paces, back and forth in time to the ticking of her wristwatch but nothing comes of it, no train, no announcement of arrivals. She leans against the empty bench, refusing to sit down in defeat. Then, just as she thinks she may genuinely lose it, that her friend isn't coming after all, a hopeful whistle blows in the distance, and the train chuffs and chugs slowly into the station, coming to a noisy, screeching halt. In clusters of ones and twos, passengers staggering beneath loads of packages and unwieldy suitcases, disembark. Isabel strains on tiptoes to see through the jostling crowd. Not one face is familiar, not one silhouette distinguishable, until there, finally, at the door of the last car a tall, gangly girl emerges, she holds no suitcase, but her traveling clothes are refined, a dark, finely pleated skirt, tailored jacket, and dark leather gloves, far more proper than anything Isabel has seen her wear before.

"Antonia!" Isabel rushes over. "I almost didn't recognize you!"

"Hello." The once robust voice is wooden, drained of life and its usual ebullience; she barely glances up, and when she does, a weak smile remains frozen on her face.

"Antonia, I can't even begin to say how good it is...," Isabel reaches her good arm wide for an embrace, but the girl stands still as a statue.

"These clothes," Antonia gestures at the tailored jacket with embarrassment, "are borrowed."

"Oh, of course. Well, come on, I'll take you home."

"No, I'm expected at work."

Isabel cocks her head in confusion. "But the café is closed, Antonia. Your father...you know he had to move away."

"My father?"

"Yes. He's staying with your cousins in Naples."

Antonia blinks in swift succession. "I don't have any cousins."

Isabel tries to act as nonchalant as possible. "Well, never mind that. You can stay with us."

Antonia continues to be someone Isabel no longer recognizes: only speaking when spoken to, refusing anything but water, and sitting in the parlor staring down at her bandaged fingers, each wrapped in thick white gauze.

By the second day, it's more than Isabel can bear.

"What is it?" Isabel stirs her spoon in little circles in the cup and the teabag bobs up and down. They are alone in the parlor, she and Antonia; Nonna and Miriam have gone to the fish market. It should be a normal Thursday. Except that nothing is normal, Antonia least of all.

"What do you mean?"

"You haven't said a word yesterday or today!"

Antonia sits up on the couch where she installed herself, her travel suit wrinkled and visibly graying at the lapels in the stripe of warm sun. She wipes a strand of her unwashed hair away from her face. Her eyes are ringed with circles and her hands, even bandaged, reveal purple bruises and dry blood-crusted nails. "What do you want me to say?"

Isabel shakes her head in dismay. "At least let me change them." She gestures to the bandages.

"I'm fine." Antonia shrugs, burying both hands beneath the sofa cushion.

"Look, I felt horribly strange too when I first got back." Isabel scoots her chair closer to the sofa. "I couldn't explain to anyone about the thoughts, the memories in my head. It was just so very awful."

Antonia gives her a look, one side of her mouth crooked up in a strange way, half smile, half grimace. "So very awful?" she says. "You mean as awful as being left to die with the skeletons?" Her face is still making the same hideous expression. "As awful as trying to claw my way out of that dark tomb for days...never knowing if anyone would find me?"

Isabel can barely speak past the hard lump rising in her throat. "We would never have left you in there like that."

"Oh really? Because I was there. The whole time." She lifts up her bruised and bloodied hands despairingly. "I was there, and where were you?"

"Antonia, if I could have gotten there, I would have found you. Surely, you must know that!?"

"Must I?"

Isabel feels her eyes fill with scalding tears. "I'm so terribly, terribly sorry for what happened."

Antonia stands up slowly and shakes her head. "I think we've probably both said enough now, don't you?" She heads down the hall, and there's the little click of the bedroom door as it closes behind her.

Isabel rubs at her wet eyes with the backs of her hands. Even at her very worst in Paris, even at the hands of those men, she had never felt this lost. This bereft. This grief-stricken. How was she supposed to live in a world like this? She had had one friend. One. And now even that had been taken.

"What do you mean *gone*?" Isabel stands in the kitchen doorway, blinking slowly.

"I'm sorry sweetheart. But she wasn't in the parlor when I looked this morning." Lila wrings her hands. "I thought she might be in the bathroom. I left her a hot cup of tea. Then I noticed she had folded the sheet."

It isn't true. Antonia wouldn't leave without first saying goodbye. Isabel runs to the parlor and finds the cold cup of tea, the folded sheet on the sofa cushion. She turns back around, Lila only a few steps behind her, and a strange new emptiness envelops her.

"But she had nowhere left to go!"

"Perhaps she's off to find her father."

"She didn't even leave a note!" Isabel's eyes brim anew with tears.

Nonna sighs. "We can't, any of us, imagine what she's been through, can we? Give her time," Lila puts a hand on Isabel's shoulder.

Isabel shakes off Nonna's gentle touch. She can only see Antonia sneaking away in the wee hours of the morning, wearing her fancy suit, a stranger, not the old friend she once knew, on an unknown path to somewhere far away. "Now she won't ever forgive me!" Isabel wipes the tears away angrily. "Why didn't you tell me about my parents? You barely said a word. And the paintings! You left me to find out for myself."

"I should have told you. About everything," Lila's voice cracks. "Give her time dear," she repeats.

Time. That's Nonna's best answer. If only she hadn't kept all those secrets. And giving it time is no answer at all. Because time doesn't march on anymore or flow as it had once done: it festers. It stagnates. If Antonia had been her link to life before, that link was now severed. Perhaps that's the lesson: friends come and go, a thunderstorm that batters until it finally resolves into an empty breeze that barely stirs the curtains.

A sad poem, that's what that is.

There's not a single person in all of Venice she can talk to and all the writing, all the poetry has gone out of her. She can't imagine ever writing again.

Isabel wipes her face with the handkerchief. No sense crying about it. No point complaining. She stares at the empty white spot on the parlor wall where the painting once hung, the canvas boxed up and sent on in crates with the others to New York.

Nothing is the same. She no longer understands anything about kindness, but now knows quite a bit about falsehood and brutality, the scorching desert of summertime in Venice, the endless, empty turnover of days and months and years.

CHAPTER NINETEEN

Lila closes the book she has been pretending to read and stares out the parlor window, listless. She never rehearsed what she would say when the time would come. In fact she could never imagine the time coming, she had simply lived, come what may, one day to the next, the days connected like railroad cars down a long track to somewhere, nowhere, to this very moment perhaps. But Lila can't help but think how things might have worked out differently if Isabel had known all along about her father and her mother. Because what had they done that was so wrong after all? They were kids, their only crime was finding love. Two babies had made a baby for Lila to raise and now she has gone and botched the job.

"Lila...your hair!" Miriam hasn't moved from the doorway.

The book slides from Lila's lap onto the floor. She didn't know that young Ilse was pregnant. In the camp the girl was barely showing when they first arrived and in the chaos it was beyond comprehension. But Lila should have tended to the girl more, been more protective. She was a lovely girl, the only person besides his mum that Leo ever loved and as such, a treasure. There was no shame in it, only survival. The shame came afterwards when Lila wheeled baby Isabel in the pram around the campo, under the disapproving stares of their neighbors, Italians mostly who had claimed Jewish apartments unlawfully, and the few Jews who had, like Lila, returned.

"I let myself in." Miriam dangles the house key.

Lila sits up straighter. She must make amends and she will, to Isabel. To Miriam. To Antonia too.

"What do you think?" Lila clears her throat. "The hairdresser called it a bob."

Miriam's blank stare gradually turns to a grin and then she giggles as though for the first time in years. She shakes her head over and over. "In all the time I've known you, you've never cut your hair. Not once. Ever." Her giggles are little hiccups that resolve finally in breathless gasps and Lila tries to quell her rising impatience.

"Really Miriam stop being ridiculous...so?"

"I think I like it," Miriam says, tears streaming down her face. "It suits you, it really does."

"Good. Because that's the first time I've seen you smile in days, Mim."

Isabel wanders into the room and stops when she sees Lila. "What happened to your hair?"

Lila shrugs. "I needed a change."

"Change can be good," Miriam says, although her voice sounds a bit dubious.

At the sight of Isabel, Lila is suddenly at a loss for words. She had thought it all out, in theory, what she would say, but now her mind is a complete blank. She stiffens. There must be no blame. Not on Leo or Ilse. Certainly not on Isabel.

"Would you sit down with me sweetheart? You too Mim dear."

Miriam shoots Isabel a quizzical look, but sits at the edge of the sofa cushion with the girl perched beside her.

Lila folds her hands. "First off. You did nothing wrong. Do you hear me Isabel? Nothing. I should have told you. About all of it. And God knows, you asked so many times but I was tongue tied. I was scared. " Lila gulps against the knot in her throat.

"Your mother was fourteen years old and liked reading and singing and loved my honey cake. Did you know she played piano as well as your father did? They would sit in the parlor for hours playing music together, piano concertos, all sorts. He loved her truly. They were first loves, you see, and he never loved anyone else like that. From the moment he brought her home he was a different person. He could be rough and brash and rude, Leo, he was only fifteen himself at the time, but Ilse made him sweeter, a kinder person, easier on the nerves. And oh he loved you, sweetheart. He truly did. He held you in his arms. He did. Imagine your dear mother, loving you so much that she held on until the very end, until there you came out on the dirt floor of that god-awful place and we scooped you up like the little miracle you were." Lila's tears roll down her face. "You'll never know how sorry I am that I didn't tell you about him. Because you should know. About Leo and Ilse and how they lived before they died. For all my faults, and I know there are many, you have been loved. You are loved."

"I knew she died in childbirth." Isabel says, crying too.

"She did." Lila pauses. "But she lived too. She lives. Because you are here."

Isabel squeezes her grandmother's hand and then wraps her grandmother in an embrace, and Lila takes the girl in, the sum of her, this beautiful young woman, her heart beating so wonderfully strong, rhythmic, alive.

"We do love you so, Isabel." Miriam wipes a sleeve across her face.

"I'm sorry I lost the apple, Nonna." Isabel hangs her head.

Lila clucks her tongue. "I always hated that glass ball. Just another ridiculous curio from Albert's collection to worry over."

"I'm so sorry, Nonna, for all of it...stealing the painting, bringing those terrible men into our lives."

Miriam leans forward. "No, no, I'm the one who should apologize. If I'd only been more careful. But I've gone over it a hundred times. Carlo seemed so generous. So affectionate." Her face flushes.

"I should have known it was an act." She stares down at her shoes in dismay.

"But you did nothing wrong, Aunt Miriam. I should never have let them take me to Paris..."

"Paris!" Lila gets to her feet quickly. "I knew there was something—" Lila stands up quickly and comes back with a letter from the foyer. "This arrived yesterday."

"It's from the Sorbonne..." Isabel tears open the envelope and reads silently, her lips moving. "They're accepting me," she says in an incredulous monotone. "What on earth? I don't understand. You said I couldn't go so I never replied."

"Well, I made a call on your behalf." Lila gazes shyly at her granddaughter. After all this time, and because she never could allow herself the risk before, the recognition is sweet: this is what it feels like to have pride in your child, like being lit by sunlight from within. "Your grades were more than good enough, and Sister Angelica was kind enough to write a letter." Her hand flutters to her new bob, her fingers both surprised and delighted to rediscover the smoothness of her new coiffure. "I mean, I really think it's time we had a writer in the family, don't you?"

The grand boulevard is fringed with peonies and daffodils, the plaza squares are stamps of trampled green, as ebullient children and sniffing dogs run about. Isabel has walked for miles, avoiding the metro, preferring the hot sun, cooling breeze, the soot and ash of traffic. By the time she arrives, the café on Saint Germain is mostly filled with students and the air is syrupy with clove cigarettes, the little bistro tables are overladen with heavy textbooks, cups and saucers. She sips her cafe au lait, holding the first letter in her hand: a literary magazine, a good one, has accepted her short story. Her arm has finally come out of the cast: she typed the pages easily on Nonna's parting gift, an Olivetti Lettera typewriter, sky blue.

A visit home for the holidays. That's what she promised on the phone. But Nonna and Miriam can wait a bit. She misses Venice but relishes these early days of fall in Paris, the swift comings and goings, the fabulous transience of the place, the imminent sense of departure postponed. She lingers on her last sip of hot café crème and doodles in the margins of her notebook, little spirals and stars, the face of a dog, the shape of a diamond. She's enjoying a precious moment of idleness for the first time in weeks. She has an exam in two days, a paper to write, and a pile of novels to read for Modern French Literature. And for the last day and a half she has been waiting. She turns the second letter over in her hand. Airmail from Naples. Draining the last bit of coffee, she steels herself. The opened envelope flutters to the ground at her feet, and her lips tremble as she reads, her throat tensed. But it's only niceties: the weather in Naples, the length of the commute to her uncle's shop in the city center, her discovery of a new outdoor market, and then finally the last paragraph, her response to Isabel's story. A short story that had been rattled off in hours, practically writing itself.

The empty coffee cup suspended, she reads on: "I'm not a writer, so what do I know? But I liked it. I liked how the characters were friends and then they sort of weren't. I mean because of all the hard stuff that happened to them in between. That had truth for me. The strange part is that it somehow didn't feel quite finished, you know? Like the two of them weren't done or there was another chapter yet to happen or something. I don't know. But I guess that's one way to find the truth. To write it down and then see what happens, right?"

At the very bottom of the page, it was signed. "Your friend, Antonia."

Isabel nods to herself, her heart in her throat, and setting her cup down, she picks up her pen.

About the Author

Susan Knecht completed the two-year Online Novel Writing Certificate Program at Stanford University. Her narrative non-fiction was published in the Write On Mamas Anthology, and her short story The Hijab in The Good Review literary journal. The Art Collector's Wife was shortlisted for The Santa Fe Writing Project's 2023 Literary Awards Program and reached the Scouting Programme at Cornerstones Literary Consultancy in London. Formerly a practicing psychotherapist in Northern California, she currently has a private therapy practice in Amsterdam. As a second-generation Holocaust survivor, she is keenly aware of the issues of exile, loss and the psychological devastation caused by being 'othered.'

ABOUT THE PRESS

Sea Crow Press

Sea Crow Press is an award-winning woman-run independent book publisher based on Cape Cod in Massachusetts committed to amplifying voices that might otherwise go unheard. We publish creative nonfiction, literary fiction, and poetry. Our books celebrate our connection to each other and to the natural world with a focus on positive change and great storytelling.

www.ingramcontent.com/pod-product-compliance
Lightning Source LLC
Chambersburg PA
CBHW031322180326
41420CB00003B/80

* 9 7 8 1 9 6 1 8 6 4 3 2 0 *